THE TINKLING SYMBOL

**Books by Phoebe Atwood Taylor
available from Foul Play Press**

Asey Mayo Cape Cod Mysteries

THE ANNULET OF GILT
THE ASEY MAYO TRIO
BANBURY BOG
THE CAPE COD MYSTERY
THE CRIMINAL C.O.D.
THE CRIMSON PATCH
THE DEADLY SUNSHADE
DEATH LIGHTS A CANDLE
DIPLOMATIC CORPSE
FIGURE AWAY
GOING, GOING, GONE
THE MYSTERY OF THE CAPE COD PLAYERS
THE MYSTERY OF THE CAPE COD TAVERN
OCTAGON HOUSE
OUT OF ORDER
THE PERENNIAL BOARDER
PROOF OF THE PUDDING
PUNCH WITH CARE
SANDBAR SINISTER
SPRING HARROWING
THE SIX IRON SPIDERS
THREE PLOTS FOR ASEY MAYO

Writing as Alice Tilton

BEGINNING WITH A BASH
DEAD ERNEST
FILE FOR RECORD
HOLLOW CHEST
THE LEFT LEG
THE IRON CLEW

PHOEBE ATWOOD TAYLOR

THE
TINKLING
SYMBOL

An Asey Mayo Cape Cod Mystery

A Foul Play Press Book

THE COUNTRYMAN PRESS
Woodstock, Vermont

This edition published in 1993 by Foul Play
Press, an imprint of The Countryman Press, Inc.,
Woodstock, Vermont 05091.

ISBN 0–88150–263–4

Printed in the United States of America

10 9 8 7 6 5 4 3 2 1

THE TINKLING SYMBOL

CHAPTER ONE

AGATHA PENROSE, my husband's peerless maiden aunt, got up from the breakfast table and gazed appreciatively out of the south window.

"This sort of day," she remarked, "was undeniably the only consolation the poor Pilgrims ever had on Cape Cod. Beverly, forget you're a careworn housewife. We're going to postpone your quince jam and Kyle's socks and the twins' buttons, and just sit the day out in the orchard, watching that superb blue ocean."

Around one o'clock, while Katy was bringing out our lunch, my young Cape cousin Giles Hopkins strode on the scene, all six feet three inches of him glowing like an oatmeal ad.

"This is the sort of a day," he announced, "that I leave dad alone at the boat yard and walk. Gee, it's more like July than October!"

At four o'clock, Eleanor Dwight and her daughter Jobyna appeared.

"Isn't it a heavenly day? Isn't it glorious? Isn't it rapturous after that horrid storm—" Eleo broke off long enough to be introduced to Aunt Agatha, and to cast a minimum courtesy nod at Giles. "We—"

"We've spent it," Jo's dark, gypsy-like face was burned even under her tan, "we've spent it driving and driving and driving in the open roadster, but we couldn't go home without gaping at your view, Bev! It's wonderful. It absolutely can't be improved on. Clouds like globs of marshmallow cream, the sand like toast with marmalade on it—"

"It rather sounds," I interrupted, "as though tea might possibly aid even the unimprovable view. Giles, hop into the house and tell Katy to scare up some food."

So, as simply and casually and spur of the minutey as all that, began the tea party that was to end with a crash on High F, with the earth quaking, volcanoes erupting, and occasional peals of thunder and chains of zigzag lightning.

Being a simple soul, I didn't even suspect it. I suppose I should have known, though, even if it was a glorious day, that something more than the weather brought that heterogeneous group together. Aunt Agatha claims that even as she sipped her tea, she saw a handful of Fates leer out from under a cloud, heard them yelp ecstatically, and proclaim loudly that North Weesit was just the spot to wind up their annual clambake and frolic. It's highly probable that she was right. The five of us would have lighted the face of any Fate, even a cold sober one.

Take Aunt Agatha, bordering on sixty, and water side of Beacon Street from her white hair to her long aristocratic finger tips. Soft gray tweeds, a crinkle of humor playing around her blue eyes—as my husband says, a mold for Aunt Agatha's kind is worth ten centuries to any man's civilization. And then Giles, with spots of paint on his blue shirt and two twisted shavings sticking to the rolled up legs of his dungarees—Giles, glaring like fury at the Dwights, whom he considers abject strangers. As a native Cape Codder, he actively resents and mistrusts summer people who've spent less than ten years in Weesit, and the Dwights have been there just ten weeks. I think he speaks to them only because Jo was a college friend of Kay Truman's, and even that doesn't make him any more lenient towards Jo's invariable scarlet shorts.

And Eleanor Dwight. Eleo, for all that Jo's twenty-two and my sons are only ten, went to school with me. The difference is that I just look a good forty all the time, except when I look older, while Eleo, even in bright sunlight, looks like Jo's sister. Hungry men forget to eat when she's their dinner partner. She is, in short, the sort of woman of whom other women say, "I wonder how she *does* it!" I don't wonder, because I know. The hours I spend over mending baskets, kitchen stoves, recalcitrant tires and floor polishers, Eleo spends with dressmakers, figure makers and face makers. Usually her aura of well-turned-outness doesn't bother me a bit, but that afternoon she looked so well that I was violently conscious of the holes in my old canvas sneakers, and the tear in my faded skirt, and the freckles on my pug nose, and the axle grease on my sweater. In fact, for a few minutes there while I pretended to fiddle with the lemon, I loathed Eleo Dwight with all my heart and soul. I was downright pleased to find that she was having difficulties with Aunt Agatha. She'd never met Aunt Agatha before, couldn't place her, and wasn't quite sure how to take her.

"You—oh, a first sentence, you say? Then you write, Miss Penrose?"

"No," Agatha said patiently, with a twinkle in her eye. "I never wrote, never shall and don't want to, but it's a game of mine to make up first lines to things I'd write if I did. You see?"

Eleo, who plainly didn't see at all, nodded. But Jo caught on.

"You mean, like 'I was only sixteen when I met Gaylord Leatherbridge' and 'Biffy Beltrano jammed his gat into the Kid's stomach'—I say stomach, because after all, it's tea—"

"That's it," Agatha said approvingly, "though I never went in much for confessions or gangsters. Yes. Well, I've been thinking of a grand mystery beginning all day. 'Four shots and a staccato shriek all rang out into the stillness of the midnight air.' Isn't that superb?"

Jo and I laughed, but Giles and Eleo seemed bothered.

"Why four shots?" Giles asked in perfect seriousness. "What's a staccato shriek? An' can a staccato shriek ring? What—"

"Let it pass, Giles," I said plaintively. "Let it pass. It's just a joke. And that's only a first sentence, anyway. Something that leads you to the next line, not something to be gnawed over like a bone."

"May be a joke," Giles hauled himself up on the

lowest branch of the apple tree, a puzzled look still on his face, "but it sounds like the stuff Porky Tavish used to write for English A. It's—say, you know what I wish, Miss Agatha? I wish you'd honestly write a real book about Kay Truman."

It was our turn to look puzzled.

"Dave's daughter," Giles explained. "I'm sure that some person—don't glare, Bev! I don't mean Dave pushed her off, only that someone else *must* have been up on the cliff that night. Kay knew every inch of that path, cold. Knew it night or day or fog or anything. She couldn't have fallen off accidentally, an' she couldn't have killed herself. It just plain isn't sensible. So—why don't you really write about all that? I—well, I've wanted someone to think about it. Maybe, if they thought enough, they'd get the answer. There must *be* an answer, too! Just think—four women found dead at the foot of that cliff! Kay last month, Rutledge's maid in June, Sherman girl a year ago, crazy Nan Dawson just before that. Nan might have jumped off, and Rutledge's girl might have fallen, and the Sherman kid might have been drunk, like they claim. But it's doggone funny, with all four! And Kay and Nan knew that cliff, cold. *Knew* that path!"

Giles closed his mouth with a snap over what was the longest speech I ever heard him make, for as a rule he confines himself to simple sentences or the briefest possible monosyllables, and sometimes he just makes grunting sounds.

Somehow none of us answered him, mostly because

we didn't know what to say. I watched him curiously as he stared across the inlet of the bay to the cliff. Crooked Cliff, it had always been called in the past, now, after Kay Truman's poor battered body had been found on the sharp rocks below, the newspaper name was used by everybody. It was Suicide Cliff to the natives of North Weesit and the surrounding Cape towns, to all the summer people from Provincetown to Hyannis, to the horrible crowd of gawking, thrill-seeking tourists who gazed and pointed and wisecracked and gossiped till I, with the rest of my neighbors, including Dave Truman himself, nearly went mad.

There was a granitey look in Giles's gray eyes as he continued to stare at the cliff, and his lips tightened till deep lines appeared on either side of his mouth. He seemed more Cape Coddish than ever; his namesake and ancestor, the first Giles Hopkins, might have worn the same expression as he stood by the rail of the "Mayflower" with his father and surveyed the bleak outlines of the new land.

I was a little afraid of his intensity. From the cradle Giles has been a lad of quick action rather than quick wits. He's not a dolt, but his mind, instead of leaping like an agile mountain goat from thought to thought, rather tussles with each new idea until he has it licked. Apparently he hadn't been able to catalogue the business of Kay Truman's death, and he'd brooded over it so long that he was seeing it a little bigger than life size. I remembered how, all afternoon, he'd looked over at the cliff from time to time, and I wondered if the rumors

I'd heard about Kay and Giles might possibly have been true—

"And Dave," Giles went on, completely forgetting the Dwights and Aunt Agatha, "honest, Bev, I don't see how he stands it! All the gossip about Kay's death, and the talk in the papers that because he started to go out to walk with her that night, he must have killed her! And Dave's such a swell man. Sterling, like dad says. And—"

"I was fond of Kay Truman." Eleo, her cheeks very red, stood up. "I liked Kay and admired her. But I simply cannot and will not listen to the praises of David Truman! That utter, complete rotter!"

Giles opened his mouth and stared at her. "But, Mrs. Dwight, Dave's a grand fellow! And with that wife of his that ran off with that nigger—"

"He wasn't a nigger, Giles," I broke in, suddenly remembering that Eleo Dwight was one of Marie Truman's dearest friends. "He was not a nigger. He was only sort of coffee-colored—"

Of course, in trying to smooth it over, I only put my foot in it twice as far. I was genuinely trying to give the devil his due, and I might have got away with it if Aunt Agatha and Jo hadn't involuntarily chuckled.

"Adrian," Eleo was clearly more annoyed with me than she'd ever thought of being with Giles, "Adrian is a Frenchman, a delightful—"

"I didn't mean," Giles cut in hastily, "I didn't mean anything about the nig—about him. I meant, Dave's had a lot of rotten breaks for such a swell man. Like Truman and Company flopping, when it wasn't Dave's fault any

more than the other officers, or the stockholders, or—"
Giles is a hereditary Republican—"or this crazy fool gov-
ernment! And they've called him a second Insull ever
since! And then Kay—"

Eleo buttoned up her white sports coat and reached
on the table for her bag.

"David Truman," she said, and every word was
carved out of a block of ice, "is a rotten scoundrel. He's
a liar, an embezzler, a common thief! He—"

Giles slid down from the tree and towered over her.

"Mrs. Dwight, I—I don't care a rap if you're older
than me, nor—nor lousy with money, or anything! You
can't talk about Dave Truman like that while I'm around,
an'—an' he's Bev's friend, too, an' you owe us an apology,
an'—"

"Come, Jobyna!" Eleo turned her back on him.

Jo, who had been watching the scene with blazing
eyes, shook her head. She loved Dave, I knew, as much
as Giles and I did.

"Jobyna!"

With a sigh and a peace-at-any-price expression, Jo
got up and followed her mother out of the orchard. One
clenched fist behind her back made numerous gestures.
I gathered that she would return.

"Well," I said when they were out of earshot, "just
what does the well-bred hostess do at a time like
this? I—"

"Gee, Bev," Giles was still breathing hard, "gee,
Bev, I'm sorry! But I couldn't help it. She hadn't any
right to talk like that!"

"Of course she hadn't," Aunt Agatha remarked soothingly. "Don't fret, Giles. She asked for it. And though I don't think you're worrying, Bev, stop it if you are. There's no necessity for bothering with ill-bred rudeness. She was your guest, and I must say she allowed the fact to slip her mind. Just ignore the whole affair."

"I'm not upset, I'm just sorry things like that have to happen. Eleo." I added reminiscently, "is a creature of firm convictions. Funny, we've talked about Dave before, but she never exploded like that. I don't understand. Anyway, Jo'll be back, probably, if she doesn't burst into pieces with rage first, and she'll tell us why her mother blew up."

"I see now," Giles, back in the tree, hurled an apple viciously at an innocent crow, "I understand, after hearin' her, how Dave might kill himself, even if I don't understand about Kay. Gee, what's a man got to live for? Wife gone—and he was a nigger. Dad saw him and said so. Money gone, business gone, Kay gone, everything he's aimed for and built up and sweated over. Even his good name's gone. Not for us and some of his friends, maybe, but look at that Dwight woman! And ask anyone who reads papers what they thing about Dave Truman! Gee, I don't see how he can go on—"

"Stop it!" I ordered. "I hate to hear you repeat the Spit-and-Chatter Club's twaddle—that bunch of Main Street bums! You've been told about the shots up here. I know. And there *have* been shots, too. Half of 'em were me potting at the muskrats that are simply ruining my garden, and the rest Dave after skunks. They're digging in under his kitchen, and John L. Sullivan, the poor dear cat, has got mixed up with 'em twice. Last time I had to wash him in a carbolic bath, and it distressed him terribly. He's a proud thing."

"So Dave kept the cat instead of the dogs?" Giles's tone indicated his disappointment. He thinks cats are sissy.

"Sully'll cost less to feed, and Dave says he's understanding without letting his emotions get the best of him. But Giles, truly, do step on this talk about Dave killing himself! He'd never dream of it, in spite of the papers and the chit-chat, and the people who feel like Eleo!"

Giles's grunt was more affirmative than not, but I knew very well that he didn't agree with me.

The three of us fell silent, and I looked over the inlet to the cliff; the sun lighted up its thick veins of clay, and the east wind swayed the tall sea grass along the path at the crest. Down below the waves pounded against the sharp rocks—I watched the spray spin up, and thought of Kay, and somehow found myself blinking steadily at the high thick hedge that separates our land from Dave Truman's. I could just see the top of his white chimney and the thin spiral of smoke winding up to the sky.

"I hate that hedge," I said, thinking out loud. "As soon as Jethro gets through digging Dave's potatoes, I'm going to have him come over and cut it down. It's no earthly use as a wind break, and it's so darn unfriendly."

"Good idea." Giles, still perched in the tree, leaned

forward. "Hey—there's Dave now. Just come out the front door—"

"Run over and ask him to tea," I suggested. "There's still some food, and Katy can bring out—"

"Bev—Bev—he's got a gun in his hand!"

"Don't be so confoundedly melodramatic, Giles! Relax. He's after his skunks or my muskrats. Or maybe the wildcat that's been bothering Sully. Come to think of it, I just saw Sully slip through the hedge, but I didn't—"

"No skunks around here," Giles said excitedly. "The wind's—"

I got up from my deck chair and walked over to the hedge. I'm five feet two inches, but even on tiptoes I couldn't see over the top.

"Damn this hedge!" I said violently. "It's going to come down!" Pulling two stalks aside, I peered through as well as I could. "There—see? He's gone back into the house. I told you."

"Uh-huh. Only he's stopped in the doorway! Bev, he's pointing that gun at himself!"

"He's putting it in a shoulder holster, stupid." I let the hedge snap together and started back to my chair. "Aunt Ag, let's go over and ask—"

"He—look out!"

Giles swung out of the tree like a monkey, leaped over the tea table and most of Aunt Agatha, and tried to charge through the hedge.

"I can't hurdle—help me crash through, Bev! Push—can't help if I—"

He was just half way through when a shot rang out.

By the time I reached the other side, with more tears in my skirt and scratches on my face, Giles was some twenty-five yards away, kneeling beside the body of Dave Truman, sprawled on his front steps, his gun still clutched in his right hand.

"He's alive," Giles said. "Opened his eyes and tried to say something—here, you're better at this. Hold his head—I'll run phone Doc Cummings to tear over here—"

"Can't we do anything?"

"What he needs is a doctor," Giles said. "Don't joggle him." And he dashed into the house as Aunt Agatha appeared, having sensibly chosen to come through the driveway opening.

Once again she proved herself by asking no questions, indulging in no hysterics, and making no banal remarks. She knelt down beside me and undid the collar of Dave's shirt.

Dave stirred slightly, and as I looked down at his face, a reel of mental pictures flicked briefly and with chronological accuracy through my brain—Dave in his uniform as brigadier, with Joffre and the Prince of Wales, Dave and the President and half the Cabinet starting out on a fishing trip, Dave reading that telegram from his wife the day she ran off with the coffee-colored Adrian, Dave at Kay's commencement the previous June, Dave as the tabloids cartooned him after Truman and Company's failure—

"Just got the doc," Giles said. "He'll be here in two shakes. Bev, he's trying to talk again—"

As I bent over, Dave half opened his eyes; his lips

moved, but even when I put my ear close to his mouth, I couldn't hear a word. Neither Giles nor Aunt Agatha had more success.

"I didn't," Dave spoke with tremendous effort, "I didn't—"

"Go on, old man," Giles said softly. "You didn't—"

"I didn't m—" the word ended in an indistinct hum. "I didn't m—" he paused, and then very distinctly formed a word. "Ink."

We all looked at each other blankly.

"Ink," Dave whispered, and then his head fell back.

Giles went into the house and returned with a soft blanket.

"Get up," he said to Agatha and me. "It's—oh, gee— if only I'd popped down from that tree when he first came out—"

"If only," it startled me to find that I could talk at all, "if only I hadn't blown you up! I was a fool to let him stay alone. Kyle didn't want him to either—"

Aunt Agatha took each of us by an arm and led us away from the front door, but no matter where I looked, I seemed to see that strong, well-tanned hand whose long fingers still clutched the pistol. Not even the sight of Dr. Cummings's car—and it's a sight that's cheered me more than once—made me feel the least bit better.

The doctor strode up the oystershell walk, swinging his little black bag. He stopped short when he saw the blanket.

"Too late? By George, I'm sorry! Poor Dave—I never thought he would, even with all the talk, but he certainly had reason. Ought to have made him stay with us. Tried, but he wouldn't listen. Giles, take this paper cup, fill it at the hose. Bev, take this pill, drink the water—that's right, Miss Penrose, sit her on that fool green seat by the zinnias."

Obediently I took the pill and the water and let Agatha lead me to the green settee.

"I want," I remember saying very firmly, "I want to scream!"

Cummings knelt down. "Scream away." His round, usually jovial face seemed to have lengthened in the last minute. "I—yes, he's gone. I'd like to scream with you," he continued as he rose. "Will you, any of you, or any-one on this earth, tell me why, with all the useless gib-bering idiots, all the crooks, all the swine who thrive and prosper and grow fat, why should Dave Truman have had such—Giles, help me take him in. I'll phone Gibson and stay till he comes. I'll take charge of things. You happen to know how this—what went on?"

Briefly, Giles told him.

"Hm. All alone, eh? Jethro gone home?"

"He's digging potatoes in the back garden," I said. "He's too deaf to have heard—took me ten minutes with a cow bell to call him in yesterday. Let Jethro be, at least until we have time to write out what's happened. I couldn't bear to howl it at him. I—I want to stay."

"Me, too," Giles said. "Bev, you and Miss Agatha wait out here till I call."

We sat on the stiff green settee and watched the gulls

hover over the cliff, swooping down, then up and up in ever widening circles till they seemed to be a part of the low hurrying clouds.

A couple of fishing boats putt-putted in toward home on the opposite side of the bay, near the great bar, and down by the inlet Tommy Dawson sculled a little sharpie with one hand, poised a flounder spear in the other. I knew it was Tommy though I couldn't see his face, for he wore one of Kyle's old cast-offs, a crimson striped jersey I'd mended so often that I could tell it in the dark.

It amazed me that familiar things should be going on in their familiar, every-day grooves. I don't know that I expected the world to stop, or anything like that, but it made me feel all the more stunned to find the bay as blue as it had been an hour before, the birds still flying, and the wind still blowing.

I wondered how Kyle would take the news, and then it occurred to me that the "Jetsam" had no radio, and Kyle wouldn't learn of Dave's death till after the little boat reached Bermuda. I'd send a cable. As for the boys, I'd telephone their head master later, and have him explain it as well as he could before the papers blared the story from one end of the country to the other.

John L. Sullivan, Dave's enormous tiger cat, mewed plaintively at my feet, and rubbed his back against my torn skirt. Aunt Agatha lifted him into her lap and hugged him tight.

"Poor Sully," I said, "why, he—he looks as though he knew!"

Aunt Agatha looked at me. "Of course he knows," she returned. "I'll take him home with me, if you don't mind. You were probably thinking of adopting him, yourself, but the twins are a bit vigorous for cats. Cheer up, Sully. You can have a basket on my hearth, and a dozen catnip mice, and fish—"

Giles appeared silently and threw himself down on the ground beside us.

"You—I guess you got a story whether you want it or not, Miss Agatha," his voice wavered. "Only—well, only Dave wasn't shot."

We stared at him. His eyes were all granite, now, and his chin jutted out till I thought it would part from his face.

"Are you mad, Giles? Are you crazy?" I demanded. "Wha-what did you say?"

"I said, Dave wasn't shot."

"Are you quite sure," Aunt Agatha asked anxiously, "that you're—all right, Giles? Are—"

"He's insane," I said. "Stark staring insane. Didn't we see him? Didn't we watch him? Didn't we hear the shot? Didn't—"

"We did," Giles agreed. "I saw him tumble, an' I saw the flash of his gun as he fired, an' I saw him point it—"

"Well, then," I interrupted, "what d'you—Giles, man alive, we *saw* everything! We heard—"

"We did," Giles said again. "We did. But he wasn't, just the same. He wasn't shot, Bev. He was stabbed in the back."

CHAPTER TWO

THREE hours later I dumped the contents of six bowl-like ash trays into my fireplace for what was by actual count the twenty-second time.

"At this point," I swung around and faced Sergeant Hanson of the state police, "at this point I absolutely and finally refuse to go over the story again! Giles and Miss Penrose and I've told you and told you—my God, man! You should know by heart every single thing anyone of us saw or thought or felt or noticed or smelled or heard! Now, please go, and take your men with you, and go quickly, before—"

"Before," Aunt Agatha said calmly, "I lose my temper, too. And I warn you, I'm inclined to throwing things with what amounts to uncanny accuracy."

"Aw, Miss Penrose, you don't mean that!" Hanson stuck his thumbs under the armpits of his light blue coat, leaned back in his chair and puffed contentedly at another of Kyle's best Egyptian cigarettes that dangled from his underlip. "You and Mrs. Penrose, you got to be reasonable. The state police has got—"

"You've got to do your duty." Dr. Cummings crisply

finished Hanson's favorite sentence for him. "You've got to do your duty, and Beverly and I and the rest know it as well as you do! But consider, if you can bear the feverish effort of exercising your brain, consider that she and Giles and Miss Penrose have not passed the easiest of afternoons. It's been no picnic for them. Give 'em a chance to rest, get some food, pull themselves together, and then you can—"

"Now, listen, Doc. I told you a hundred times—"

"A hundred and forty-one," the doctor snapped. "And it's passed the stage of being even a dress rehearsal! Call it a day, Hanson, and start in fresh again to-morrow morning, can't you?"

Without answering, Hanson reached for another of Kyle's cigarettes, and as he did so, he deliberately scratched his puttee straps across my best maple footstool.

That was the last straw, and I started to boil over in earnest. But before I could say a word, Aunt Agatha picked up a small cut glass vase from the table and pitched it at him. It caught him neatly on the ear, bounced off and smashed into smithereens against one of the red-coated Hessian andirons.

Hanson's mouth opened and closed with great rapidity, but the words mercifully remained stuck in his throat. His two men made valiant attempts not to laugh.

"The next vase," Aunt Agatha informed him pleasantly, avoiding the twinkle in the doctor's eyes, "is one Bev particularly cherishes, but it's coming in one minute by the clock, and your nose is *so* ample! Arrest me for assault and battery if you want, but keep in mind that I've a brother who's a supreme court judge—"

Hanson spluttered a few incoherent bits under his breath.

"Just give it up for the present, Hanson." Dr. Cummings tried to soothe him. "She's likely to toss the baby grand at you next, and I'll testify that you disregarded a highly hysterical condition. Oh—has it occurred to you, by the way, to do any outside sleuthing at all, or d'you intend to spend the rest of your days wearing out Mrs. Penrose's most comfortable chair?"

At that Hanson got up, still muttering, and slashed out of the house with much slamming and banging and thumping. His men followed more leisurely, both grinning broadly. I gathered that Aunt Agatha had made friends of them by her display of pseudo-temperament, even if Hanson was her enemy for life.

"A very pretty piece of pitching, Miss Penrose." Half the doctor's smile was appreciation, and the other half sheer pride in his alliterative sentence. "You were entirely right. A little show of feminine violence always goes farther than polite pleading and withering sarcasm. Nothing balks a man more than to have a woman throw something at him—and hit him! Whole trouble is, Hanson's promotion's gone to his head. Whippersnapper! Never did have any use for him, not after the way he treated Asey last spring. And Asey got him his stripes, too. Let him take all the credit for the Frost business over at Sandbar. I'm speechless, Bev, just speechless!"

"Say, Bev," Giles, who had been busy groveling in

the fireplace, stood up and held out the pieces of the broken vase, "I can mend this all right, so you don't have to feel bad—"

"Dear boy," I said, "it was a wedding present from Kyle's fourth cousin in Des Moines, and I've been dying to find a legitimate excuse for breaking it these twelve years. Thank you, my aunt—you wretch," I added, as I watched the corners of her mouth turn up, "you heard me moaning over it yesterday! Doctor, did you call Asey? I assume you did, but with that man scattering questions like confetti, I've had no chance to ask."

"I called Asey Mayo just two split seconds after I found that wound," the doctor replied. "He's off somewhere, because we couldn't rouse him. But the girl in the phone office promised to ring him every five minutes, calling in order every other place he might possibly be, in between times. He'll get here sooner or later. But I want—"

The front door opened, and Jo Dwight, her cheeks glowing and her brown eyes throwing off sparks, strode into the room and planted a huge wicker hamper at my feet.

"Those asses!" she said, tossing her scarlet beret deftly on the head of Kyle's bronze bust of Napoleon, "I've been spitting tacks at that sergeant for hours. Seemed like hours, anyway. He's that same chip on the shoulder that's always stopping me for speeding—Bev, isn't this all ghastly? Mother's taken to her bed, she's that worked up—but that's a long story. Anyway, I remembered you said Katy was taking to-night off, so I cleaned out the ice box and Martha dolled the mess up—look, am I getting in your hair, and d'you want me to leave, or may I sit in the corner like a mouse and hear all?"

Giles's stern-and-rockbound-coast look came over his face as Jo rattled on. He never did understand her vivid good looks or her vivid, expressive language, and I knew it would be some time before he let her mother's outburst against Dave retire from his thoughts.

Jo felt his unspoken disapproval, and bit her full red underlip.

"Don't look daggers at me, Giles!" she lighted a cigarette with fingers that shook. "And don't be so funereal. I know what you think about mother, but I don't agree with her and you should know it. And I understand what's happened, and I feel as badly as you do. I loved Uncle Dave more than any of the real uncles nature foisted on me, and since Kay—oh, dear, it's like trying to explain relativity to a bathtub! Bev, tell me!"

"My dear," I said, "I've told the estimable Hanson a million times and it still doesn't make sense. I—"

"The stuff in the hamper," she interrupted, "is food. You know. Stuff you eat. Like drumsticks and sponge cakes and coffee in a thermos. Snare some before you get going."

"What happened," I took out a packet of sandwiches, "won't really take long to tell. And maybe you, with a fresh open mind and a sane viewpoint, can grasp it. It's just so many words to me, now. I can rattle 'em off like 'Thanatopsis' or 'The quality of mercy is not strained'—"

So, between bites, I told it over again.

"And," I wound up, "strange as it may appear, Jo, Giles and Aunt Agatha and I all concluded that Dave had shot himself. We didn't—and this slew Hanson— we didn't look to see if he'd been shot, poisoned, stabbed, gassed or hanged. We just thought, in our simple fashion, that he'd committed suicide. We called the doctor. Dave died before he got there. And the doctor found out, believe it or not, that Dave had *not* been shot!"

"But Bev!"

"Just so. Dave had been stabbed in the back by some person or persons unknown. After still more travail, Hanson has figured out that the person who did the stabbing must have been inside the house, because there's a rip in the screen door—"

"Should think Dave would have heard it," Jo commented. "I mean, heard the knife go through the screen before—"

"Perhaps he may have," the doctor told her, "but of course it would all have happened in a split second. And there wouldn't have been any time for him to have done anything about it. Chances are, if he heard any noise of the screen tearing, he would have thought it was Sully sharpening his claws. Go on, Bev."

"Well, there must have been someone in the doorway behind Dave. I didn't see anyone, because I was sitting down most of the time, except for a minute or so that I pulled a couple of branches of the hedge apart. Didn't look for anyone then, naturally. Neither did Aunt. Giles didn't see anyone any part of the time. You see, it was brand new copper screening, and sort of glared—"

"Besides," Giles interrupted, "I wasn't looking for anyone lurking behind the door, any more than the others were. And honest, the more I think of it, the more I don't understand any of it at all. I never saw a soul. And from where I was sitting, you could see everything. No one could have come through Bev's driveway without us seeing, no one could have gone through the hedge without our knowing, and I'd have noticed anyone going towards Dave's house from the left or right. Only place I couldn't see would be directly behind the house, and you go about fifty yards, and there's that swampy low garden that leads to the swamp, and no one could cross that. And since Bev's drive is the only way to come to Dave's by land, I'm thinking the person must have come by boat."

I sighed. That was another point we'd gone over, ad infinitum and ad nauseam. Hanson and Giles agreed on the idea, and I thought it was silly.

"Why someone had to come while you were watching," I said wearily, "is still beyond me. Why couldn't it have been someone who came to the house this morning, or yesterday morning? Any time you please. Someone who just came, and stayed. After we found Dave, we didn't do any looking around for murderers. A battalion of people might have sneaked around the house and left the place, by boat or plane or anything, while we were out there with Dave, and we'd never have noticed them. God in heaven, we weren't thinking about murderers!

We were thinking about Dave! And then, Giles, while
you and Eleo—I mean, you *did* get down from the tree,
once, and you weren't watching like a hawk *all* the
time!"

Jo scratched the tip of her nose, a habit of hers whenever she's really puzzled.

"Why'd Dave's gun go off?" she demanded. "Was
he shooting at someone? Or at one of your skunks or
something? Or just for fun? I don't get it!"

"Do you," the doctor inquired, with his mouth full
of apple turnover, "think *we* do? Anyway, to add my bit,
I can tell you that Dave wasn't shot, but stabbed, and
stabbed with terrific force. I can't see how the man lived
the few minutes he did. And I think the knife was one
of those hunting knives—the kind Simeon Smalley buys
by the gross, like every other hardware dealer around
here. Not a thin blade, at all. Need a lot of force to drive
it the way this was driven. And of course, there's no sign
of the knife. That gripes brother Hanson a lot, too. He
always wants a weapon littered with fingerprints right
plunk on the scene, so's to give him a nice start."

"How about footprints?" Jo asked. "What about
hunting Dave's place for tracks of someone else? Did
they do that?"

"Hanson looked the house over in a perfunctory
fashion," I informed her, "and phoned for some sort of
print experts and photographers. Then he left a man
there and moved us all over here. Dave's house was cold-
ish, and everyone in this country seems to know that we

had an oil burner put in last week. Deary me, I wish Asey would hurry up and get here!"

"Asey? Look," Jo said seriously, "who is this Asey, this admirable Crichton, this general Mr. Fix-it? I've never dared ask, not after the things I've asked about and got yelped at for—"

"Everyone knows Asey." Giles spoke with finality, insinuating by his tone that anyone who didn't was more of a chump than he had suspected.

"They said that about the snipe hunt," Jo remarked sadly, "and they said even louder and funnier things about qua-qua—quahaugs not being clams."

"No." Giles corrected her. "It's clams not being quahaugs—"

Jo looked at him. "Don't! It's like beer on wine I must decline, or wine on beer—or something. I never remember and regret both anyway. I'll learn the Cape Cod language and customs as the years roll on. I'm already calling lakes ponds, and sometimes I only have to think as little as ten or fifteen minutes when someone lands me at another strip of beach and says, 'Now where's Boston from here?' But tell me about Asey Mayo. I admit it's like standing on Thirty-fourth Street and asking where the Empire State is, but tell me anyway—"

"But the Empire State *is*—" Giles began.

"Let it pass, cousin," I said. "We haven't time. Tell her about Asey."

"His great-great-grandfather," Giles began briskly, "married my mother's great-great-grandmother. She was a Freeman, and—"

"What he means, Jo," I didn't dare let Giles go completely genealogical on us, "is that he and Asey call each other cousin in much the same way Giles and I do. Also, I'm related to Asey through the Higgins family, and from that you ought to be able to gather gently that Asey is a real Cape Codder. He talks and looks more like one than Giles does. He's been a sailor, and a mechanic, and he—"

"Drives a Porter sixteen roadster," Giles took up the recital. "Used to pretend to work for Bill Porter and his folks. He's got plenty of money, but he likes to tinker around. Why, sometimes, he—"

"Sometimes he cuts my lawns," I said, "and sometimes he carpenters with his cousin Syl, and—well, the big point is, he's solved five cases the police couldn't. Why, Jo, he's famous as a detective! You must have heard all about him!"

"And he wears corduroys and a Stetson," the doctor didn't give Jo a chance to speak, "and a hunting jacket —oh, know him, do you?"

Jo turned red, and seemed embarrassed for the first time since I'd known her. "I—no. No, I was thinking of something else. He sounds amazing."

"He is," the doctor assured her. "He's a combination of Scheherazade and David Harum, and he's got a mind like a steel trap. Oh, I could talk about Asey all night long, but you have to know the man. He—"

"How old is he?" Jo demanded.

"No one knows," Cummings shrugged. "Least of all do I. He looks forty, moves like a younger man, and— Lord, I wish he'd come and settle this business!"

"You don't honestly think," Jo emptied the ash trays again, "that he'll be able to step in and say, 'So-and-so's the guilty one,' like a book or something, do you?"

The four of us, in unison, said that we did.

"No doubt about it," the doctor said confidently. "No doubt at all. Sooner or later, that is. And certainly he'll get places before Hanson does."

Jo smiled. "I hope he lives up to your ideas of him, but from what you've told me, I'd say your jack-of-all-trades was going to be in a tough spot for any lo-and-behold-business. Yessiree, as Giles says, it's going to be a case of 'Asey Adverse'—"

She stopped as Giles held up his hand.

"That's the Porter horn," he said excitedly. "Hear—yup. He's coming up the drive. I'll go—"

"Wait and let him get the story all at once," I suggested. "Let's see if we can't give him a decently connected narrative, not just a burst of littered phrases. We have, God knows, time enough."

Giles, with rather bad grace, went back to his chair. We heard the roadster stop, then the knocker sounded Asey's pet knock. "All po-licemen have big feet!"—Rat-tata-tata-tat—Tat—TAT—T-A-T! And then Asey came into the living room.

He was dressed as I knew he would be, in corduroys and a heavy duck hunting coat with countless pockets, and in one hand he gripped one of the biggest lobsters I've ever seen.

"All yours, Bev," he said cheerfully. "I been outside lobsterin' with Nate— 'Do, Miss Penrose, hi, Doc. Hi,

Giles—" He looked briefly at Jo, and a flicker of a smile passed over his face. Then he turned to me. "What's wrong, Bev?" he asked quietly. "Nothin's happened to the boys, or Kyle?"

I shook my head. "Not—"

"By all that's holy," Cummings cried out, "d'you mean that you came here of your own accord? You don't know—haven't *any* of those phone calls hit you anywhere?"

"Nope." Asey sat down on the couch. "But I can tell—huh. I thought that was Hanson's car down the road. Begin at the beginnin', Bev."

I told the story again, a longer and more nearly complete version than I'd given Jo. When I finished, Giles added his bit, Aunt Agatha delivered hers, and then the doctor polished off the story with his few remarks.

"Poor Dave," Asey said. "An'—huh. Let's see. Dave's land comes off yours just like the thumb of your right hand. Only half a thumb, I guess. Your hedge runs like the line of your forefinger carried straight down to your wrist. The cliff's off the first joint. Can't get to his house legal-like, 'less you go through Bev's drive. None of you seen anyone. Well, prob'ly the someone who was in the house been there some time. Might of used your drive, might of come by boat. Sim Smalley's cousin Ike can tell us all about that. Where was old Step'n-go-fetchit? Wan't he workin' over to Dave's to-day?"

"Jethro? He was digging potatoes. I saw him all the time in the back garden," Giles said. "He couldn't have gone near the house without my knowing. You can tell his walk a mile off."

"Swayin' like a dory in a no'theaster," Asey said with a chuckle. "An' he's so dum, all fired deaf! Anyone told him yet? He'll feel bad. He liked Dave. Used to snap back at the town talk."

"One of Hanson's men bellowed the news to him half a dozen times," the doctor said. "It was a high spot of the afternoon. Bev told him to stay over at Dave's till Hanson's experts got through, and all, and then to bring Sully over. Miss Penrose's going to take Sully and keep him."

Asey smiled. "That's what she thinks. Won't be a week, Miss Ag'tha, before Sully's keepin' you. Very demandin', that cat. I know. I got him for Dave. One of Skim Milk's kittens—oho, I hear Jet comin'."

"Skim Milk?" Jo asked, as Jethro limped into the room, with Sully in his arms.

"Can't be beat," Asey explained, and turned to Jethro.

I suppose, in his way, Jet is more famous than Asey; he has a wooden leg, one of the old-fashioned wooden peglegs, and with his stubble of black beard, he looks pretty much like a movie conception of Long John Silver. Newcomers to the Cape, new summer people and the great crowd of artists, all go mad over him. He's been painted at least three times by every sort, class or species of artist that exists, and as everything from "Davy Jones" and "Moby Dick" to "St. Thomas Aquinas"—that was just a portrait, without the wooden leg, and as "Peter,

Peter, Punkin Eater." The last was done by a cubist with a hare lip.

Anyway, artists and newcomers go crazy over Jet, and they've talked so much about what a picturesque salty character he is that sometimes he believes it himself. But natives and semi-natives like me, and dyed in the wool summer people, are all inclined to see the funny side. Actually Jet has never set foot inside a boat, rarely strayed more than a hundred miles off the Cape, and lost his leg in a very commonplace way; a horse car ran over him some thirty years ago while he was on a binge in Boston. At first he had a very respectable-looking substitute leg, the sort of thing you'd call an artificial limb. When the artists began coming to the Cape, though, Jethro got his pegleg, and a lot of fancy tattooing on his chest for additional flavor, and he's cashed in on both ever since. In the fall, when the artists scatter, Jethro goes back to being an ordinary gardener and man of all work. During the tourist season, he's a landmark along with the Town Pump and the wreck of the "Jefferson" on the back shore.

"Can I stay in your woodshed to-night?" Jethro asked me as Sully made for the fireplace. "Heavy fog comin' up, an' I don't want to walk all the way over to my shack. B'sides, I ain't had time to git in my Franklin stove yet, an' b'sides, I'll be able to start in work for you early to-morrer. Ain't it awful about Mr. Truman? What say? I didn't get that."

"You can sleep over the garage," I howled. "It *is* awful about Mr. Truman, isn't it?"

I said it three times, and then Jethro got out his trumpet, and Asey finally made him understand.

"My golly!" Asey was hoarse by the time Jet left, "it's pretty nerve-rackin' to carry on any lengthy conv'-sation with him, ain't it? Just small talk wears me out. Well, to get back, you know what I think? I think some-one was hidden in Dave's house, an' I sort of got a feelin' —y'see, I had a long talk with Dave last week. He called me over an' said he was sort of scared—"

"What?"

"Yup. 'Bout a lot of things. Kay's death, for one. He didn't think she killed herself, or that it was an ac'dent. An' he said someone was follerin' him around. He thought, an' I think maybe he was right, that it was some crank that'd lost money in Truman an' Comp'ny. You know, the sort of feller that sends fake bombs to the pres'-dent, an' threatenin' letters to prom'nent folks when he gets mad at anythin'. Dave'd got a lot of threats, but he said he thought there wasn't much use to worry about anyone that'd warn you with threats. It was the fellers that wouldn't that made him nervous. First off I'm goin' to call Bill Porter's brother Jimmy. He was one of Dave's board of d'rectors, an' he can get hold of what Dave called their crank list. See if we can't get somewheres there while we're doin' other things here. Other things right now bein' Ike Smalley. He's spent half his life with a pair of binoculars lookin' out over the bay—"

"Why?" Jo asked interestedly.

Asey grinned. "Hadn't nothin' else to do, an' I guess it seemed as nice a life work as any. Anyhows, he can maybe tell us if they was anyone scurryin' around in boats on the other side of the cliff, or near Dave's landin' there, 'cause he's usually down to his fish house on Thursdays. Cranks was Dave's hunch, an' it's as good a hunch as any. Course, ain't no tellin' what Hanson'll think of, now his headsize's increased. He'll be sore if I seem to butt in, too. Got to go at things easy, but I can't set back an' let Dave's—well, I'll be startin'.'"

"Can I come with you?" Giles asked. "I want to see dad and tell—"

"I'll tell him. Rather you'd park here with Bev. Got to go, Doc? Well, I'm goin' to stay over here a few days. Drop in when you can. Bev, draw your curtains, please, an' lock your doors—"

"Asey, don't be silly! What on earth for?"

"'Cause, if they's a crank around, I want you safe. Told Kyle I'd look after you, too," he added. "An' I bet we hear plenty from him when he—well, Pegleg'll be in the garage, an' Giles here till I get back, an' Miss Dwight's goin' to get in her car now, an' I'm goin' to trail her home."

Jo started to protest, but she didn't. Crushing on her scarlet beret, she walked to the door.

"Ready, sir," she said. "And who, may I ask, is going to protect you?"

"I'm proof," Asey told her with a grin. "Lots of folks has tried to do away with me, but none of 'em's been successful yet. Cape Codders don't die, you know. They just dry up an' blow away."

Giles and Aunt Agatha and I stood shivering in the

doorway while Asey put Jo into her car, slammed the door and exchanged a few good nights with the doctor. The fog was rolling in, and the air was damp and cold.

"You'd better put up the top to your car," I called out, as Asey slid behind the wheel of his long roadster. "It's no—"

The rest of the words froze somewhere on the roof of my mouth.

A shot rang out, and Asey slumped forward over the wheel. With the meager aid of the electric lantern above my head, I watched him, too stunned to move, as he slid limply sideways to the floor of the car.

CHAPTER THREE

I DON'T know who reached the roadster first, but Giles, Jo, Dr. Cummings and I swarmed over the seat like one big locust.

To my, and everyone else's blank and utter amazement, Asey spoke. Softly, almost in a whisper, but there was a hint of laughter in his voice.

"I ain't even touched, but you pretend so, hard! Not goin' to have any afterthoughtin'. Doc, you'n Giles carry me in. Bev, you'n the girl fuss around real anxious. Miss Ag'tha, take your hank'chief an' hold it to my side."

We didn't have to pretend very hard. Jo and I were excited and fuddled enough to twit around in circles without half trying, and even Agatha's cucumber coolness seemed to have thawed. Giles and the doctor had their hands literally full with Asey; he let himself slump, and his head rolled weakly from side to side. I found myself thinking that it was really a more convincing scene than the actual murder in the afternoon.

The doctor and Giles, both very red in the face, started to put Asey on the couch before the fire, but he jerked one finger toward my bedroom. I rushed in ahead, pulled down the shades and drew the curtains, and the men dumped him on my bed.

"Sure," Cummings's panting breaths sounded like the first hot air engine we'd had to pump water for the house at North Weesit, "sure you're okay, Asey? Lord, you can weigh a ton when you—say, are you sure you're all right?"

Gingerly, Asey removed his hunting coat, and looked thoughtfully at the hole in the left shoulder.

"I'm okay," he assured us. "Huh. Miss Dwight, they was a second there when I wondered if I hadn't sort of bragged too much about my charmed life. Luck—whew! Y'know, the seat adjustment on that car's a flop. I've told Bill Porter a thousand times he'd ought to change it. Anyhow, when I slid in behind that wheel, that seat bobbed forward. Just b'fore I shifted, I leaned forward a mite to get hold of the lever, so's to slide the seat back. N'en, in just that second, just that second I leaned, that bullet thudded into the seat b'hind me. If I'd been leanin' back, it'd of gone plumb through what you might call my vital portions. Huh. This is worse'n the time the 'Nellie K. Piper's' cook went nuts an' started hackin' around reckless at folks with an ax in either hand. Least, you could see him comin'. But this—nope, I don't like this. Nosiree-bob!"

"Who did it? Shouldn't I go see if I could find who did it?" Giles demanded. "I—"

"Don't know who 'twas, Giles, but I wouldn't advise huntin' him right now. Ever see a rabbit pop out of his hole to 'vestigate a gun shot that he didn't get regretful real quick? Well, you just stay right in your hole."

"But shouldn't we call Hanson over from Dave's? And why'd you have us carry you in? And—"

"I sort of think," Asey said quizzically, "that Hanson won't shed much light. If I know him, he's prob'ly got a headache already. An' I had you carry me in, b'cause if ole Shot-in-the-dark seen I was all right, it was just hum'nly poss'ble it might irritate him into shootin' again, an' you can't count on more'n one miracle a day. There are some times when I don't care a lot for this world, but I got a kind of long, lingerin' desire to stay in it as long as I can."

"But why should the person who killed Dave want to kill you?" Giles demanded. "Why—"

"What makes you think it's the same feller? Doc said Dave was killed by a huntin' knife. Most anyone with a strong arm could have stabbed him in the back, but who ever shot me was a pretty cool hand, an' a darn sight better shot. I—y'know, an' almighty thunderin's thought's come to me. Pegleg's brother, Nehemiah Black, used to be a fancy shooter with Barnum an' Bailey's. An' they was a time, b'fore his accident, that Jethro used to help him. Used to be a real fancy trick shot. Still is the best shot I know of in this part of the Cape—"

"You *can't* mean you think that limping, deaf old haddock—why, Asey, he may *look* sinister, but you can't possibly think—"

"Right now, Bev, I ain't thinkin' much anyhows," Asey said. "I'm still too busy offerin' silent prayers of gratitude. Huh. Let's see. Let's do some mullin'. That shot come from the bushes to the left of you an' Giles, an' Miss Ag'tha, Bev, as you three stood on the doorstep. Either there, or still more left. Not very far, or the bullet'd of gone through the windshield. Um. Left side of your house's got a dinin' room door—"

"Then you can easily tell if Jethro came out of it," I said. "The door and the steps were painted only this morning. The Logan boy did it, and the paint won't be dry, not with the fog."

"Um. Pegleg know it was painted? Oh, he got the paint for you. Well, they's the garage doors—"

"And both of 'em padlocked on the outside," I told him triumphantly. "We haven't had either car out to-day. And as for the kitchen door, on the other side of the house, that's been stuck tighter than a drum ever since the storm. You've wrestled with that door yourself, and you ought to know that when it sticks, it sticks for at least a week."

"Just the samey," Asey said, "s'pose you go look around quiet like, Giles. See where Pegleg's keepin' himself. Don't rouse him particular, but if you can make it take a peek at his leg. It's wet out underfoot, an' loam sticks."

The very thought of Asey suspecting Jethro, who's done odd jobs for me for years, looked after the twins, and spent any number of nights in my woodshed or over the garage—the very thought of it hit me like a ton of bricks. In a sense it shocked me more than Dave's death or Asey's near murder. Somehow our conversation pro and con Dave's bad breaks had taken the sharpest edge off his death. And although it doesn't sound quite right, it was a relief to know that he had not killed himself. I really hadn't been much moved by Asey's talk about cranks, and though the shock of seeing Asey slump after that gun shot was terrific, his miraculous escape had cancelled that bad moment.

Now the whole wretched business was coming home with a vengeance. For the first time I began to think of the hullabaloo that would follow—newspaper reporters milling about, still more Truman headlines, inquests, courtroom scenes, more of Hanson's infernal questions. I fell rather than sat on the cushioned window seat.

"Jethro!" I said weakly. "But we *know* Jet, Asey! Why, he's someone we know!"

Aunt Agatha gave me a cigarette and lighted one herself.

"Probably," she observed, "the smallest town murderer in Timbuctoo has friends, Bev. After all, my cousin Ruth Blake once went to school with Lizzie Borden."

"And Creel Friar," Jo added, "once spent the night in the same tourist camp with Dillinger. You—you can't tell who may get mixed up in this before it's over and done with."

"Yes," I said, feeling rather nettled, "but Jethro— Asey, he couldn't have had anything to do with Dave's death! Giles saw him up in the potato patch all the time he was looking around, from the tree. And Jethro never came *near* the house!"

Asey admitted that it might not work out at all.

"Maybe he didn't have a thing to do with what happened to Dave. But far's this evenin's concerned, Pegleg happens to be the only expert shot around that we happen to know about. Well, Giles?"

Giles reported that the garage doors were padlocked from the outside, that the paint on the dining room door and steps was still wet and sticky and without sign of footprints, and the kitchen door still refused to budge.

"Jethro's up in bed in the garage loft," he concluded. "I turned on the light and asked him if he was all right. His leg's hung up over the wall bracket—looked all right to me. And besides that, Asey, he was up in the potato patch all afternoon. He didn't come near Dave's house till long after Hanson got there."

Asey pulled out a villainous looking corncob pipe.

"Well," he said, "seems silly now, but it was a good long shot. Huh. Well, I'll get on to what I was goin' to do b'fore the explosion occurred. I s'pose I can phone Jimmy Porter about that crank list from here, an' call Ike about who was out this way in boats just as easy as seein' him. Rest of the things I had in my mind can wait till to-morrow. Somehow I ain't got much of a hankerin' to go outdoors again to-night. I—"

"I can't see," Jo interrupted, "why you don't make some effort to find out who fired that shot. It seems to me you should call Hanson and have his merry men—"

"Scour the neighborhood?" Asey suggested. "Like they do in the papers? 'P'lice scoured the neighborhood with riot guns an' searchlights for a man with a black mustache.' I wonder, Miss Dwight, if you'd linger in a

neighborhood after shootin' at someone the way someone shot at me to-night? Prob'ly before you got out of
your car, an' the doc got out of his, an' the three others
come down from the top step, that feller was on his way.
I know I'd be. Take an av'rage runner just about fifty
seconds to get to the lane, ten more to get into a car an'
be off. An' he knew he was safe for a couple minutes,
'cause it was only human nature for all of you to see how
I was. If Giles, say, had spotted where the gun was shot
from, an' dashed then, he might of stood a chance of
gettin' the guy. Not much of a chance even then, with
the fog. I sort of yearned to do some dashin' myself, but
it didn't seem such a sterlin' thought when you 'plied
common sense. R'minds me of old Reuben Snow; Rube
used to jump headlong out of the nearest window every
time he caught his wife even glancin' at the rollin' pin.
After he busted his right leg three times, ole Doc Stone
asked him why he kept the custom up. 'Matter of self-
pres'vation,' Rube says. 'I got two legs but only one head.'
I—what's the matter, Miss Ag'tha?"

Before answering, Aunt Agatha carefully knocked
my work basket off the table with such force that the
entire floor was frosted with a mess of spools, and hooks
and eyes, and pieces of elastic, and odd buttons, and hideously gnawed stockings of all lengths and colors.

"There seems," she said placidly, as she knelt down
to help salvage, "there seems to be—and don't any of you
dare look up, now that I've taken this stringent method of
getting you all out of range and on the floor—seems to
be a face firmly glued to the window nearest the bath-

room. In the crack where the curtain stuck out, and the drapes were pulled away toward the center of the window. Jo, scramble for that pink silk that rolled under the bed, and don't dare crane your neck. What's to be done, Asey?"

"Has he seen me?"

"Don't think so, from that angle. What a mercy that Bev and I spent yesterday rearranging all the furniture out of sheer boredom! You'd be shot at again if the bed was in its old place. Any suggestions?"

"Sure it's not one of Hanson's men?"

"From what little I could see," Agatha said, "he looked like a fox terrier. Ferrety. I'm sure it's not any of the police I saw. I don't suppose you have a gun?"

"Nary a gun. Bev, have you?"

"Top drawer of the bureau," I said. "I'll be in sight, but I can ostensibly be getting a handkerchief. And then what?"

"Then Giles takes it, sticks it in a pitcher, and goes in the bathroom. Don't put on the lights, run the water loud, an' creep into the other bedroom. See if you can snake out the east window an' circle round on him—but no risks! Any sign of trouble, an' you fall down an' play dead dog like I did. You're too valuable to the Hopkins fam'ly. An'—"

"How would it do," Agatha asked, "if I were to slip upstairs and observe?"

"Fine. An' the doc can cover the front of the house. I'd say to call Hanson at Dave's, but Bev's phone rings like a fire alarm, an' she'd have to ring it to call up.

Scatter an' be careful an' do your best. I feel like a shirker, lyin' here, but I got what you might call a gen'ral r'luctance to get in the line of that feller's fire again to-night."

Jo and I, with the perspiration oozing gently on our foreheads, continued to pick up spools and needles as Giles, with the revolver in a Wedgwood pitcher, started into the bathroom. The doctor stood beside Asey, still on the bed, and Agatha, with a towel over her arm for atmosphere, made her way jauntily out into the hall.

The water in the bathroom tap began to cascade, and I remember hoping that the electric engine, always a variable and eccentric performer, wouldn't choose that time to show off.

"I can feel those ferrety eyes," Jo mumbled. "They're boring into the seat of my shorts, the old fox terrier!"

I could feel the eyes boring, too. It was definitely awful. Worse than having people on subways stare at your feet, or at the tip of your ear. Worse than the time I'd subbed for Kyle at a lecture and known suddenly in the middle of it that my slip was coming off. Four hundred eyes, then, had watched its descent, a thousandth of an inch at a time. But none of the four hundred had a gun in his hand—

Outside there was a thud and a crash, and Asey and the doctor leaped out of the room. Jo and I scurried after them; it would of course have been far simpler to have raised the shade, pushed aside the curtain and looked out, but wild horses and a threat of the Iron Maiden wouldn't have driven me to doing that. I'm not an abject coward, but I felt, with Asey, that it was a matter of self-preservation.

As we rounded the corner of the house, Giles steamed up from the rear. Asey and the doctor were standing over a crumpled figure outside the bedroom window.

"How'd you manage to lay him out, Giles?" Asey inquired.

Giles shook his head. "I didn't, Asey! I heard the crash just as I managed to crawl out—Bev, you certainly have your screens in to stay! Who—how—"

"I'm afraid," Agatha appeared on the scene, "I'm afraid I'm to blame. I got the window open—there wasn't any screen up there, and he was standing right in the shaft of light below. I—well, I'd just stumbled over it, and I really, as I told Hanson this afternoon, I really hurl things with what borders on uncanny accuracy."

Asey leaned over, picked up from the ground a triangular piece of earthenware with a handle still attached, and proceeded to laugh till I thought he'd never stop. All of us, except Giles, joined him. Giles had to fit three more pieces together before he got the general idea.

"Oh," he said. "Oh. A—a chamber!"

Asey wiped his eyes with the back of his hand.

"Miss Ag'tha," he said, "if you can lick Hanson with a vase, an' this feller with a chamber, I'd just like to give you a set of two-three hundred pieces an' watch you 'lim'nate public enemies. It's—oho. He's comin' round. Lift him up, Giles, an' we'll take him in."

They put him on the couch in front of the fireplace,

and we all got in the doctor's way while he neatly affixed iodine and plaster in clearly indicated spots.

It rather disappointed me to find that even in the glare of the three lights focussed on him, the little man didn't look a bit gangsterish or crankish or ferrety. His face was small and pointed, which undeniably accounted for Agatha's fox terrier label, but otherwise he wasn't at all menacing.

"For the love of mud!" Jo said disgustedly. "He's the spitting image of my Uncle Bert! Yes, sir. Reindeer toe nail or whatever it is on his watch chain, pince-nez on a black ribbon, one slightly ecru front tooth—I'll wager he's got two needle pointed pencils in his vest pocket and a black book with addresses, and a flap of matches besides a cigar lighter! Bev, it's—"

"But I don't smoke," the little man said plaintively. "I—oh, dear, my head!"

There wasn't anything sinister about his voice, either. I placed it mentally as suburban Boston, about fifteen miles out.

Asey reached into the man's breast pocket and brought out a well worn, and very thin wallet, and a black address book—

"With addresses, even," Jo said triumphantly, looking over Asey's shoulder. "I knew it!"

"Includin' his," Asey said. "With—say, with all these cards, you'd ought to be able to get one insurance comp'ny out of the bunch to pay for that bump, mister, 'less they sp'cifically state that large earthenware vessels is excluded. Well, Mr. Luther Charles Grosgrain—"

"That," Agatha said firmly, "is carrying it too far, Asey Mayo!"

"I ain't kiddin'," Asey protested. "That's what it says. Mr. Luther Charles Grosgrain of Dolphin Avenue— five foot three, blue eyes, gray hair, born—let's see. He's fifty-nine years old. Single. In case of accident, notify Walker, Adams, Meredith, Jones and Levy. Huh. One at a time, or all five together?"

Mr. Grosgrain sat up rather groggily, and I didn't in the least blame him for the way he looked at us.

"You don't need to notify the firm," he said. "I—I'll come—I'll be all right in a minute. It—it was very good of you to take me in. I—I really don't know what happened. All of a sudden something seemed to—why, a black cloud just descended on me."

That, of course, set us off again.

"Fund'mentally," Asey said, "you're wrong, but I can see where you might of got that impression. Honest, is your name Grosgrain?"

"I am the fourth of my family, the fourth Luther Grosgrain, in this country," the little man announced with pride.

Jo was the only one who didn't laugh at that. After all, Asey and Giles and Aunt Agatha and I all had pretty well-established families on Cape Cod twelve or thirteen generations ago. The very house we were in has been in my family over one hundred and fifty years.

"I'm afraid," Asey said in response to Mr. Grosgrain's lifted eyebrows and hurt expression, "that's a sort of a Cape Cod joke. Now, would it be troublin' you too much

to ask you to tell us just why you happen to be playin'
Peepin' Tom outside Mrs. Penrose's window?"

"Why, why, but I wasn't!"

"Your face and your wounds," Agatha observed, "are
distinctly against you. You've been staring outside that
window for easily half an hour."

"It couldn't be that long—I—well, to tell you the
truth, I was on my way to see Mr. David Truman. I had
directions, but I must have become confused. I got to
what I thought was Mr. Truman's house, and two men
yelled at me and started running after me. I thought I was
in the wrong place, and—well, when some one runs after
you, yelling, and cursing, you just naturally—why, you
run, too!"

"An' you run here?" Asey asked. He was using his
suavest tones, and I felt sorry for Mr. Grosgrain. When
Asey butters his voice, he's carefully and elegantly laying
a methodical trap.

"Just so, just so. I—my previous experience had
frightened me, and I thought before I knocked that I'd—
well, that I'd investigate. You all seemed," he rather ac-
cented the word, "you seemed such friendly looking people, that I thought I'd come in and ask you the way to
Mr. Truman's."

"Didn't you take rather a long time makin' up your
mind?" Asey asked.

"Why—"

"It was my shorts," Jo said. "I told you, Bev. Just
like Uncle Bert."

"You a stockholder of Truman an' Comp'ny?" Asey demanded.

"Yes," Mr. Grosgrain said sadly. "Yes, I was. But it wasn't that which brought me here to see Mr. Truman. I had written him several letters about my hobby, asking if I—but I do not see why I should tell you all my affairs. I'm—very grateful to you for caring for me, and perhaps you'll be good enough to tell me where Mr. Truman lives?"

"We'll take you there," Asey promised. "I—oh, you was the feller that wrote him about takin' pictures of—" Asey hesitated, "um. His rock garden, wasn't it?"

"It was the cliff." Mr. Grosgrain bit. "I'd seen pictures of it in the paper, and they said the cliff belonged to him. It seemed to me, from what I'd read, that the cliff might possibly be the original home of the Weesit Indians. I've some very interesting papers about the Weesit Indians that a friend of mine left me in his will, and now that I'm retired, I spend a great portion of my time working on those papers. It is my hope to complete his work."

"Oh, then you've r'tired from," Asey consulted the card, "from Walker, Adams, Meredith, Jones an' Levy?"

"I worked for them forty-five years," Mr. Grosgrain told him proudly. "I began as an errand boy when I was—"

"An' worked up to head bookkeeper," Asey said. "Yup. Don't ask me how I knew. You have a lot of Truman stock?"

"The failure of Truman and Company," Mr. Grosgrain admitted, "rather seriously affected my income. But as I told Mr. Truman in my letter, it seemed to me that the fault was definitely not his. Now, if you will be good enough to show me to Mr. Truman's house?"

There was a certain simple dignity about his request and about the little man himself which rather made me ashamed of the way we'd treated him. I felt, as I had about Jethro, that Asey had definitely made a mistake. His story was sound, told without hesitation, and it was just silly enough to be true. At least, it went with the man. He actually did look like a retired bookkeeper with a yen for delving into the innermost secrets of the Weesit Indians. He didn't look one bit like anyone who'd stab Dave Truman or shoot at Asey from a clump of pyrus japonica.

There was only one thing about him which bothered me; he kept his right hand in his coat pocket, and he seemed to be clutching something with all his strength. I could see his arm muscles—well, they weren't exactly leaping, because Mr. Grosgrain didn't have the physique for leaping muscles. At all events, they moved. And curiously enough, Asey didn't appear to notice it at all.

"My mother," Asey informed him, "had an Indian nurse. I got a lot of things over at my house at Wellfleet that I think might interest you. Delilah—that was the Indian's name—was a c'nverted Meth'dist, an' from what I heard tell of her, she wa'n't one of them slim Indian maidens you read about. Quite sizable, Delilah was, an' she had—no, don't bother—" Asey, pipe in hand, reached over Mr. Grosgrain for the bowl of matches. "I—oh, thanks."

But he didn't take the matches. Instead he held Mr. Grosgrain's right wrist in a grip of iron, stuck his pipe in my hand, reached into Mr. Grosgrain's right coat pocket and brought forth an automatic pistol.

"Deary me," he said. "I thought you was goin' to hang onto this till—it was such a nice story, an' for a time you had me goin', Mr. Grosgrain. Now, just for fun, explain away this gun, an' tell us where the bullet went—just what you shot at with the one that seems to be missin'—"

CHAPTER FOUR

MR. GROSGRAIN'S eyes blinked and his mouth quivered and he made gurgling noises in his throat.

"Go on," Asey said. "Git to it. Who was you shootin' at?"

"But the gun isn't mine!"

"Ah," Asey said. "Just keepin' it for a friend while he went to get a cup of coffee, huh?"

"But it isn't mine! It isn't! And," he unsuccessfully attempted a show of spirit, "and even if it is, what business is it of yours?"

Asey released Mr. Grosgrain's wrist and moved back to his seat by the fire. Perching the pistol on his knee, he lighted his pipe.

"You heard me!" Mr. Grosgrain bristled a little more. "What business is it of yours?"

Asey, smiling faintly, puffed at his pipe.

"I'm not going to stand for any more of this nonsense!" Mr. Grosgrain rose somewhat unsteadily. "I'm going to leave!"

"You ain't goin' to leave now," Asey said in conversational tones, "b'cause your head's buzzin' like a hive of bees, an' you know 'tis. Just set down. Does it seem to you that I'd be delvin' into your comin's an' goin's without reason, Mr. Grosgrain, or does it seem to you that I'm a reas'n'bly sane sort?"

"I—why, you're all right, I suppose." The little man sat down, shook his head as though to clear it. "But—but I don't understand all this—this hitting me over the head and asking me questions!"

"While your head's convalescin'," Asey said, "you might as well answer 'em. Tell me, who'd you fire that gun at?"

"I tell you I didn't fire it! It isn't my gun! I picked it up out behind this very house, just the way it is! I—I was going to give it back. Really, if it belongs to any of you here, I hope you don't think—oh, I see! It belongs to one of you, and you think I stole it!" Mr. Grosgrain almost relaxed, and something resembling a smile—about a third cousin, as Agatha said later—flitted across his face. "Oh, so that's it! Well, I'm glad to get something explained— I'm really sorry. I never even touched a gun before, and it was making me nervous, and I didn't quite know how to offer it to you. I mean, I didn't know what to say."

Jo stuck a finger on Agatha's sleeve. "Add first lines," she whispered. " 'They laughed at me when I sat down with my pistol' "—

"Yup." Asey played with his pipe. "I know how 'tis. They wasn't much of an op'tunity in the conv'sation to work in the gun easy an' graceful an' fluent—"

There was a great banging and knocking outside,

and I knew, even before he swaggered in, that it was Hanson—and very much on the warpath. He looked at Asey, tried not to change his expression, and succeeded only in achieving a sort of fixed, sour grin. Some of his swagger departed, too.

"Uh—glad to see you, Asey," his greeting was perfunctory. "Say—found the little beggar, have you? That his gun? Oh, boy, you got a gun on him?"

"He says it's not his gun," Asey passed it over to Hanson. "He says he picked it up out back, behind the garage."

"They always do." Hanson tipped his hat on the back of his head. "It's always two other people's—say, one shot fired. Huh. You hear any shot?"

Asey grinned. "Got Forman with you? Good. Tell Bob here to go get Forman an' have him dig out a bullet from the back of my roadster seat, an' see if he can't mate it up with that gun. I got more'n a notion that he can find it without no trouble at all. I—"

"Back of your car? Back of your car?" It took some time for Hanson to catch on. "Beat it for Forman, Bob. Take the automatic. Say—he—this little beggar here, he shot at you? You mean he tried to kill you?"

"Wa—el," Asey drawled, "someone did, an' this is the only stranger we found, an' the only gun. He missed me by what my father used to call a hair's breath. If you ask me, it was somethin' more like the one hundred an' sixty-third of a very small hair's dyin' gasp. Yup, me an' death had a little fracas to-night, but I fooled him."

Hanson looked at Mr. Grosgrain, and his grin turned

to a broad smile. Personally I should have hated to be smiled at like that. I've seen Sully look just that same way when he's found the end of a mole track.

"I—I found the gun, officer," Grosgrain began nervously. "I—I really did."

"I know. Found the knife you killed David Truman with this afternoon, too, didn't you? Found—"

"Mr. Truman—dead? Killed? Oh." Grosgrain turned white and then a sort of sickly green. "Oh. Oh, but I was in the bus this afternoon. In the bus—"

"Sure," Hanson went on. "I suppose you just found the knife you killed Dave with, too. Laid low around here somewhere till you seen Asey Mayo come—"

"Is he—is he Asey Mayo?" There was a shade of reverence in the little man's voice, and he put on his beribboned pince-nez. "Asey Mayo himself?"

Hanson laughed. "Little one, you're good, you are. Yes, Asey Mayo. You seen him, figured out your chances with him around, an' decided to get him while the getting was good. That's where you made your biggest mistake. You might be able to murder Dave Truman, but it takes more than a canary bird like you to kill Asey Mayo!"

"But I didn't," Grosgrain insisted. "I didn't even know he *was* Asey Mayo! I wasn't even here this afternoon! I was on a bus. On a bus, I tell you!"

Hanson looked around for the box of Kyle's cigarettes which I'd carefully put into a cabinet and locked away, and finally accepted one of Jo's.

"Asey," he said, "you've done it again. Believe it or not, I'd got it most all doped out when he barged over to Truman's a while back. We chased him, but he gave us the slip. I knew we'd get him eventually—I got everything blocked below here. It was just a question of time—"

"I was in a bus!" Grosgrain shrilled. "I was in a bus! In a bus. A bus!"

"Looks to me," Hanson returned, "like you was going to bust in another minute—ha ha!" He laughed heartily at his own joke, and continued to laugh at intervals during the next twenty minutes, when Forman, the ballistics expert whose picture I'd often seen in the papers, finally returned. He looked to me more like a rising young bond salesman than anything else.

"I've got the bullet," he said briefly in response to Hanson's eager questions. "Is it from the same gun? Oh, I wouldn't say so definitely, now. Some very marked similarities, very marked—here, take the glass and gape at it yourself. Now look at this bullet—I just fired it from that pistol. See that mark—and that? And this? Now—"

"We didn't hear any shot," Jo said. "How could you have—"

"Over at Truman's, in a wadded box for that purpose," Forman barely noticed her. "There are six points of similarity there, Hanson. I'll run along and check it. Paul's got all the pictures. Be seeing you."

Hanson nodded. "Thanks, Forman. Now, come along, shrimp—"

"I—you can't arrest me! You can't! I picked that gun up—"

"Attempted murder," Hanson said. "Clear as the nose

on your face. Suspect in the Truman—well, Asey, you think I'm rushing this. Sit down, shrimp. Here, Asey, I'll show you I wasn't bluffing when I said we were on his track."

From an inside pocket he brought out an elastic banded packet of letters.

"Here," he said, "are seven letters from this fellow—name's Grosgrain, isn't it, all right?"

"Yes, but I was on a bus, and I picked up that gun, and I demand—"

"Here's seven letters he wrote Truman, Asey, saying he wanted to come down and look at Suicide Cliff for Indian relics. Ain't that a nifty?"

"It's possible," Aunt Agatha rose to the little man's defense, "it's entirely possible, sergeant, that those letters mean just what they say."

Hanson paid no attention to her. "Pretty nifty camouflage," he said. "See his main point in all of 'em? He wants to meet Truman personally, was a Truman stockholder, but thinks Truman still is a wizard of finance. Don't bear any grudges, great interest in Indian relics. Why, with that handwriting and the way he's said it, you'd think he meant it!"

"Maybe he did," Agatha said. "Maybe he still does."

"I do," Grosgrain shouted. "I do! I've told you the truth! I—"

"Cinch," Hanson said. "This guy's clever. He could turn up and ask to see Truman, and Truman'd see him rather than keep on being bothered. Think he was a harmless lunatic. And all the time—yessir, that's a nifty."

"It's one way of working it out," Agatha told him with a sniff, "but—"

"But," Asey interrupted, "don't you think you got some loose ends?"

Hanson hooked his thumbs under his armpits and teetered back and forth on his heels.

"Now, Mrs. Penrose, and Miss Penrose, and you," he jerked his head toward Giles, "now, what was the last thing Mr. Truman said before he died?"

"Ink." The three of us told him promptly, with a sort of Gilbert and Sullivan chorus effect. "Ink."

"Yeah. And—now, get this! On Truman's desk is a letter he never finished, see? He must have been writing it before he went outside this afternoon. And it begins, 'Dear Mr. Grosgrain'—see?"

"No," Asey said, "I don't."

"Yeah? Well, longside it is an inkwell. Get it now? Truman couldn't say 'Grosgrain'—God, I can see where he couldn't! And he wanted to tell you who'd killed him, see? And he's been writing a letter to Grosgrain. And he can't tell you that. He knows he can't. So what does he say? Remembering the inkwell and the letter on the desk? He says, 'Ink.' Perfectly simple. Now, come along, shrimp."

"I was in the bus this afternoon," Mr. Grosgrain was nearly on the verge of tears. "I—"

"Y'know, Hanson," Asey said, "he seems awful def'-nite about that bus. Mightn't be a bad plan to call up an' do some checkin'. Make you surer, if he's lyin', an' keep you out of trouble if he ain't. Might as well play safe. It won't be no great effort. Call P—town or Hyannis. Bill Hardin' or Pete Brady, either one could tell you, an' Bill specially. Nobody comes on that train he couldn't tell you about years after."

"I got enough for one night," Hanson said. "Y'see, there's one more thing. About a week ago Truman came up to the station and had a little talk with me. Said frankly he was afraid some crank or other that'd lost money in his company might come down here and decide to shoot him. So we got up a plan. He wouldn't have a man stationed here, and he didn't want to bother having a man call every day, so he arranged to telephone us every night at ten. If we didn't get that call at ten, someone was to come in a hurry. Well, here's your crank. Come on, mister. Night, Asey. See you in the morning— oh, I'm leaving a man over at Truman's—"

"An' one here, too," Asey requested. "If you'll be so kind."

"Absolutely no need for one here," I said. "I don't want any state policeman—"

"Sure." Hanson was in an expansive mood. "Sure, I guess I better leave one here anyway. You folks had a hard day, and you might get nervous. Okay. One at Truman's, one here and a couple down the road. You'll be all right. 'Bye."

And he swept out, with Mr. Grosgrain sort of tagging along in the dust. Asey followed them to the door, and I noticed that he gave the little man a pat on the shoulder before the two of them disappeared out into the fog.

From the door Asey went directly to the phone and called Bill Harding, as I knew he would. At the end of a ten-minute conversation, he reported to us.

"Bill, he says the little feller was on the train to Yarmouth, an' on the bus from there to here. Alibis him perfect as far's Dave's death's concerned. Gee, he even told Bill Hardin' about Sludgebox, Ackroyd, Beelzebub and Cohen, or whatever that firm was, an' the Indian relics. Yup, it would sort of seem that maybe Luther might possibly of been tellin' us the truth."

"Of course he was," Agatha said scornfully. "You knew it all the time. A man like that couldn't lie. Poor thing, I'm sorry for him! He'll never be able to get rid of Hanson."

"You should have thrown a vase," I suggested. "It might have worked again—"

"But if it wasn't him," Giles protested, "then who fired that shot at you, Asey? Besides, it's got to be him!"

"Bill Harding may think he's the same man," the doctor added thoughtfully, "but there's a nice loophole there, don't you think, Asey?"

Asey nodded slowly. "Yup. It *was* a swell op'tunity to pull a fast one. I thought so when he first come in. Nice, in'cent, casual—if he was actin' a part someone'd written, he couldn't of done better. Yup, I thought then, it wouldn't be hard to alibi someone like him. But I dunno. Maybe—"

"What's all this nonsense?" Agatha demanded. "What on earth are you two babbling about?"

"Friend Luther's a commonplace lookin' bird," Asey

explained. "Even Miss Dwight here said he looked like her uncle, an' I can think offhand of half a dozen folks he reminds me of. All right. Now, s'pose one commonplace feller comes down on the bus an' train, takin' care to talk to Bill Hardin', an' tellin' him about that comp'ny, an' from office boy to bookkeeper, an' the Indian relics. Course, it ain't ever hard to talk to Bill, but them details is just dif'rent enough from the ord'nary so's Bill'll remember. I bet you that you could stick half a dozen people in pepper an' salt suits, dress 'em half way like Luther, an' Bill'd say any one of 'em was the feller that come down with him this afternoon. Anyway, carryin' it all on, they's one in the train, an' they's one here. See?"

With a great deal of honest and righteous indignation, Aunt Agatha admitted that she saw. "But it's like confusing a rampaging lion with a Pekingese. It's a lovely idea, and it's all very clever, but Luther told you the truth. He hasn't the wit to think up anything like that."

"Just a thought," Asey said. "But you can't never tell. Maybe—"

The telephone rang with energetic persistency. My ring is five, and the operator never considers she's done her duty unless she's rung five at least four times.

"Answer it," I said. "It's either a reporter or Hanson. Undeniably something unpleasant."

Asey obediently picked up the phone and said "Hullo" in his sweetest tones. For the next ten minutes, while a wide grin overspread his face, he said nothing but yes, yes and yup, and uh-huh, at odd intervals.

"Uh-huh." He said. "Yup. Okay. Night." He hung up the receiver and turned to us. "That," he announced, "was—"

"Don't tell me," Jo broke in, "I guessed hours ago. It was mother. A bit off the handle, I gather?"

"I didn't want to make cracks about your own kith an' kin," Asey told her, "but that's about the size of it. If the lady had paddle wheels, she could make Liverpool easy, she's that steamed up. Gen'ral idea is, she wants you to leave your low 'sociates an' get the hell home. I'm pract'cally quotin'."

"I'll go." Joe sighed. "Deary me, I foresee a long hard night ahead. Mother doesn't get wrathy more than once a year as a rule, but when she does, I lose a good five pounds without effort. Whoosh! Second time to-day, this is. Giles, come along. I'll drop you, or you can escort me, and take the car home with you, and bring it back to-morrow. I'm beginning to get a bit scared of this murky outside darkness. In fact, the principal reason I've hung around so long is that I'm too scared to go home alone."

Without much enthusiasm, Giles said he guessed he could see her home if she wanted.

"You won't have to," Asey remarked. "Mrs. Dwight's sendin' someone for you."

"Sending—? Oh, probably Creel Friar. Seems to me I had a date with him to-night. That means another temper to combat, and at least a million more explanations. Creel Friar—"

"Just who is this Creel Friar?" Asey asked. "I keep

hearin' an' hearin' about him, seems to me, but I don't know's I ever met him."

Dr. Cummings smiled, Aunt Agatha sniffed, I grinned, Giles wrinkled up his nose, and Jo looked slightly embarrassed.

"Creel," I said finally, when it became apparent that no one was going to present him with any details, "is a tall sallow youth who has an artistic limp, a very slight lisp, and he drives a very old but still aristocratic Mercedes. He—"

"Oh, him. Huh." Asey nodded. "I seen that around." I couldn't tell whether he referred to the man or the car. "Yup. Uses an empty champagne case for a baggage rack on the rear. What's he do?"

"I don't know." I proceeded with caution. Creel was Jo's friend, and I didn't know how she might react to criticism. "I really couldn't tell you, but I believe he writes."

"He'd have to," Asey commented. "Only thing left for a fellow that looks like that. First time I seen him was in P—town. I sort of wondered then if he hadn't grown up under the mossy side of a pebble."

"He isn't such a bad sort," Jo defended him against our raucous shouts. "He—have you met him, Miss Agatha?"

Aunt Agatha let her upper lip curl slightly. "I had that misfortune," she said. "He may not be, as you say, a bad sort, but to me any young pseudo-snob—"

"He's not!" Jo said hotly. "He—"

"My dear," Aunt Agatha was very bland, "any young

man with such a broad 'A' and a scalped—what d'you call it? A crew haircut. Well, any young man with those attributes who pretends to have gone to Harvard—"

"He *did* go to Harvard—"

"He likes to make you think he did," Agatha said patiently, "but when you force him to the very last ditch, he admits to a state university. Idaho or—oh, some place near it. I remember asking him nastily where the place was, exactly. Anyway, Jo, any young snob who divides the world into bitches and bastards exclusively, lacks, in my estimation, a certain luster. For my part I can call the most unpleasant person I know a 'leering cockroach' and achieve on the whole more lasting results than Mr. Creel Friar does with his stable chatter. But let's drop him. I rather resent wasting words over him. Asey, just what d'you think Dave Truman was trying to say, at the end? Ink doesn't make sense, even with Hanson's elaborate train of thought."

Asey, with true New England shrewdness, turned the question to Jo. "An' what's your idea, Miss Dwight?"

Jo, who had really been quite completely squelched by Agatha's comments on Creel, told him huffily that she had no ideas on the matter at all. "The obvious thing," she added, "is to figure that he meant to say that he didn't mean to shoot his gun, and that he thought—well, something or other. 'I didn't mean, I think'—or something like that."

Asey looked at her closely. "An' that's your best guess?"

Jo nodded. "Why not?"

"Why'd your mother get so mad this afternoon, when Giles was talkin' about Dave?"

"She was a friend of Marie Truman's," Jo was rather glib. "She just believes the other side of the story, that's all. I mean, for all that I liked Dave, I've got to admit that he didn't pay much attention to Marie. When he wasn't all tied up with business, he was always getting a bunch of bankers, or governors or senators together, and going off on a fishing trip somewhere. With just one or two reporters and a couple of the rotogravure boys. Kay used to go with him, but Marie wasn't that sort."

"Yet your mother's been over there to see Dave," Asey countered, "as late as—let's see. Tuesday of this week. She was over there havin' lunch with him Tuesday, when I come over with some fishin' gear. An' I've seen 'em talkin' an' chattin' real friendly on Main Street any number of times this summer."

Jo shrugged. "After all, she couldn't toss rotten tomatoes at him with all Weesit society looking on. At least, not with people she thought mattered, all gaping in the distance. Mother's not above trying to impress people even at this stage of the game."

"But she was alone with him, Tuesday."

"See here." Jo looked Asey in the eye. "I know nothing at all about my mother's comings and goings! If you've any more questions, ask her!"

"I shall," Asey promised. "Now, what d'you think about Kay's death?"

"I honestly don't know what I think. It's incredible to believe she was killed, but it's just as hard to think she killed herself. I think it was what they said. Just an accident."

Giles got up and began to pace the floor.

"It wasn't any accident," he said. "She was murdered! I thought so, and now I'm sure of it—"

"Was Kay a friend of this feller Creel Friar?" Asey ignored Giles.

"No more," Jo said coldly, "than she was a friend of Mr. Hopkins, your Cape Codder—"

In the flash of a second, with the agility of a cat, Giles was across the room, towering over Jo's chair.

"Say that again," Giles warned her furiously. "Just you say that again! Say it, so I can change the shape of your face till your own precious mother's own private face-lifter couldn't make it look like anything human again. Just give me—"

"I mean it." Jo was trembling, and I didn't blame her. Giles was mad through and through. "I mean it. And you leave my mother out of this, d'you hear? I won't have you—"

Asey grabbed Giles bodily and shoved him down on the couch.

"For a Hopkins," he said, "you got the sense of a new-born sand flea, sometimes. Shut up, both of you. Keep quiet! Now, Miss Dwight, I want you to tell me what you think David Truman meant when he said 'Ink.' This time, tell me—"

Before Jo could answer, Creel Friar breezed in without disturbing the knocker.

"Your mother's in a drizzly sweat," he told Jo, apparently not noticing the rest of us. "Poor Pink, she's—"

"Who," Asey asked, "is Pink?"

Creel, jingling some change in his pocket, looked at Asey as though he were some far-away, particularly unpleasant odor.

"Pink? Mrs. Dwight. Jo-jo, come—"

"Thank you," Asey said courteously. "Thank you. I thought as much. Pink. Ink. Yup, by all means, remove Jo-jo before she boils over."

CHAPTER FIVE

BREAKFAST in my household the next morning was not only a very late, but also a very ragged meal.

The state troopers had apparently scared off the milkman; the kitchen stove smoked hideously and over-ran into the living room; Katy, the cook, was completely disorganized. We'd given her full details, or as full details as her intelligence warranted, when she got in the night before, but time had only added to her state of general upheaval. Contrary to fiction, Aunt Agatha and I had slept like logs and were fiendishly hungry, and so of course we hurried and harried Katy, with the result that even our bacon's carboned edges were dotted with salty tears.

Asey sauntered in during the worst of it, and sat down and laughed until he, too, cried. Somehow he cheered Katy up and got the stove working, but it was long after eleven before we were really fed.

"This business," Aunt Agatha remarked as she set down her empty coffee cup, "reminds me of the time just after the war when I went to France with Rowena Winters to reclaim her château. It wasn't much of a château to begin with, and after five years of being shot at—well, we spent eight weeks sitting on camp stools and staring at the remains, wondering where to begin. Have you any new notions since last night?"

"Heaps," Asey said. "I got my best idea 'bout six this mornin' an' been playin' it ever since. Roused Giles out of his downy cot an' pulled a Hanson on him b'fore he got his eyes unstuck."

"You don't mean that you made him tell his story all over again!"

"Yup. I been sort of wonderin' how an' why Dave's gun went off. Whether he was shootin' at someone or somethin', or what. Giles's story works out with what I been thinkin', an' the doc says it's prob'ly right."

"Did you pull the doctor out of bed, too?"

"Didn't have to. Creel Friar wandered over to his place round four this mornin' with a busted arm an' the r'mains of an awful drunk. Doc'd been patchin' him up. He seemed to think, 'cordin' to the doc, that he'd run into a phone pole somewhere, but he wasn't sure. I'm 'fraid it ain't a bit fatal. Anyhow, Giles is sure to a point of bein' pos'tive that Dave was pointin' that gun at himself. Least, with Dave wearin' a shoulder holster, he feels sure that if Dave wasn't pointin' the gun at himself, he was puttin' the gun back in the holster. In other words, the muzzle of that gun was pointed either toward Dave himself, or toward the front door, or the front hall, or the top step. So, when the gun went off—"

"But what made it go off?" Agatha demanded. "Did he fire it at something, or what?"

"I was gettin' to that, but we might's well clear it

up. My idea was, that when he got stabbed, he prob'ly give a c'nvulsive sort of start, an'—doc can tell you about it right, all about reflexes an' nerves an' all. Anyway, durin' that process, his finger pulled at the trigger enough to shoot the gun off. B'cause if he'd been shootin' *at* somethin', his right hand'd of been outstretched, not close to him, an' from where he was standin', if he'd been tryin' to shoot at somethin' to the left of him, the bullet could only of gone through the door, an' the heavy door was hooked back, against the lattice. Get it?"

We got the idea, but we didn't get the point, and I told him as much.

"It's all the long dreary process of 'lim'nation," Asey said. "He wasn't shootin' at somethin' in front of him, nor to the left of him. Gun went off—well, you might call it by mistake. Only way the gun could of been pointin', as I said, was at the door or hall b'hind him, or at himself. Or down, toward the threshold. But the funny part of it is, they ain't no bullet in him, or in the hall, or the woodwork, or anywhere it should be. An' Giles an' Bob Raymond—he's one of Hanson's men, an' a darn nice feller, by the way. College boy that couldn't find any bonds or can openers to sell, an' like he says, couldn't even play football well enough to get a job. Well, the three of us has fine tooth combed that place. House, hall, every place within the limits of reason an' beyond even that, an' we can't find the bullet, an' a bullet certainly did come out of that gun."

"So what?" I said.

"You got me. They's only one pos'bil'ty. That the

bullet struck the millstone on the top step an' ricochetted. We think that's what happened, b'cause they's a mark there where it might of hit. An'—"

"If there's no hole in the screen door where it might of ricochetted inside," Aunt Agatha said, "then it must have gone outside. And—"

"Yup. Only there's this—an' it seems crazy. But Dave always had a hole cut in the screen door for the cat to come in an' out. He said a few flies didn't bother him half so much as havin' to get up an' let Sully in an' out when he scratched at the screen. So it's perfectly an' hum'nly poss'ble that that bullet hit the top step, bounced, as you might say, popped through Sully's hole, seein' that the door's a high step up, an'—"

"And went into the person who was doing the stabbing!" Aunt Agatha said delightedly. "Isn't that superb!"

I planted my hands on my hips and stared at her.

"You bloodthirsty creature!" I said. "Superb indeed! What would the Browning Club say to that?"

"Retributive justice," Agatha went on. "Why, all you've got to do now is find someone with a bullet hole in his leg—"

"'Cept," Asey said, "you can't tell if the bullet'd have force enough to do anything of the kind. An'—"

"And Mrs. Dwight," Agatha continued, "took, in the expressive words of her daughter, to her bed last night. Asey, what about that 'Pink' business, by the way?"

He shook his head. "Later, when I get somethin' on her, if I *get* anythin' on her, I'm goin' to look into that. Dave happened to call her Pink that day I was over.

Tuesday. I wanted to make sure, so that's why I tried to bully Jo. Anyway, my ideas is sort of long drawn out, about the bullet, but it has a nice sound, an' leastways we got somethin' def'nite to hunt for in the line of a bullet. Let's go over an' hunt some more. It kind of has got me, that lost bullet. An' b'fore I forget it, Bev, I want a nice safe place to put some of Dave's stuff. Bob Raymond an' Giles an' I decided that we'd take his pers'nal papers an' make off with 'em b'fore Hanson hands 'em over to the tabloids. Dave's diaries make kind of pers'nal readin', an' they ain't nobody's business. I—"

"What about the reporters?" I asked. "Are they here?"

"They sure are. Like flies. I figgered on 'em, an' took Pegleg over with me. They fell for him plenty, an'," he grinned, "carryin' on a conv'sation with him ain't easy. They ought to be pretty hoarse by now. While they was bellowin' at him an' takin' pictures of him in the potato patch where he was durin' it all, I just slipped around an' done what I wanted. Oh, an' here's a bunch of keys, an' some of his pictures an' letters, an' Giles has put all Kay's things he could find in one of your trunks out in the garage. 'Cept for Dave's books an' clothes, that house is as impers'nal now as a hotel bedroom."

The keys jangled as he dropped them on the table; Aunt Agatha picked them up and stared at them in a puzzled way.

"Silly," she said. "The jingle of those keys makes me think of—oh, it's foolish, but I knew there was something wrong about our stories, Bev, for all that we went over them so many times yesterday. I almost thought of it when that Friar boy jingled change in his pocket last night, but I got sidetracked. D'you remember, Bev, just after the Dwights left yesterday, and just before Giles saw Dave come out, that Sully went through the hedge?"

"Yes," I said promptly. "I saw him, and I said so, I think, and—oh, I know what you mean! I didn't hear his bell. The silver bell on his collar. It always tinkles. Always!"

Agatha swung the keys on her forefinger. "It didn't tinkle then," she said. "I started to say something about it—"

"So did I. But that was when Giles went into action. And—but Aunt Agatha, Sully's bell was on his collar when he rubbed against me, when you and I were on the green settee. Asey, isn't that strange? That bell snaps on. I know, because the twins gave the collar and bell to Sully, and Dave, for a birthday present last July. I bought the thing. And it always makes a noise. And if it didn't sound yesterday, before Dave was killed, that means it wasn't on, or the collar wasn't. But it *was* on later. Who could have taken it off? And who put it on again?"

Asey rubbed his chin with his hand. "Is sort of p'culiar, ain't it? Ord'narily it's the sort of thing you'd let pass with a snicker, but right here, it's p'culiar. I'll whistle the cat in an'—maybe it ain't the same bell."

It took a lot of whistling and tapping on plates with spoons before Sully could be enticed into the house. But the bell was securely fastened onto his collar, and it was the silver bell that belonged on it. Nor could we tell if the collar or the bell had been tampered with.

"Huh." Asey let Sully jump down from his arms. "Missin' bullet an' a bell that don't ring! An' that's all."

"It's a lot," Aunt Agatha said, "if—"

"Yup. If the bell's got anythin' to do with it, an' providin' this ac'dental bullet bounced through a cat hole—y'know, the whole thing's screwy. Sully, go sick Hanson! He's comin' here—"

Sully, with a disdainful flick of his tail that amounted to a thumb on his nose, jumped onto the window seat, sat himself sedately in the sun, and proceeded to wash his face.

"That's all you care for Hanson, huh?" Asey murmured. "Okay. I'll go see what's to be seen. You two comin', too? Just don't tell Hanson about the bullet, please. Let him have the fun of dopin' it out all by his lonesome."

I doubt if Hanson had been forced to cope with creamless coffee and burned bacon and clouds of wood smoke, but clearly something had happened to annoy him vastly. He was pretty much subdued, too. There wasn't any swagger at all in his walk, and his voice sounded like Budge's—Budge is the pug-nosed twin— when Budge knows he has to make an apology. It was penitent, puzzled, and faintly hurt.

"Parker," he announced, "says for God's sakes will I come to you and learn how to spell cat, Asey. And he says for God's sakes will you teach me. He's sending down O'Malley, he says, if you won't, but otherwise not, because he needs O'Malley in town. Boston. He also says you got a date to take him fishing."

Asey smiled. Parker was Hanson's boss, and a friend of Asey's. I'd once heard Parker try to persuade Asey to go into detecting as a business—

"S'matter, Hanson?" Asey inquired. "Friend Luther flew the coop?"

"Adams, Meredith, Meredith, Whatever-it-was and Levitsky," Hanson controlled himself with difficulty, "the firm that bird said he belonged to—they're lawyers!"

"Yup," Asey said. "I had a sort of notion they was."

"And all sixty of 'em," Hanson went on, "got up out of bed and pulled on their pants and run for the Governor the second we let Grosgrain phone. I just wish that people with friends that can pull my stripes off would wear a sign, or tip me off! I do my duty as good as I can, and—gee, a runt like that! They got Bill Harding to swear he was on the train to Yarmouth, and on that damn bus, and they got Pete Brady to swear it, too. And they got three Portygees from P-town, Harry Jones from Chatham—say, I didn't know the New Haven had that much business! Then—"

"What about the bullet from my car? Did it match up with the gun?"

"You know Forman, Asey. He doesn't say yes and he doesn't say no. Just says there's forty-eight points of similarity—sure, it's the gun, all right. But what of it? Those lawyers, they had papers saying Grosgrain didn't know one end of a gun from the other, couldn't see the side of a circus tent at ten feet, and had been refused a driving license on account of bad eyesight!"

"Where's Luther now?" Asey asked sympathetically.

Hanson shrugged. "I don't know. I don't know anything, Asey. Last I seen of him, he was strutting out of— I just hope to God he stays of my sight! There's one bird I don't ever want to see again—"

It was probably the same Fates who had leered at us the day before who sent Mr. Grosgrain walking up our driveway at that exact same moment. Hanson looked at him, made snarling noises in his throat, and started off on a dead run for Dave's.

"Good morning," Mr. Grosgrain greeted us pleasantly. "I—perhaps that officer told you I'm entirely cleared of all his ridiculous charges?"

"He's told us," Asey said, "at what you might sort of call some length. Now you're out of it, what you doin' back here?"

"I'd planned," Mr. Grosgrain said mildly, "to look over that cliff, and I didn't think, now that Mr. Hanson knew I was all right, that he'd object to my carrying out my original plans. Do you?"

"I think," Asey told him, "Hanson'd probably give you the sand in his shoes, if you even so much as hinted that it'd help your peace of mind. You got Hanson right under your back molars."

Mr. Grosgrain blinked and smiled politely, but he didn't get what Asey meant.

"There," Agatha said proudly. "I told you he was all right, Asey. And be sure, Mr.—er—Grosgrain, that you take care, if you're really going over the cliff. It's a treacherous place. Caves in sometimes eight or ten feet from the edge."

Mr. Grosgrain promised that he would be very careful, and trotted off.

Asey watched him reflectively. "It still don't seem quite human," he murmured, "that one man—no matter. I'm goin' to call Parker, an' then I'm goin' over to see Ike Smalley. Want to come?"

We did, but I thought suddenly of the reporters.

"They'll trail all over the house," I said. "Katy could never stave them off. And I hate having things messed up—"

"I'll have Bob Raymond hold the fort," Asey promised.

Half an hour later, Agatha and Asey and I set off in his long roadster; he didn't seem even to notice the rips and tears, and the chunks of leather bitten out of the back of the seat, where Forman had probed for the bullet. I must confess, though, that I was still uncomfortably aware of the fact that whoever had shot at Asey was still at large, and that, after all, I had a husband and two children dependent, to some extent, on me. And Asey, particularly when he's at all preoccupied, drives with a swift, urgent abandon. Sort of a modern Paul Revere spirit. During the tourist season he slows down some, but the rest of the year he just whizzes. Of course he knows the roads like a book; once, on a bet, he drove from Wellfleet to Orleans blindfolded, and got there intact. My stomach didn't feel at all happy, but Aunt Agatha, beside me, seemed to be having the time of her life. I think she was even mildly disappointed when we drew up at the traffic light at the town four corners.

As we waited, Jo's roadster slewed to a stop beside us. She didn't turn her head our way, or give any sign of knowing we were there, even though she must have. Asey's car isn't one you don't notice.

Asey's eyes twinkled as he looked at the pompon on her beret, and he spun the wheel. When the light changed, Jo had to yank on her emergency to keep from barging into our fender. And was she mad!

"Mornin'," Asey said cheerily. "How are you this bright an' shinin' day?"

"Hi." Jo spoke through clenched teeth. "Never mind pulling off. I'll back."

"Just a sec. I hear tell that Mr. Friar had a crash early this mornin'—"

"We weren't—he's not hurt," Jo said, and stepped on the accelerator.

We slid forward, but she missed the light and had to wait.

"An' what she's sayin'," Asey remarked, "ain't fit for me to hear, even lookin' in the mirror. Huh. So she was out with that Friar, was she? Doc said he thought she was. Said he thought someone'd walked Creel to his doorstep an' dumped him there. Didn't think he would of been able to make it by himself."

"I suppose," Agatha said, "that, being faced with the prospect of her mother letting off steam, she thought Friar might be the lesser evil. Hm. On the whole, I think I should have plugged my ears with cotton and stayed at home."

We swung off the King's Highway onto an untarred

side road I knew well. It's one of the old wagon paths, bordered by scrub pines and scrub oaks and a great deal of poison ivy, and I make a point of taking newcomers to the Cape over it for atmosphere. I don't know how many haunted houses and gibbets and pirates' haunts I've planted along that lane, or how many bits of stone I've gravely got out and picked up, and given to guests as genuine pieces of Indian arrow heads or flints. Long ago I gave up trying to show people the Cape Cod they expected, for it really doesn't exist outside of fiction. Instead I present them with small, intimate glimpses of dried up swamps, dinky ponds, top heavy sand dunes, and abandoned fish weirs. I also throw in a great amount of history and anecdote, practically none of which could stand verification. There are some yarns I've told so many times that there's occasionally some doubt in my mind as to whether they're not true, after all.

After stopping several times to grind through the sand, still soft in spite of the rains the week before, we came to Ike Smalley's house. That house would be local color anywhere, but it never occurs to me to display it. The Smalleys are remote cousins of mine, and I know perfectly well that strangers would never understand them at all.

Take the orchard. Under the trees were the twisted remains of dozens of old broken down buggies and carry-alls, and strewn carelessly around were enough rusty model T Ford parts to build at least three, complete. Hens and chickens and turkeys and guinea hens hopped from buggy shafts to battered rear axles, and a goat chewed industriously on a rusty fender.

The front yard was given over to a potato patch and a lot of withered cornstalks, and practically no one would have denied that the house was languishing for a coat of paint. It was, at first glance, pretty messy, and I wondered what Aunt Agatha, who'd never happened to go there before, would say. With what my father used to call the true instincts of a lady, she ignored the confused untidiness and spoke of the front door.

"Superb," she remarked pleasantly. "I'd give anything to have a leaded glass fan like that. And look at those melons—they make my mouth water! How sane to have a garden in your front yard. Much better land." She cast a swift look around. "Much better than that strip in back. I—what are you laughing at, Bev?"

"Just thinking of the opportunity some in-law relations would leap at. After all, the Smalleys are cousins of mine, and you've a swell chance to murmur things about the Cabots and the Lowells and Beacon Street. Point is, Ike's God's laziest man. That's why the garden's in the front yard. Convenient like. Saves steps. And though his sister Sophy pretends to be a human dynamo, she runs Ike a pretty close second. The polite explanation of 'em both is in-breeding. Aunt, just cast your eye over that big elm—"

Agatha grinned as she read the signs, and so did I, even though I know 'em by heart. The oldest and most weather beaten one said simply, "Blacksmith." Underneath and above it were eight or ten shingles which announced little items like "Wagon Springs Mended. Harnesses neatly sewd. Hand wove Horse Blankets." "Fords Fixed. Ford Parts. Cheap." "Beach plum Jelly for Sale." "Also Herring Dried or Salt." "Scallops, oysters, lobsters." My favorite of all was the newest: "A Nice cemetery lot For Sale, also a Cobbler's Bench."

"Optimists," Agatha commented. "Opportunists, too. They don't appear to have missed a chance. But you said they were lazy, Bev. Those signs sound like a beehive of activity."

"Cam'flage," Asey told her. "Helps 'em feel good. This place is a mile'n a half from the main road. How many folks you think ever see them signs? Oh—h'lo, Ike."

Ike, looking more or less like an Old Testament patriarch in overalls, ambled out to the car.

"H'lo, Asey. H'lo, Bev." His voice was as weary as though he had just personally finished the demolition of something quite large—New York City, say—with his bare hands.

He looked at Aunt Agatha and waited sleepily until I introduced her.

"Kyle's folks, I guess," he said. "H'lo. Sophy an' me was just settin' down to dinner."

"Can it wait a few minutes?" Asey asked. "I wanted to—"

"Can't wait. It's on the table."

"Then we'll do the waitin'," Asey said. "Hustle in an' git it over with, Ike."

Ike nodded and proceeded with increasing slowness to the back steps, where he came to a dead stop.

"He's thinkin'," Asey murmured. "S'pose I better go catch him b'fore he falls?"

Ike retraced his steps. "I s'pose," he said listlessly, "you could come into the settin' room an' set."

"We won't trouble you," I told him. "We—"

"You better come into the settin' room an' set," Ike repeated.

Apparently he had no intentions of budging an inch until we went into the settin' room and set, so we did. And for one solid hour we squirmed around on the horsehair seats of the walnut furniture while Ike and Sophy leisurely consumed their dinner.

After the first thirty minutes I got to hate that room. I can look at just so many glass covered, fly-specked funeral wreaths, and just so many anæmic Currier and Ives children. Two of either, in fact, is distinctly my limit. The Smalley settin' room had fourteen wreaths and nineteen Currier and Ives lithographs, and three steel engravings, and four shell covered boxes—

"One thing to be said for this dust an' d'struction bound age," Asey said as he replaced two copies of *Harper's Monthly* for 1890 on the marble topped table. "Least ways the ads is readable. 'Course the folks in 'em may be pinin' for fresh coffee an' lots of bran, but at least they don't all look like they was slowly dyin' of cancer. Thank God, Ike's lightin' his pipe. They must be through. Maybe they still cling to fletcherizin'. That's all I can think of that'd make 'em take so long. Sixty-one chews to every swallow—"

But it still took Ike ten minutes to saunter in from

the kitchen. Asey waited until he had deposited himself in the most comfortable chair, and then asked if he had heard the news of Dave Truman's death.

"Yes-yes," Ike said. "Washy Wheeler told me." He clucked his tongue. "Bad business. Know anythin' about it?"

Asey gave him a bird's-eye view, accurate, but not very detailed.

"Now what I want to know, Ike," Asey added, "is, did you happen to be down at your fish house yesterday afternoon? I thought maybe if you was, an' happened to of had your binoculars with you, perhaps you might of seen somethin' out of the ord'nary."

"I was there all right," Ike said. "Plenty of time to look 'round, too. Fish business is as slack as I ever seen it. Honest, Asey, I don't see where the country's comin' to. What I say is, you take these war debts. Now, how you goin' get good times without—"

Asey interrupted Ike before he worked up any momentum and repeated his questions about the boat house and the binoculars.

"Didn't see nothin' out of the ord'nary," Ike shook his head. "Not a—by gum, I forgot my sody—"

We squirmed another fifteen minutes while Ike and Sophy tracked down the soda to the woodshed and bickered plaintively as to who put it there.

"Nary a thing," Ike continued when he finally got settled in his chair again. "Tommy Dawson was putterin' around after flounders with a spear, an' Pegleg Black was up there in Truman's potato patch—no, sir. Not a single thing I can think of. Asey, just what does Bill Porter think about business?"

"Bill says he give up thinkin' about business back in nineteen-thirty," Asey told him patiently. "He says he begins the day by seein' if any sheriff's waitin' for him, or any subpeena servers, an' then he sticks his head into the plant to see if he gets shot at. If nothin' happens either way, he knows he ain't bankrupt yet, an' his men ain't strikin', an' then he goes off an' gives his caddie a sales talk on Porters for eighteen holes. Look, Ike, give us a blow by blow d'scription of your goin' from here, gettin' to the fish house, lookin' 'round. Just give us the works till you come home again. P'raps somethin' happened that didn't seem p'culiar at the time, but might in the light of what's happened. Go on. We need you."

Interrupting his narrative with a great deal of praise for McKinley, Teddy Roosevelt and Calvin Coolidge, and a greater number of distinctly unpleasant cracks at the Democratic party, Ike led us down the lane through the orchard, past the low garden to the shore. Laboriously, we heard him sell two lobsters, a bushel of oysters. Between war debts and Japan, we watched two liners, two tramp steamers, a tug and four barges, all pass by the harbor entrance, and listened to a discussion of new-fangled boats versus clippers.

"Think of Uncle Lisha," Ike said, "bringin' the 'Pride of Asia' 'round the horn to New York with a fire in her hold. Saved half his cargo, not a man hurt, an' the boat back home to the owners. An' look at the way they manage now'days, with their fancy liners. Huh. Well, soon's that tug went by, Washy Wheeler dropped in to pass the time of day, an' just b'fore he come—'twas 'round four— four-thirty, I guess, I seen that girl whose mother's got the Henderson house. Girl that wears them red pants."

"Jobyna Dwight?" I asked.

"Yup. She come down to the shore, walked down from the road, I figgered, an' took Dawson's oldest sharpie an' rowed across to Truman's, an' clumb up the bankin'. But that won't help you none. She often does."

"Often?" Asey raised his eyebrows.

"Oh, I see her do that two—three times a week. Bold piece, with her cigarettes an' her short pants. Kay Truman brought her over here once. Now Kay, she was a nice girl. She—"

"See the Dwight kid come back?" Asey wanted to know. I knew he was thinking what I was thinking: the direct route to Dave's necessitated the use of my driveway. If Jo chose to call on Dave via back roads and someone else's sharpies, obviously she didn't want me to see her or know about her visits to Dave.

"Yup," Ike said. "It was just after Washy—no, sir. I was goin' to say it was after he decided to go back, but it was later. He'd come in his truck, an' I figgered he might as well take me along an' save me the trouble of walkin' back. Just as I was closin' up, it was, I took a look around. Nate's boy hadn't come in the harbor, an' I r'member thinkin' if he didn't make the inlet inside of ten minutes, he'd lose the tide. Well, he was right off the shoals, an' then I swung the glasses over to Truman's.

Pegleg was still up in the potato patch—he's slowin' up, Pegleg is. An' then the Dwight girl come limpin'—"

"Limping?" I demanded. "What—how—"

"Bold piece," Ike said. "Limped down to the head of the bankin' there, an' took off her red sweater an' pants an' went in swimmin'. When she come out, she took her handkerchief an' bound up her leg. Hip, I guess. Guess she'd fell an' hurt herself on the rocks. An' Washy said—"

"So you give the glasses to Washy, too?" Asey asked with a twinkle in his eye.

"Sure," Ike said. "Bold thing—what's she doin', hangin' around Truman's all the time?"

"You're certain of all this?" Asey asked. "Sure she seemed to of hurt herself?"

"Ask Washy. He seen—"

"Asey," Agatha said, "I rather think you've found your bouncing bullet, don't you?"

"I think," Asey said, "we'll look into this, anyhow."

We tore ourselves away from the Smalleys' as quickly as we could, and made for the car. Asey opened the door for us, and then leaned forward and looked into the roadster.

"Y'know," he said quietly, turning back to us again, "this is gettin' to be kind of annoyin'. We ain't, as Queen Victoria used to put it, amused one bit. No, siree!"

Plunged into the seat behind the wheel, between the tears of the bullet the night before and the slashes where Forman had probed, was a particularly grim and business-like hunting knife.

CHAPTER SIX

I DON'T suppose, looking back on it later, that there was anything else for Asey to do but to pack us into the car and start off, after removing the knife.

Ike and Sophy wouldn't know who had been prowling about any more than we did, and certainly it would have been futile and dangerous to go wandering about trying to find the person.

The knife itself, a common hunting knife of the variety the doctor had thought responsible for the murder of Dave, was gleaming as though it had recently been rubbed with an oily cloth. And the person who thrust it in the back of the seat had without doubt worn a glove. There wasn't even the sniff of a fingerprint.

So off we went, along the sandy lane. The sun had gone in behind a cloud, and somehow the lane, instead of being a funny tourist item in my mind, took on a distinctly sinister aspect. I saw from ten to fifteen figures behind every scrub pine, and imaginary knives sung by my ear till they reached grand opera proportions.

I hoped I didn't look as frightened as I felt. I tried hard to be nonchalant and casual like Asey and Agatha, but an inch of neat agate type danced in and out of my line of vision. "Penrose, Beverly (Nickerson). Wife of Kyle Penrose. Services—"

Or would Kyle say, "Beloved Wife"? Probably. He was a conventional thing. "Beloved Wife of Kyle Penrose. Survived by her two sons, Peter and Noel." Or would anyone ever remember, without my personal prompting, that the twins had proper names? Probably not. Still, "Survived by her two sons, Budge and Snuffles," would hardly seem decent in an obituary notice. "Services at"— Where on earth would they hold services? Kyle is an official Episcopalian. My family were just passive Christians, without any tags. Perhaps I couldn't have services at all. Maybe—

"If you know anythin' as chuckly as you look, tell us!" Asey demanded.

"I was only thinking, who makes up obituaries? And—"

Asey threw back his head and laughed. "Come, come, Bev! I ain't dead yet. An' my obituary won't amount to a row of pins. I ain't a Mason or a Bison or an Elk or anythin'. Dunno's—"

"I wasn't thinking about you, selfish!" I said indignantly. "I was thinking about myself. I mean, suppose they missed you and—"

That time both Asey and Agatha yelled immoderately.

"If the person who wants you out of the way so badly," I observed, "could see you now, he'd probably go commit suicide in sheer despair. The most rollicking murderer in the world couldn't bear up."

"I been hopin' for ten minutes that he'd spot my happy grin," Asey said.

"Just what," Agatha inquired, "d'you think was the purpose of this last bit of drama?"

"Just tryin' to scare me, I think. Voodoo. Black magic. I seen a nigger carpenter once—he was a Haitian on the barque 'Cecelia,'—I seen him curl up an' die real happy an' r'signed one afternoon in his hammock, after he spotted a few chalk marks an' curlicues on the top of his sea chest. Huh. Sort of dumb, when you come right down to it. Whyn't the feller haul off in that orchard of Ike's an' hide under a wagon wheel or a spare tire or a piece of horn, an' pot at me like a gentleman? Same as he done last night. I'd of been a dandy target, an' you'd no more chance of gettin' him, or of him gettin' caught, than last night, either."

We swung off the lane onto the main road, and I heaved an unconscious sigh of relief. Anything could happen on that back lane, but there was a merciful air of civilization about that tarred road.

At the four corners Asey stopped and called the traffic cop, Peewee Hastings, over to the car.

"Say, Peewee," Asey asked, "you hear anythin' about that ole Mercedes gettin' smashed last night?"

Peewee laughed shortly. "Yeah. Friar smashed it up on the S-curve before you come into town. And does it burn me up!"

"Can't you get him?" Asey asked sympathetically.

"Nope. No one saw the accident. Least, no one did who's going to come and tell me about it! He didn't damage anyone's property but his own, didn't even graze the phone pole, though he must have circled about it for an hour, by the tracks. He was drunk when he came to the doctor's, but I can't run him in for drunken driving. I didn't see him. Maybe he wasn't driving. And," he wound up bitterly, "I'd given fifty dollars to have got him before he left this town. Honest, Asey, I'd give any money at all to get him yet! Remember that, will you? Any time you get a chance to get him for anything, just let me know, and I'll come running. Run—hell, I'll fly!"

Asey promised to do his best, and we drove on.

Before we reached the turn-off to North Weesit, Jo's roadster went tearing by us in the opposite direction. Jo was driving, and Creel Friar was beside her.

Asey frowned and slowed up.

"If you want her, why don't you chase them?"

"I could get 'em soon enough, Bev, but I got a kind of feelin' that if I do, they'll try to give me a run for my money, an' in that car of Jo's, with her drivin' well, no need to murder 'em both. I guess we'll go call on her mother instead."

"Look, Asey," I said as we flew up the beach road, "just why was Dave killed?"

"D'you want a phil'sophical d'scussion on motives?" he returned, "or d'you think I know more'n you do?"

"There are only two motives for killing anyone," Aunt Agatha said. "At least, that's the theory, isn't it, Asey? Love and money?"

"Make it r'venge an' money," Asey said. "An' money's out of this case."

"Why?" I asked. "Dave was broke according to his standards, but it would mean abject wealth to most people. Why couldn't you consider the money angle of it?"

Asey looked at me with an expression I couldn't quite fathom.

"Because," he said, "Tuesday evenin' I witnessed Dave's will. He'd left everythin' to Kay, b'fore, an' didn't change it till then. He made me read it through. So did Pegleg, who was the other witness. I mailed it off to Steve Crump myself, along with his life insurance pol'cies that'd been changed an' a lot of other stuff."

"Well?"

"Well, it ain't my business to tell you, but you'll know sooner or later, an' it won't make much diff'rence. Everythin' 'cept a set sum of money for one other person, goes into a trust fund for your sons. So you see, the money—"

"Asey, you don't mean it! It—oh, dear!"

"Don't see why you feel that way, Bev. It pleased him to do it. He said he'd thought the whole thing over, an' he didn't know two nicer kids. But the other," Asey saw the tears in my eyes and hastily changed the subject, "the other—oh, I might as well tell you the works, now I begun. I forget the exact sum of money, but it's what was Kay's, an' Dave wanted Jo to have it. So you can't call that a motive, either. Dave himself said that Jo's father left her more money than he did Mrs. Dwight. It don't seem sane to think Jo'd kill Dave for a few thousands."

"That leaves revenge," Agatha said thoughtfully. "Such a broad heading, somehow. And a man like David would have had so many enemies! Not just the cranks, but business men and politicians and bankers, and his wife's friends, his own group of friends, men and women —it's a hopeless thought!"

"Yes'n no." A network of wrinkles appeared on Asey's forehead. "Only, people go about r'venge in so many dif'rent ways. Cranks wrote him threatenin' letters; they don't hurt. Business men an' pol'ticians used the publicity angle—"

"You don't mean, you think all those attacks on him were not just reporters—"

"Usin' up their adjectives?" Asey smiled wryly. "Nope. There was one feller, a friend of Dave's in England, who believed in him an' asked him to start a new business. Like Truman an' Comp'ny, with his backin'. Dave told me about it, an' said he sort of hesitated; he said once he accepted, an' people found out how many millions was b'hind him, all but one or two of the papers'd start in to scratch his ears friendly instead of tryin' to scratch out his eyes. Y'see, just his name threw weight. An' when Truman's flopped, all the fellers who didn't like him seen their chance, an' took it. An' passed on the word. Upshot of it was, word got passed finally that when Truman's name was mentioned in certain papers, nothin' nice an' pretty was to be said. The ole

game of kickin' someone's teeth out after they slipped on
a b'nana peel."

Agatha nodded. "I begin to see what you mean. Yes,
it has been that way. But you think that's just business
revenge, and trying to keep him from staging any come-
back?"

"In a way. Dave thought so, too. But, once they found
out the extent of his new backin', they'd have to change
their tune. Dave said he missed bein' in the thick of things,
but for the first time since he was a kid, he had time
to enjoy himself. Didn't think he wanted to go back to
it again. Anyway, as to his wife's friends—somehow,
havin' seen her, I think they'd confine themselves to a
mess of dirty cracks. An' as for his own friends, Dave was
pretty close-mouthed, when you come right down to it."

I knew what Asey meant. In Weesit, Dave talked
about Weesit people and Weesit problems. In New York,
about New Yorkers. And so on, in whatever group he
happened to be. But he never mixed groups. Many times
I've met people who knew Dave, or found old friends of
mine who knew him, but I'd never had the slightest notion that Dave knew them.

"Then," Asey went on, "there's the method of approach. I think the feller that's after me is choosin' the
nicest method of r'venge I know. Leastways, he would
be if I was the harryin' kind. Lot more intel'gent, harryin'
folks, than killin' 'em. Killin' don't hurt, an' harryin'
does. I'm wonderin' if—well, if maybe it wasn't somethin' Dave might of told, or might of done, rather than

somethin' he did do or say. 'Cause all this is the work of someone with a brain or two."

"This new business," I suggested. "Perhaps someone wanted to prevent him from—"

"Don't think. Only three people knew of that. Dave, this Englishman Amborough, an' me. Well, we'll go see Mrs. Dwight. By this time," we'd been stopped outside the driveway for ten minutes, "she'll of told the maid servant or the butler or what not that she's not at home."

Agatha and I giggled when the white-coated Filipino said just that.

"I'll wait," Asey assured the boy. "I've plenty of time."

The boy didn't know when Mrs. Dwight would be back, didn't think she would see people when and if she did come back.

"I'll take a chance," Asey said. "Cheer up, brother. It's just a contest of wills, an' she shouldn't of told you so loud. Sure, I heard her at the end."

He came back to the car, parked it squarely across the drive, pulled out his pipe and began to fill it leisurely.

"Wish I had a German band," he muttered. "Just somethin' to while the time away. Got any s'gestions, you two?"

Agatha pointed to the radio on the dash.

Shortly one of the harshest, shrillest, most utterly awful female voices I ever heard over the air, filled the front yard with friendly suggestions about cleaning garbage cans with a quick cleaner.

"Spelled, home makers, Q-U-I-K-L-I-N-O. You simply can't beat it for quick cleaning. Remember the name when you have some quick cleaning to do. Q-U-I-K-L-I-N-O. Quiklino comes in three sizes, big, medium and small, and the big container contains just five times as much as the small container, and costs only twice as much. So you see, home makers, it's a real saving to buy Quiklino in the big containers, because it contains so much more. Now, girls, we come to this afternoon's recipe. Got your paper and pencil handy? Of course, if you'll just send in the top of a Quiklino package, with your name and address, printed, to me in care of this station, you'll be sent a handy pencil and pad with the compliments of Quiklino, the quick cleaner that really cleans quickly. Now, got your pencil and pad, home makers? To-day's quick recipe is one I've been asked for again and again, and it's just as simple as it is delicious. And it *is* delicious. All ready, then, for Creamed Deviled Ham on Toast, and if you Quiklino fans, spelled Q-U-I-K-L-I-N-O, don't agree with me that it's the quickest, most delicious—"

The Filipino appeared in the doorway and dashed, as though in agony, out to the roadster.

"Mrs. Dwight say, she iss sorry she do not know it iss Mrs. Penrose and friends. Will Mrs. Penrose and friends please come in?"

Before he got out of the car, Asey pulled an old letter out of his pocket and scrawled on it hastily.

"Is that the recipe," Agatha inquired in a voice that shook from suppressed laughter, "for creamed deviled ham on toast?"

"It's a mem'randum," Asey informed her as he gallantly helped her out, "to buy a case of Quiklino. Can't never tell when it might come in handy again—"

Eleo was, if anything, slightly more consumed with rage than she had been the day before. But to-day she had herself in hand. No one who hadn't known her for a long time, or who was not quite as shrewd and quick-witted as Agatha and Asey, would have even begun to suspect that the charming woman who reclined on the chaise longue, looking the perfect hostess and sounding it as well, was actually longing to knock our teeth out and stamp on them hard.

"Bev, my dear, I'm so ashamed! I thought it was that tiresome—you'll forgive me for not getting up, but my head is simply in a torment! Everything's such a perfectly frightful mess, with Jo absolutely possessed of demons—no two ways about it, and dear Creel! That hideous car of his turned over last night and nearly killed the poor boy! I can't see why everything has to happen at once—and Bev, dear, I've never really met Mr. Mayo, though of course I know all about him!"

I introduced Asey, who'd been listening to her airy chatter with the straightest of sober, interested faces, though his blue eyes couldn't help twinkling.

"Sorry to disturb you when you ain't feelin' so good, an' with everythin' botherin' you, Mrs. Dwight, but I had some questions I wanted to ask you about Dave Truman, an' I—"

Eleo's perfect hostess attitude melted as if someone had applied a blow torch to it.

"You have some questions to ask *me?*" she inquired icily. "You—*you* have questions to ask *me?* And by what right, Mr. Mayo, and by whose authority?"

Without answering, Asey pulled a sheaf of papers from an inside pocket of his canvas coat and passed them to her.

"What do I care for papers?" Eleo barely glanced at them. "I absolutely refuse to be questioned by—"

"'Course," Asey returned the papers to his pocket, "'course, I thought, what with you bein' so bothered an' upset an' everythin', I sort of thought we'd just do this the easy way. But if you want to make it hard, I'll make it hard. I'll call over Sergeant Hanson an' half a dozen troopers, an' drape 'em all over your driveway an' your front steps, an' I'll bring over the r'porters an' we'll do the whole thing up real crisp an' brown an' formal-like. 'Cordin' to Hoyle an' Em'ly Post. Only I didn't think you'd want your neighbors—well, the Shepherds is nice folks, but it's just hum'nly poss'ble they might not under-stand, an' maybe even figger you had somethin' to do with Dave's death—"

That was a master stroke. The Shepherds are the Astors of North Weesit, and they hadn't begun to pay Eleo the attention she thought she should have.

"So," Asey sounded plaintive, "I just thought, I'll go see Mrs. Dwight with Bev an' Miss Penrose, an' then if the Shepherds see me come, they'll just think it was a friendly little call. But I—"

"Now you're here," Eleo interrupted, "I suppose you

might as well get it over with. What do you want to know?"

"Tuesday," Asey frowned at a bilious, lop-sided landscape in the modern manner, "you was havin' lunch with Dave Truman, friendly as could be. Just what was it that happened b'tween then an' yest'day that would make you as angry at him as you seemed to be when you an' Giles had your little flare-up?"

Eleo hesitated, and shot a quick look at Asey, still absorbed in the landscape. She didn't realize that every wink of her eyelashes was beautifully reflected to him by the tiny mirror beside the painting.

"I may as well tell you the whole story, I suppose." Her sigh was just a shade too artistic. "I bought a lot of Truman and Company stock years ago. When the market began to act up, I intended to sell it along with a lot of other things, but Dave persuaded me not to. I thought he honestly expected Truman's to come back with a bang, but I realize now that he just didn't want such a large block sold. Anyway, when Truman's finally went under, I had a telegram from him personally guaranteeing any losses of mine. Tuesday, at lunch, I asked him what he was going to do about it, and the—well, he pretended that he knew nothing whatever about it at all! He said Marie must have sent it; of course, he was simply backing out, and I don't know what I can do about it. He says he was in Toronto the day the wire was sent, and the wire was from New York. It's all a matter for my lawyers, as I told him. He said he believed my lawyers might convince me that the president of any corporation hardly sent such all-inclusive telegrams to his stockholders, personally guaranteeing their losses. So—well, you can picture my feelings, after thinking Dave would of course stand by his word!"

"Didn't ever mention the wire to Dave this summer, any time?"

"But no! Why should I? Dave had promised, and that was enough for me. I'd no intentions of dunning him, or whatever you call it. Of course Dave sent that telegram, even if his name wasn't signed the way he said all his personal wires were signed! Code word, or something. I never realized, when I finally gave in and told Jo we'd spend a few months down here, just what terrible things we'd get into. I knew she wanted to be near Kay, but I'd no idea that Dave himself was to be here. He seemed to hold the most uncanny fascination for Jo. I finally had to forbid her going there alone, after Kay's death. People were talking—but of course, you knew all that."

Asey chewed his under lip reflectively and said nothing.

"She met such strange people there, too," Eleo went on. "That uncouth Hopkins boy—oh, I'm sorry, Bev dear. I keep forgetting that he's one of your Cape Codders. Anyway, though I suppose Dave's friends were all right in their way, they were hardly Jo's type."

I thought briefly of the night before, of Creel Friar, and his smash-up and his broken arm and all the rest, and wondered by what mental process Eleo arrived at the conclusion that Creel *was* Jo's type.

"Did Jo tell you what Dave was tryin' to say b'fore he died?" Asey swung around and faced Eleo.

"All that frightfully mysterious stuff about ink? Yes. Amazing, isn't it, how people wander. Of course, he was wandering, wasn't he?"

"Doc didn't seem to think so. S'posin', Mrs. Dwight, s'posin' Dave was quite sane an' tryin' to tell somethin' about the someone who killed him. What's your guess as to what he meant?"

"My guess?" Eleo gave a trilly little laugh. "Oh, Mr. Mayo, you're simply perfect! As if I'd know! But—don't you suppose he tried to say that he wanted a drink? I mean, if he knew what he was talking about, 'drink' seems awfully sensible to me. But there are so many, many things that it might have been!"

"That's right." Asey rose. "They sure is a lot of words that fit in. Think, drink, mink, pink, an' so on. Sorry we bothered you, Mrs. Dwight. Comin', Miss Ag'tha an' Bev?"

We left Eleo still lying on the couch, and were let out by the Filipino, who slammed the door behind us with heart-felt cheer.

"Enlightening interview," Agatha commented as we rolled out the drive.

"Enlightenin' in some ways," Asey said, "if not what you'd call glowin' with truth an' accuracy an' the mighty beam of honesty. 'Course, you wouldn't expect a woman like her to show a lot of sense, but why, when she knew she was cornered, couldn't she of made up a better yarn than that!"

Aunt Agatha chuckled. "What were those papers you thrust on her?"

"Them? Oh, a license to fish, an' a license to hunt, an' a license to catch lobsters, an' a license to carry a gun, an' a license to drive a car, an' a license to let the car be driven, an' a motor boat license, an' a few other odds an' ends of licenses I have to cart around. I didn't think she'd look much farther than the Indian on the seal. It ain't what's in a paper that counts. It's the seals on 'em. I know a feller that rode in a special train all over Central America, just on a handful of cigar store coupons that'd been dabbed lib'ral with sealin' wax. Real comf'table, it was, too. I—anyway, they worked."

Agatha laughed. "Asey, d'you realize she didn't get up off that chaise longue? Couldn't it have been Eleo in Jo's clothes that Ike Smalley saw?"

"Never," I said. "Eleo Dwight never rowed a boat in her life. She wouldn't know an oar from an anchor. Don't you feel that way, Asey? And tell me, how are you ever going to get the truth from her?"

"Wait. Catch her up some day when she ain't got the footlights lit an' the backdrop down. She measured me up just now an' d'cided I was a fool. It's an awful good plan to let someone like her think you're dumb. They get a lot more expansive-like. Wa-el, we'll just let her run loose, an' then catch her up some day."

I began to feel quite sorry for Eleo.

Up in the village the station agent hailed me and demanded eighty-four cents for a day letter.

"It's from Budge an' Snuff," he said. "Nope, they ain't been kicked out of school yet."

I didn't know whether to laugh or cry about the garbled message, which was intended, I gathered, to comfort me about Dave and to add their own feelings on the matter. It ended up characteristically: "Take care of Sully we will pay for his keep out of our allowance. Snuf lost a front tooth yesterday but it was loose you know the one and please send hockey stick in boat house locker we think."

While Agatha was reading the message, Hanson's car slowed to a stop beside us. Bob Raymond, the good-looking trooper of whom Asey had spoken the day before, hopped out and jumped on our running board.

"I've hunted you through three continents—Asey, did you go to Ike Smalley's?"

"Yup. Why—"

"Listen. Hanson was burning up about that Grosgrain laddie and told me to trail him. He went up on Crooked Cliff, poked in a few swallow holes, and then sat down behind a rock. Out of sight of us all, he thought, and had a nice quiet little smoke. And—"

"He told Jo he didn't smoke," I said. "He told her so distinctly when she was kidding about her Uncle Bert carrying a lighter as well as matches—"

"Maybe so, Mrs. Penrose. But he lay there and smoked and seemed mighty pleased with himself. Every now and then he'd grin and sort of chuckle, and he didn't even seem to see a piece of flint at his elbow. Weesit Indians, hell!"

"Deary me," Asey said. "So Luther—"

"Just wait'll you hear. After half an hour or so, he got up and went down behind Truman's house. And just about that time, I saw your car scudding along the beach road. So did he. He took one of Truman's dories and set out rowing. I couldn't very well follow him by boat, so I dashed back to get a car and keep him in sight from the road, and Hanson and the boys had taken everything, so I had to run it. I got mixed up on one of the wood lanes, and came out—well, God alone knows where. Anyway, Grosgrain was just shoving off from Ike Smalley's boat house. I walked down from the woods to the beach, about a hundred yards down, and got my breath and watched him row back. Then I walked through the bushes to the path, the one that leads from Smalley's boat house up to his place, and—just wait'll you hear what brother Grosgrain left behind. He was the one that left it, too, because I couldn't find any other footprints. Look—"

Triumphantly, Bob held out the leather sheath to a hunting knife, as spanking new as the knife plunged into Asey's car had been.

CHAPTER SEVEN

BEFORE you could comfortably say "Luther Charles Grosgrain," Asey swooped us and the roadster back to my house, found Hanson, and learned from him that Grosgrain was in my orchard.

"Sitting there like he owned it," Hanson added bitterly. "*I* can't help it if you don't want him there, Mrs. Penrose. I learned my lesson with that guy! If he wants anything, he's going to get it, and from now on I treat him—"

"With p'liteness," Asey finished. "Don't know's I blame you. Raymond told you about that knife sheath he found?"

"Yeah. But if you come and show me a slow motion picture, showing Grosgrain in the act of murdering Dave Truman, I'd know it was a fake somewhere."

"Then you don't mind, Hanson, if I do the dallyin' with him?"

"Mind?" Hanson laughed shortly. "Mind? All I got to say is, if you don't, no one will."

We found Luther puffing placidly at a cigar that was

nearly as large as he was. He jumped up at our approach, and waved his hand apologetically at the ocean.

"It was so—so lovely here," he spoke to me, "that I asked the officer if he thought you'd mind my trespassing until you returned—Mrs. Penrose, isn't it? I'm sorry I didn't hear you come back. I'll go at once."

"Mrs. Penrose," Asey said smoothly, "is always d'lighted to find strangers lurkin' in her orchard, settin' on her chairs an' gen'rally makin' themselves to home. Don't leave, Mr. Grosgrain. Don't even fidget like you'd like to go. Seem's if they was a lot of things I want to ask you. Last night, f'r example, you told us you didn't smoke. Sort of surprises me to find you smokin' to-day."

Mr. Grosgrain clucked his tongue. "Tsk, tsk! I—I— why, really, Mr. Mayo! I've no recollection of saying that! I—you know, I'm afraid my whole recollection of last night, from the time I was—er—knocked out, till the officer came, is really very hazy anyway. Very hazy indeed! If I said that I didn't smoke, I can assure you that I didn't know what I was talking about. I've always found tobacco a great comfort and solace."

And if Luther didn't feel it, he put on a very good imitation of a man very anxious to set things right.

"Hunted any Indian war whoops to-day?" Asey asked.

"This Cape air!" Luther sighed. "I intended to, but I just went up on top of the cliff, and it was so comfortable up there in the sun, I just sat and lazed. I shouldn't have, because I've only funds for two weeks down here, and I ought to make every minute count—"

"Two weeks!" Hanson threw his visored cap on the ground and kicked it. "Two weeks, he says. Two weeks I got to have that under my heels and in my sight! Two weeks—two weeks, for God's sakes—Asey, can't you do something about it? Two weeks—"

"And after I'd wasted time up on the cliff," Mr. Grosgrain went on, "I walked over to Mr. Truman's landing and borrowed one of his boats—"

"Borrowed?" Asey raised his eyebrows. "Borrowed, Mr. Grosgrain?"

"Perhaps I shouldn't have. Perhaps—but d'you know, as a Truman stockholder, I thought it might be within my rights to borrow one of Mr. Truman's boats for a brief time—"

"Sure," Asey murmured. "Sure. Own a share of steel, an' ride around in Schwab's limousine. Buy a gov'ment bond an' borrow the M'rines. Sure, I get it. Go on."

"I rowed over to the shore of the opposite neck of land, and then I found I was tired," Mr. Grosgrain went on, "so I beached the boat and rested for a while. Then I came back. Truly, Mr. Mayo, I didn't hurt the boat one bit. I took great care to leave it exactly as I found it, and I think I may even have left it in better condition. I bailed it out, and scraped numerous shell fish from it, and removed several clams that had clearly—well, they could never have been used for bait."

We just sat there and stared at him. If he was ad libbing until he found out how much we knew of his comings and goings, he certainly was doing what my tailor calls a class A, number one, no shoddy material job.

"An' when," Asey inquired, "did you lose your huntin' knife an' the leather sheath?"

Mr. Grosgrain positively beamed. "Oh, did you find that? My, I'm glad. I lost it out of my coat pocket last night when I was running away from the officers at Mr. Truman's. In fact, it was while I retraced my steps in an effort to find it in all the fog and wet, that I came upon that gun. You see, there's a youngster who lives at my boarding house, and he's taken a keen interest in my research into Indian lore. He insisted, when I told him of my projected visit here, that I should take his knife with me. It was a brand new birthday present of his. You see, he's quite young. Only eight. He had an idea that I might run into some Indians and need to defend myself. I know I could get him another knife, but it wouldn't be the same, and I hated to have to tell him that I'd been careless enough to lose it."

"There," Hanson said to Asey. "There, see? I told you, it wouldn't make any difference. Ain't it slick? Ain't it a nifty? Ain't it a natural? And if I could only get him into some court long enough to tell that to a jury! Deary me," he mimicked Luther's tones, "my, my, wouldn't I just be glad! Wouldn't the judge just love it! Peachy, that's what."

Asey got up and shook Mr. Grosgrain by the hand.

"Whether it's God's gospel truth," he said gravely, "or the expert shellackin' of good, toothsome lies, I hand it to you. It's genius. It's got polish. It's got—"

"It's got everything," Aunt Agatha said. "But what are you going to do about it, Asey?"

"He's going to do what I got to do," Hanson jammed his cap on. "He's going to take it and like it. There's just one hope. I told Parker what you said, Asey, and he promised he'd have one of that firm this bird worked for come down and identify him for sure. Maybe—but there ain't a chance. He'll be him, and that story'll be true."

With a weary sigh, Hanson left. There was something funereal about his slow, labored march to the house, and all of us watched him in fascination, almost keeping time with our heads.

"I'm afraid," Grosgrain turned to Asey, "that the sergeant doesn't believe me even now. Do you happen to know, Mr. Mayo, which member of the firm will be coming here? That is to say, whom the firm is sending? Of course, it's not possible that Mr. Montgomery himself—Mr. Montgomery Walker, the senior partner," he explained parenthetically, "it would be impossible for him to come. Mr. Montgomery only consults in the most important cases, and then only from his own home. He never bothers to come to the office any more. I suppose young Mr. Meredith will send his clerk. Though maybe," Luther's eyes gleamed, "maybe they'll send young Mr. Meredith himself. I don't expect I could hope for anything better. Yes, I shall be very interested to see just who—"

He was so excited thinking over who would be sent to his rescue, and just how important his rescue might be in the eyes of his former employers that he might as well have been in Tibet for all he noticed us.

"I'm damned," Bob Raymond said to Asey. "Damned and befuddled. Here I thought I had this whole thing settled with my little hatchet, and my God, Asey, you have to believe the man!"

"Yes, Peter Pan," Asey murmured with a grin, "I b'lieve in fairies! Oho—here comes your boss, Bob, with Hanson leadin' the way like a drum-major."

Parker, loose-jointed and amiable, was strolling over towards the orchard, but I hardly saw him after my first glance at the stranger with him. He was portly in size, bearing and complexion, and he could have officiated as a best man or even as a bridegroom without the slightest alteration. Silk hat, lavender tie, gardenia in buttonhole—beside me, Luther let out a yelp.

"It's Mr. Montgomery!" he shrilled. "Mr. Montgomery! Mr. Montgomery himself! HIMSELF!"

"Dam' nuisance, comin' down here to pull you out of scrapes, Grosgrain," Mr. Montgomery told him severely. "Dam' nuisance. Just goin' into the club, I was, and young Meredith stopped me. 'Grosgrain's in trouble,' he says, 'and you better handle the matter yourself.' Dam' nuisance, tearin' all the way down here this afternoon. Missed my golf. Missed my golf, mind you!"

"Oh, Mr. Montgomery," Luther was practically on the verge of tears, "oh, Mr. Montgomery, you shouldn't have done it, sir. You—"

"There, there, Grosgrain! But mind you, keep out of scrapes from now on! It's the last scrape I get you out of,

my man! Fiddlin' with murders at your age! You ought
to be ashamed! Told you when you left. I said, Grosgrain,
find yourself a hobby. My very words. Thought you'd
have sense enough to play golf. What other hobby is
there? And you pick on Indian relics! Indian relics, pah!
See where they get you? Did I ever get mixed up with
murders playin' golf? No. Lot of nonsense, the whole
business. Throw your Indian relics out of the window
and buy a set of golf clubs. Better—no, I'll send you a
set myself. And a card to the club. And I'll have McNabb
take you out. Mind you don't take his dither about—yes,
yes, Parker, of course it's Grosgrain! Don't twitch my
elbow. You keep a straight left, Grosgrain, keep your eye
on the ball, and follow through!"

Mr. Montgomery demonstrated with his cane, and
Luther nearly fell all over himself.

"I'll do my best, sir, I—"

"Better had. Got to live this down. Don't like it—
don't like this business at all. As I told Parker, if the
feller had a hobby like golf, he'd be all right. Indian
relics—hullo, Agatha. How's your game?"

A little weakly, Aunt Agatha told him her game was
rotten. "Neuritis," she added.

Mr. Montgomery shook his head. "Pity. Great pity.
Have a twinge myself now and then. Need me any more,
Parker? If I hurry back, I may be able to catch them before they leave the club and see how Hunter's new mashie
went. Too whippy, if you ask me. Too whippy—yes,
indeed, Parker, I knew it was Grosgrain. Good feller,
completely reliable, absolutely honest, but no judgment

about hobbies. Mind you, Grosgrain, no more scrapes! Can't have my day ruined for a feller old enough to know better. You stayin' down here? What's that? Two weeks? I'll send your clubs down, and mind you use 'em! Indian relics—"

With shaking shoulders, Parker escorted Mr. Montgomery back to the town car parked in the drive.

"Dachshund," Agatha said. "The car, I mean. Long and low—I've got to sit down. This touching rescue of an old servitor has been too much—my, watch Luther scamper to hold the door! Asey, are you still here?"

Asey wiped his eyes. "I thought I'd seen all sorts, but I'm just in the kind'garten. I wish I had a glass case to put Mr. Montgomery in. Miss Ag'tha, did you ever really know him? Whyn't you say so?"

"Because," Agatha said promptly, "in all the years I've known Monty Walker, I never knew he had any business other than golf. It just didn't connect. Asey, Parker's beckoning to you."

We continued to laugh, in spasms, till dinner. And through dinner—during the course of which Luther appeared and borrowed all of Kyle's golf books, an old mashie and a crocheted practice ball. Even after dinner we were still giggling.

"At least," Asey said at last, "we can be pretty sure that brother Luther is out. I suppose that's an achievement, when you come right down to brass tacks. It's somethin'."

"Something, yes," Agatha replied, "but it still doesn't answer all the questions that have been vexing me. Who killed Dave? Who shot at you? Who planted the knife in your car seat? Where was the cat's bell, or his collar, just before the murder? How'd either or both get back on him, just afterwards? Why is Mrs. Dwight so wrathy over Dave? What was Jo doing at Dave's yesterday afternoon? What happened to the bullet that came from Dave's gun? Those are the things that bother me."

"All I can tell you," Asey grinned, "all I can tell you is that Luther ain't at the bottom of any of it. I was thinkin' we might track down Jo an' see—"

"You don't have to." Jo spoke from the doorway into the dining room. "Jo's here. I snuk in the back way. At least, Creel Friar dumped me on your back door step. He's mad—"

"Is he drivin' with one arm?"

"Yes, he's driving." She paid no attention to the terrific crash that followed her words. "That is, I guess he was driving. His idea, all of it."

"Ain't you goin' out to see what that noise was?"

"No, Asey, I'm not. I can tell you. We just missed the stone wall coming into the driveway, and I'd say, offhand, that he wasn't so lucky going out. I—"

"Whose car? Not his?"

"Well, it was mine up till dinner time, when mother presented it to Creel. So I suppose it's his. Was his. I don't really care."

"What," Agatha looked at Jo curiously, "what's happened, my dear? Has Creel—"

"Creel," Jo lighted a cigarette with perfectly steady hands, "is a Nasty Word. I came here in the fullness of my heart and the first—well, practically the first flush of my girlhood, to tell you that you were right and I was wrong. Asey, don't jitter so! If you want to go out and see if Creel Friar's killed himself, run along. All I have to add, Miss Agatha and Bev, is that I haven't been dashing around with him since last night because I wanted to, because that's not so. I more or less had to. And if you don't give me a bed and some pajamas to-night, I'll have to sleep under a pine tree in some one of God's open spaces or another. The thought repels me."

"But Jo, Eleo—"

"Eleo and I," Jo said pleasantly, "have had what promises to be an understanding. A parting of the ways. It's been brewing a long time, and it came to a head yesterday, and to-day. Eleo's a model parent in lots of ways, but she and I don't always see eye to eye on a lot of subjects. And to be terribly honest, I can't say that her judgment is mature enough, often enough, for me to bow down to it. Do I get a bed? I'm free, white and over twenty-one."

"Of course you do, my child," Aunt Agatha said quickly. "And if Bev doesn't provide it, I'll share a pine tree with you. I—what happened, Asey?"

"Other arm," Asey told us as he phoned for Doctor Cummings. "Changed your mind about Friar, Jo?"

"Uh-huh. Just been confessing. 'Had I only believed people when they told me Creel Friar was a cad and a rotter'—there's a swell true story beginning, Miss Agatha."

"Look here," I said. "You and Asey, you didn't tell

us the truth when you said you'd never met him. Hadn't you met him before, Jo?"

"Hanging her head in shame, the young woman confessed such was the case. Yes, Bev. Wednesday night. Creel was drunk, and we were having the hell of a time getting home. What with one thing and another. Asey roared along in his low backed car and spanked Creel—"

"He didn't," Agatha said delightedly. "Asey, how splendid of you!"

"He did a very thorough and workmanlike job," Jo smiled at him. "I thought for the moment that he was going to spank me, too, but he just carted me home and gave me a few well-chosen words of wisdom. So Creel's only broken the other arm? What about the car?"

"Gravity was agin' it," Asey said. "Like ole Lem Swett said when he turned atheist and tried his dumdest to pull down the Meth'dist church. Matter of fact, grav'ty done a neat job here. But Friar ain't suf'rin' any. He's too boiled to feel. The doc'll be over an' look after him. Now you've r'formed, Jo, what about yest'day?"

"You mean, why was I over to Dave's? How'd you find—well, I went over to see him. I often do. If he's busy, I just sit around and read, or dig in the garden. I like that house and I like being there, and I was fond of Dave. And after Kay's death, he was awf'ly lonely. It— oh, you know."

"But you didn't go into the house yesterday, did you?" I asked. "Giles never saw you."

"I started to, but the shades were crooked in the living room. That meant Dave was having company, or busy, or just plain didn't want to be bothered. So I plowed around the swamp to Kay's lean-to. You know where it is, up on the cliff. I sat there and read. She and I always kept a mess of books in a box there. And then I went along home."

"Ike Smalley seen you," Asey said. "Tell me how you hurt your leg."

"Hurt my—oh. Was Ike peering through his binoculars? The old eel! And I forgot all about him, and stripped and took a dip. Deary me! But I haven't hurt my leg, Asey."

Briefly, he told her his theory of the ricochetting bullet.

"An' Ike said you limped, an' bound up your leg or your hip."

Jo leaned back in her seat and laughed. "I'm forced to believe, Asey, that he and Washy Wheeler weren't watching the binding process much. I was limping. I had a stone in my shoe, and I hated to bother to stop and take it out. But the wound—I'll show you." She started to peel off her sweater, but Asey held up a restraining hand.

"I'm no eel. An'," he chuckled, "I hear the doc's car. Nick of time. You show Bev an' Miss Ag'tha, an' I'll take their word for whatever it is."

The wound turned out to be an ugly blotch of poison ivy on Jo's hip.

"Sun bathing," she explained. "I didn't go near a scrap of poison ivy. Not within ten miles, but apparently it leaped from the ground and fastened itself on me somehow. It itched like fury yesterday. That's half why I took that dip. Then I slapped some salt water on it, and covered it with my white scarf. I'd lost the bandage swimming. Look, Bev, you haven't anything to eat, have you? This argument of mother's and mine took place just as I bit into my soup. I marched out soupless and gee, clothesless, too. S'pose mother'll dump my things on the lawn, or will I have to spend the rest of my life in these shorts? Thank God I remembered my check book!"

Asey and Dr. Cummings came in.

"I'm speechless," the latter announced, "speechless with disgust. Every time I see that Friar boy, I want to rub him against a nutmeg grater. I told Bob Raymond to take him to the hospital, and have them set his arm, and sober him up, and bring him back to Nellie Howes's place. He's fighting, now, and I'm still black and blue from the way he carried on this morning. At least, he can't drive a car for a while unless he decides to use his feet. What was Jo's wound?"

"Poison ivy," Agatha and I told him.

"Glad to hear it," Asey said heartily. "Jo, your mother reclined all aft'noon while we was there, on a couch. You think—"

"Look, Asey, I've just left mother behind me. Don't let's go into the subject."

"I know, but d'you think—"

"Think your bouncing bullet is lodged in her anatomy somewhere? I do not. She just sprawled on the chaise longue because it's picturesque. She does look well, lying there in a tea gown. And besides all that, Asey, she and I had an argument yesterday afternoon practically before we hit the end of Bev's drive. I got out, and she went on alone. Creel said he'd been waiting over at our house yesterday for years, and mother came straight home from here. You could check up on the time she left here and the time she got home, and make sure, but I know darn well she never went near Dave's. And I'll practically swear she hasn't any bullet holes."

"You don't think Dave meant 'Pink' when he said 'Ink'?" Agatha asked.

"He might have, but I don't think mother had anything to do with killing him. I really don't. She can ruin anyone's reputation in two sentences, and she lies fluently, and she is definitely unpleasant when crossed, but she hasn't the courage for murder. Nor the strength to wield a knife. Mother might try to poison someone, but nothing more vigorous than that."

"What about Creel Friar?"

"His being mixed up in this? I doubt it. Murder requires a more or less sober hand. But I've wondered sometimes if perhaps he didn't have something to do with Kay's death. You know, Giles was right yesterday. There's a lot more to Kay's death than has ever come to light. And all the rest of those suicides from that cliff, too. Somehow I can't get over the feeling that there's some connection with all that, and with Dave. But—I almost forgot. Whatever became of Luther?"

We told her about Luther and Mr. Montgomery, and about the time we were beginning to recover Luther himself walked in, beaming gently behind his pince-nez.

"I do dislike bothering you," he greeted me apologetically, "but there are some terms here which I find I do not understand, and Mrs. Howes's boarding house has no dictionary, nor does my pocket edition cast any light. I wondered if Miss Penrose—Mr. Montgomery said she was a fine golfer—with a splendid swing—I wondered if she could tell me, what is a bogey, what is a dormy, what is a stymie—" he pulled out his little note book and consulted it anxiously, "what is—oh, I know mashie, now. What—"

"Perhaps," Agatha said, "you'd best come in the dining room with me while I define terms. Jo, aren't you a golfer? Come help."

Talking in either ear, they led Luther into the other room.

"I'm beginnin' to feel sorry," Asey remarked, "for all the little arrow heads an' flints over on the cliff by the clay bank that'll never find a home. One thing I promised myself: I'm goin' to carry Luther up to Boston after this is over an' treat him to a pair of plus fours. Ever since Monty begun to preach golf, I been wonderin' how Luther'd look in plus fours. Bev, this business is a mess."

"Mess?" I picked Sully up from his basket and held him in my lap. "Mess is too mild a word. Asey, didn't Hanson's men find anything? With all their experts and photographers and what not? What does Parker think?"

"Wa-el, Parker's sort of come to the same conclusion that I have. It wan't no casual crank, like we thought at first. It's nearer home. Someone who knows the lay of the land, an'—providin' whoever's so crazy to get me out of the way is the same one that killed Dave—someone who knows me more'n by name. I still can't see—y'know, somehow, somewhere, we must know somethin' that matters. At least, I must, or they'd lay for you an' Giles an' Miss Ag'tha, Bev. But hell's bells, from the time I come here till I started to leave last evenin', that's too short a time!"

"If you ask me," I said, "there's a maniac loose. The whole thing isn't normal."

"Yup, but if it's just someone that wants to kill for the sheer an' utter joy of killin', why does he pick on me? 'Course, he might have a single track mind, but with so many other folks lurkin' around this place, you'd think he might take a pot shot at some one of you, for a change."

"He's just aiming high," the doctor said soothingly. "Just—"

"If that's a bad pun," Asey said, "you ought to be ashamed of yourself. An' that r'minds me, all day—in fact, ever since I met Luther, I been dyin' to—"

"I've watched you try to work it in," I said. "And I've watched Agatha try to work it in, and Bob Raymond very nearly has. Probably even you, doctor, have been rolling it over your tongue."

"You mean, it goes against my grain? I have," he admitted cheerfully, "and I did, too. I've got to see that Smith boy who stepped in the cold frame over at Pamet. If Friar gets drunk again, Asey, send for Collins. I'm tired of seeing those pig eyes."

At midnight, we pried Jo and Agatha and Luther

from the dining room, which was by that time a shambles of golf balls, golf clubs, diagrams, broken flower pots that had got in the way of follow-throughs. The floor was scratched and a pane of glass broken, but I knew better than to get worked up about it. My husband has been an enthusiastic golfer since he wore short pants, and I still shudder to think of how the house will look on the day that he really breaks seventy-eight. I still remember the carnage of his first ninety-nine.

Eventually we all got to bed. Jo slept in my room downstairs, and Agatha had the connecting room. It was around five o'clock that I woke to hear something bounce in the room above, upstairs, but as it was followed by the tinkle of Sully's bell, I thought nothing more of it and dozed off again.

Then I moved a toe. And then I broke out into a cold sweat. Sully was curled up in a ball on the foot of my bed.

CHAPTER EIGHT

ANOTHER slight thud sounded in the room above, and Sully pushed against the sole of my foot. But I heard no further tinkling of the bell.

Wide awake, now, I closed my eyes and listened so hard that my ear drums nearly burst. There were all the thousand-odd familiar noises which I've listened to and mentally catalogued every summer for forty years—the tapping of the white lilac bush against the side of the house, the little bang of the south honeysuckle trellis no carpenter has ever been able to still, the slap-slap of loose shingles near the chimney, the clatter of a shutter from Agatha's room, the creak of Jo's spool bed as she switched around restlessly, the rustle and scrunch of a mouse in the wainscoting—

The wind suddenly blew a strident blast around the corner of the room, bringing with it the beating of the trees in the orchard and the dull pounding of the surf beyond, so clearly and so evenly that I seemed to see it smash against Crooked Cliff, throwing off curls of foam that slithered around the rocks at the foot.

But those, and all the other sounds, were familiar

ones that I knew by heart. Most of them were too faint for a stranger like Jo even to notice. There wasn't any creak or squeak I couldn't place. There wasn't any soft tinkling of Sully's silver bell.

I began to wonder if I hadn't been dreaming, and perhaps imagined it all. Leaning on one elbow, I stared out at a lopsided moon and tried to remember the dream. As usual, I couldn't. But I did begin to recall Kyle's often repeated advice about noises at night.

"In all probability, Bev, it's not a burglar. Not down here, anyway. If I were a professional burglar, I shouldn't make noises. If I were an amateur, my first noise would send me streaking like a greased pig. Now, if it isn't a burglar, there's no sense in worrying. If it is, just restrain yourself and your impulses to grab a gun and go for him. I pay insurance enough so that everything in this house is covered. There's nothing valuable anyway except the books and some of the prints and a mess of antiques, and the drabbest idiot of a burglar would never think of snaring away the mahogany lowboy—"

"Just the same," I said, "a woman with a gun, a woman who looks as though she knew how to use the gun, should be—"

"Should be and is in more danger than a woman with a gun who doesn't look as though she knew butt from barrel. If I were a burglar, and thought there was some chance of a bit of shooting, I'd jolly well shoot first."

"Burglars," I retorted, "aren't supposed to carry guns. They—"

"My dear, there is no book of etiquette for burglars. Perhaps in the past they didn't carry guns, but in these days most of 'em do, and it's considered quite smart to use your little weapon. No, Bev, if it isn't a burglar, what of your noises? If it is, let him burgle in peace. After all, with the house unoccupied most of the winter, there's plenty of opportunity for burglars to burgle without disturbing us. The whole damn thing is simply that you're afraid of the dark!"

And he was pretty much right. I am. My hand itched to pull out the gun I knew was in the dressing table drawer where Giles had put it after his chase for Mr. Grosgrain the night before, but somehow I did nothing about it. The spirit was perfectly willing, but the flesh was against the idea. Besides, I remembered that Asey himself had locked all the doors. He was sleeping somewhere in the house—I think the living room had been his final choice, and the yard and back of the house held quantities of state troopers. If there were any intruders prowling around, Asey or the police would know it.

So, after cocking my ear once more, I rolled over and definitely went back to sleep.

Furthermore, odd as it may sound, it never entered my head to see if Sully actually had on his collar or if the bell was attached.

I didn't mention the interlude the next morning. In the clear light of day and reason, my behavior seemed stupid even to me. But after breakfast, I slipped away from the rest and took a hasty glance around the second floor. Everything was in its accustomed place, and I couldn't find a trace of any prowler.

Aunt Agatha followed me up after a few minutes.

"I want that tennis ball Sully was chasing yesterday," she said. "I left it on the maple bed while I took my bath up here last night. Oh—did you take it?"

We found it, after much groveling about on our respective stomachs, wedged underneath the bureau.

"Amazing," Agatha said breathlessly, "how cats can get—it's funny. He must have come up here in the night and played with it, because he came downstairs when I did, and spent until at least two o'clock on my bed. I say, Bev, you didn't happen to hear any strange noises in the night, did you? I thought—"

Jo, who had just clattered up the stairs, burst into the room in time to hear Agatha's question.

"Don't tell me," she laughed uneasily, "that you two heard noises in the night, too? I was—well, I waked up once myself, but you two seemed to be sleeping like a couple of logs, so I thought nothing of it. I decided it was Sully after his catnip mouse, or a real one, or something. Say, let's go tell Asey, and see if he heard any sounds or saw visions—"

We found Asey in the living room, almost obliterated by the smoke of his corncob pipe. He listened to my story, then to Agatha's and Jo's.

"I didn't think to see what time it was," the latter concluded, "any more than Miss Agatha or Bev. But if Bev says Sully was with her, and she heard the bell, and the rest of us heard the noise—honestly, Asey, I'm getting scared! S'pose someone took it into their head to come at us with knives?"

Asey puffed at his pipe, and a little smile played around the corners of his eyes.

"Don't retire under your eyebrows or behind your old pipe," I admonished. "Tell us what you think. D'you suppose there was someone parading around?"

"Wa-el," Asey drawled, "I was on the couch in the settin' room here. I didn't hear no one. I already talked to Hanson an' Bob, an' they said everythin' was okay outside. I locked the front door, chained it, an' it was all right this mornin'. Same way with the dinin' room door. That wasn't chained, but it was locked. Kitchen door's still stuck, Katy says. Garage doors is padlocked. All your lower windows is screened. So're most of your upstairs windows. I don't hardly think, Bev, that what you heard was anythin' more'n a chipmunk on the roof, or a lot of 'magination. B'sides, what'd be the idea of bustin' in here anyhows? Where'd it get anyone?"

"It's just what you call hum'nly poss'ble," I remarked, "that your boy friend of the gun and knife might have been trying to get you."

"But he didn't. An' Sully's bell is on his collar, an' his collar's on him, this mornin'. Who'd take the chance of tinklin' a bell, not knowin' where the cat was? No, Bev, I guess not."

"Very well," I said. "Very well. But if you ask me, I'd say that all of us in the house had a very near escape from something last night. I know it's my fault for not yelping bloody murder, but if all three of us, if we all heard a noise, Asey, there must have been something behind it!"

His benign, slightly ironic smile annoyed me so that I stomped out of the room, and Jo followed me.

"Huh," she said. "Bev, I agree with you. But just the same, maybe—oh, hell! I'm going to borrow a car from you, if I may, and run over to the house. Mother won't be up, and maybe Pablo or someone'll swipe some clothes for me. If they won't, I'll have to go up to Hyannis and get an outfit. Now that I'm your house guest, whether you like it or not, I'll have to dress like a lady. Can't rook your good name. Mind if I take the roadster?"

"Go ahead. Keys are on a hook in the kitchen. All tagged. Better take the whole bunch for the roadster. A rear tire is funny, and you might need the spare. It's locked. Come to think of it, I'd better see what there is left in the ice box and do a bit of meal planning. In fact, I might break down and make some pies. Katy is beneath pies, or pies are beneath her, depending on how you look at it."

Jo laughed and strode into the kitchen. I heard her exchanging pleasantries with Katy while I watered the plants by the dining room door. I hate to water plants almost as much as I hate having plants inside a house— they belong in gardens—but my grandmother and my mother were accustomed to keeping plants in the alcove by the dining room door, and they made plants a tradition.

As I snipped off a dead leaf from a gloxinia, I heard Agatha's voice, carefully muted, coming from the living room. I'd slammed the door behind me, but apparently it hadn't latched.

"Of course there was someone, Asey."

" 'Fraid so." Asey sounded worried. "Hanson an' Bob both thought they caught sight of a figger in the moonlight. Chased around, but didn't get anyone. Honest, I don't get it. I know this house, known it since I was a kid an' used to play with Bev's father in the attic. It's an ole place, but it ain't got no trick panels. It ain't got any trick ways in an' out. But no one could of come in this floor without almost walkin' on top of me, or comin' in through your room or the other bedroom. An' even then, they'd have to be awful good to get the screens off without makin' a racket, not to speak of the trouble of gettin' 'em back on again later. But for Heaven's sakes, don't let Bev an' the girl know I think they was anyone. Jo feels bad enough, with Kay an' Dave, an' all this mess with her mother. An' though Bev don't scare easy, they's no sense in gettin' her worked up."

I sat down in the far corner of the alcove. Eavesdropping isn't usually in my line, but I resented being treated like a small, vacant-faced child.

"Why the bell?" Agatha asked.

"Good sense. Noise is explained. Just little kitty, careenin' around. 'Course, they's the chance that the cat might show up, but it's still good sense. Av'rage person don't count on cats sleepin' on the foot of folks's beds. Though if anyone knew Sully, they'd ought to know he wan't no common cat, the kind you stick out in the g'rage or the barn or the woodpile."

"Hm. Then it would seem that the person wasn't so very familiar with Sully and his privileges. Asey, what d'you really think about this whole mess?"

I could almost see Asey shake his head.

"Honest, I don't know. They's been no strangers seen around. No one seen around at all, when you come right down to it. 'Cept Jo. An' I believe her. I b'lieve Grosgrain, too. Both sort of—what's the word? Means sort of child-like, somehow—"

"Naïve?"

"That's it. Giles alibied Jet, an' he's out. You'n' Bev is out. Jo's mother—wa'el," Asey spoke very slowly, "I don't know. Seems like she might of had a finger in the pie, but she wasn't around, an' somehow I can't see her shootin' an' stabbin'. Like Jo said, if she ever set out to do any murderin', poison'd be her line. Just one thing's ranklin' in my mind now. That's the idea Hanson an' Bob got. Though I'll admit I kind of toyed with it my-self."

"Giles?"

I nearly fell off my chair.

"Uh-huh. He bought a new sheath knife last week. Bob's been checkin' up. One here, an' one in Wellfleet. So you thought about him, too?"

"I did. But there are plenty of fallacies. Plenty of loopholes."

Giles! I could feel myself getting hot and wrathy, and it took practically all my self-control to keep from yelling out unpleasant words at the two in the living room.

"Uh-huh." I heard the short scratch of a match being

lighted for Asey's pipe. "Bev says the shot was fired while Giles was half way through the hedge. That bein' the case, if Dave was holdin' his gun, an' his shot was a kind of reflex action, then he was stabbed while Giles was in the hedge. But we only got Giles's own story of what Dave was doin' beforehand. P'raps Dave wasn't pointin' the gun at himself, or puttin' it in a holster. He might of been pottin' at a skunk or a rabbit—"

"He might even have shot *at* Giles. And of course it was silly for Giles and Bev to plow through that hedge. Giles could have run to the driveway and dashed over in half the time. But to get back—Giles could have leaped through and stabbed Dave before Bev or I appeared. She admits she had eyes for nothing but the hedge."

"Yup, but the—"

"The slash in the screen? I myself didn't notice that till long afterwards, Asey. Plenty of time to stab Dave, he had. Plenty of time to conceal the knife. And then there was that business of calling the doctor."

Asey made an exclamation of impatience. "I know. I already talked about that to Cummings. He says he told Giles to try to stop the flow of blood. An' while Giles was in the house callin', he could of fixed things as he wanted. An' Giles ain't been around."

"And then there's that missing bullet. His motive," Agatha went on, "would be Kay, I suppose. He probably believed that Dave killed her. Played against Eleo to state his case. Really, Asey, if you let your fancy wander, you have a beautiful mess."

As I listened to her complacent tones, I watched the

knuckles of my clenched fists grow whiter and whiter. Asey and Agatha—and they could talk like that about Giles Hopkins!

Jethro appeared at the dining room door and beat a tattoo with the knocker, but I made no move to get up and see what he wanted.

"Only thing," Asey said, "is about that shootin' at me. Giles was in the doorway—"

"He'd nothing to do with that," Agatha interrupted. "I was standing beside him. But of course, it's possible that the person harrying you and the person who killed Dave are two very separate and different human beings. Now I—"

"Mis-sis Pen-rose!" Jethro was bellowing now. "Mis-sis Pen-rose!"

I went to the door and bellowed back laborious in-structions regarding dahlias to be taken up and wood to be chopped. Just as I shrieked out the last word into the ear trumpet, Bob Raymond dashed up the walk, nearly knocking down both Jethro and me in his haste.

"Asey—I want Asey!"

I jerked my finger toward the living room, still too annoyed with Asey and Agatha and Bob and anyone else who had the audacity to think Giles a murderer, to answer in words. Besides, my conversation with Jethro had left me gasping like a fish.

But curiosity got the better of me. After a second's indecision I followed Bob Raymond into the living room.

He stood before the table, and pointed to a pair of binoculars lying there. I recognized them as belonging to

Giles, for the strap was missing and the leather case bore his initials.

"Listen, Asey," Bob said earnestly, "this may be another flop, but it fits in with what we were talking about. I mean the Hopkins lad. I found these out over the kitchen sink at Truman's, see? And—"

"And there's no earthly reason why you shouldn't," I interrupted angrily. "Giles gave them to Kay after he lost hers overboard sailing one day. That happened months ago, and they've been over at Dave's ever since. They don't mean a thing."

"Only," Bob said, "that they were over the sink. Don't you see? Sink—ink."

"D'you mean to tell me—you mean, you're trying to say that—what utter nonsense!"

"But really, Mrs. Penrose," Bob Raymond flushed, "I haven't any idea of trying to prove your cousin guilty! I'm just trying to find the answer to the words Mr. Truman said before he died! Maybe he meant sink, and if he did, then—"

"Maybe," I banged my fist on the table till the binoculars leaped, "maybe he referred to the clams that Grosgrain dumped out of the dory yesterday! 'Stink' does very nicely! Maybe he was speaking about the Peerless laundry. He left two cuff links in a shirt last week. Think how beautifully 'link' fits! And 'mink'! Think of that. Maybe he was shooting at a mink! And he used to call the ex-secretary of the treasury 'Bink.' Let's get a rhyming dictionary and see what we can do. Get all the possibilities down on paper, and cross them off, one by one. Then—"

"But I already have." Bob was so plaintive about it that I had to laugh. "I did. Honestly, Mrs. Penrose, he must have meant something by that!"

"If you ask me," I said, "he said 'ink,' and 'ink' was exactly what he meant. He said it twice, as distinctly and as clearly as ever I heard him say anything. And if Dave Truman said 'ink,' he didn't mean Giles Hopkins's binoculars! I, oh dear, Asey, I'm so mad!"

"I know," he stroked my shoulder, "but don't be, Bev."

"And," I moved away from him, "and I heard all that you and Agatha had to say about Giles, and—"

"All?" Agatha asked.

"Every bit."

"Then, my dear, you must realize what we both said, that it was a beautiful hypothetical case, which no one in this world could prove. At least, we've no proof. And really, Bev, we probably would have said the same things had you been in the room. And really, my dear—"

She didn't need to finish her sentence. I knew from that faint smile of amusement just what she was think-ing, and so I hurriedly left before she could think any further along the same line. I remembered the first time Kyle and I had found the twins listening in on a con-versation which didn't concern them in the least, and I vividly recalled Budge's comment to me later. "We won't listen again, mother. You made us feel silly."

I don't suppose I ever felt sillier.

Out in the kitchen I found Mr. Grosgrain, who dis-played two blistered palms and beamed apologetically.

"I'm disturbing you again. I wanted to bring back your mashie and the books, and your cook said you were busy with Mr. Mayo, so I waited."

"Given up golf so soon?"

"No. But the clubs Mr. Montgomery promised me came this morning by truck, special delivery. I—I think I shall wait until to-morrow to practice with them, though. I seem to have some blisters. The green book with the white stripe said that if you got blisters, you were probably gripping the club too hard. Really, there's quite a lot to golf, isn't there? Am—am I bothering?"

"Not at all." I found flour and butter and motioned for Katy to take down the rolling pin and board. "I'm just going to make a pie. Katy, will you peel the apples— no, on second thought, run over to Logan's and get some eggs. When you get back we'll make out a list and begin to stock up. No, you're not bothering, Mr. Grosgrain. I'm just a little chagrined, and I'm going to take it out on a bit of cooking."

He reached for a bowl and the apples. "Do let me peel," he said. "I used to for my mother, and later for my sister. Mrs. Penrose, do you know this Creel Friar who is staying at Mrs. Howes's place with me?"

"Briefly. Has he broken any more bones or cars?"

"I don't think so. They brought him back from the hospital last night, and my room is next to his, and really, I was glad I had my books and golf club to keep me amused during the night. I—"

"You don't mean that you practiced golf all night?"

"I had to," Luther sliced an apple with an expert

hand. "I had to. Late as it was when I left here, and much as I wanted to sleep—I really hadn't slept much the night before when I was with Mr. Hanson—really, I couldn't sleep at all. Mr. Friar had some friend of his there, a gentleman, that is," he coughed, "a man from Provincetown, I gathered. They spent the night drinking."

"Noisy, I gather?"

"Oh, very. Very. They sang and yelled, and Mrs. Howes was spending the night with a cousin in Orleans, and the other guests couldn't seem to do much about it. I don't think it bothered them much, anyway. They were all in the other wing. But towards dawn, Mrs. Penrose, they began to get confidential. Some of it was really very —well, I tried not to listen."

Luther's face was very red, and I had a pretty good idea of the sort of thing he'd been forced to listen to.

"But then he spoke about Mr. Truman's daughter," Luther went on, "and then I really listened in earnest. He—well, he compared both Miss Truman and Miss Dwight very unfavorably with a young person whom I took to be a well known character in Provincetown," he mentioned the nickname of a model whose personal generosity was an unquestioned byword, "and then he began to talk about the people who'd been found dead by the cliff. The—uh—I—he said—I mean, I gathered that his general impression of it all was that some gentleman or gentlemen might perhaps have been responsible for the deaths of those young women. Of course he was very drunk, but I wondered—"

"Not one of the four," I helped him out, "had been

attacked, if that's what you mean. That was Dave's first thought. There'd been a road gang at work near here. Not a very pretty bunch. They stirred up a terrible hornet's nest in town. Their shacks weren't far away. But all that was ruled out. And in the cases of the others, there just wasn't even a road gang. But what else did you hear?"

It appeared that after they spoke of Kay and the others, Creel and his friend had dissolved into tears and become very mournful. Luther had heard nothing but a quiet series of sobs, and finally they became quiet enough for him to go to sleep.

"I couldn't help wondering," he concluded, "if that Friar hadn't something to do with this case. He—he was —well—"

"Politely speaking, such a swell person to be at the bottom of such a thing," I suggested. "Yes, he is. I can't think of anyone who had anything to do with him after the first week he was here, except a few of the younger crowd who thought he was smart, and a bunch of rough necks down the Cape. And Eleanor Dwight, who enjoys young men about her. Got the eggs, Katy? Good. Have we anything left about the house that we could cream, or run through a meat chopper, or bake with bread crumbs, or somehow disguise for lunch?"

"The fruit man left a basket of mushrooms yesterday," Katy said. "You told him he should, last week, so we'd have 'em for Miss Penrose. You said somethin' about broilin' some, an' makin' soup of the rest. There was some nice big—"

"Get 'em," I ordered. "I'll start and—what's the matter, Katy?"

"Gee, that's funny." Her round, rather pasty face wore a puzzled expression as she dumped the mushrooms out on the kitchen table. "I thought there was more big ones—"

Luther leaned over the table. The color drained out of his cheeks as he stared at the mushrooms.

"You—Mrs. Penrose, you weren't going to cook those? My God!"

He struck at my hand as I started to pick one up.

"No—no, don't even touch them! You—you'd best call Asey, quick! Those—they're amanita phalloides— they're the Death Cup—"

CHAPTER NINE

THE echo of my dazed bellow had hardly died away before Asey was in the room, with Agatha, Bob Raymond and Hanson tagging along behind him.

"What's wrong?" Asey demanded.

I wagged a feeble finger at the mushrooms.

"Those. Mr. Grosgrain says—"

Asey picked one up. "That's—my God, that's what my cousin Syl calls the Destroyin' Angel. Poisonous— but how in time'd you get hold of this mess of 'em?"

"They wasn't the ones Mack left yesterday," Katy said. "I thought they looked funny, when I first took 'em out. They—"

"Where'd you put 'em?" Asey demanded. "Where they been since yest'day? Where'd you leave 'em? After you got 'em, an' since?"

Katy isn't the type to answer direct questions directly —Kyle says I'm a sucker for long-windedness—and it took some time before we got the matter straightened out.

She had taken the mushrooms from Mack in the afternoon, the day before, and put them in the small old-fashioned ice box we use for fruit and vegetables. She had moved them once, later, when the ice man came. She hadn't touched them again until a few minutes before. And no saint in heaven could make her think they'd been touched the day before, or the night before.

"Why?" Asey demanded. "Why?"

Katy took refuge in tears.

"Come, come," I said, patting her shoulder, "Mr. Mayo isn't going to leap down your throat and pull your hair. Why don't you just say that you ate some last night? Did you broil 'em, or fry 'em in butter?"

They had, it seemed, been fried in butter—Katy hates washing the broiler. All because, come half past twelve last night, Katy had got hungry. And every scrap of bread gone, and cheese, too, what with them in the dining room playing golf and being hungry, and no eggs, and—

"Okay," Asey said. "If you ate the mushrooms last night an' ain't dead yet, chances is—who's been in the kitchen to-day?"

"Not a soul," Katy said. "No one of you but's here now, an' Miss Jo."

"Huh," Asey said, "an' if Mrs. Penrose'd told you to cook them things, you'd prob'ly gone ahead an' cooked 'em without sayin'—"

Katy wanted to know who would think a body could expect mushrooms to change themselves over night. "An' me just—"

"Okay," Asey said again. "I don't blame you for feelin' that way. Now—what's wrong?"

Katy sat down limply in a chair. "That noise," she

whispered. "Mother of Mary, it wasn't that cat! An' me thinkin' I heard his bell, an' the cat drinkin' water out of his basin, next the ice box—"

That, of course, told the story. There *had* been someone in the house the night before, and he *had* used a bell to cover any possible sounds he might make, and he most certainly and assuredly *had* a purpose in his visit.

"And if it hadn't been for Mr. Grosgrain," I felt wobbly around my knees, "we would have sat down and cheerfully devoured mushrooms—the ones our pal substituted. Asey, that's not murder. It's a massacre—"

"How'd you know about 'em?" Asey asked Luther.

"Mushrooms," he announced with a touch of pride, "were once a hobby of mine. I—"

"Thank God," Agatha said devoutly, "you kept golf for your later years! Go on and tell us all about the little Death Cups. How unpleasantly should we have expired? Of course, it would have been unpleasant, wouldn't it?"

Luther nodded. "Yes, I'm afraid so. Very, very—dear me! You see, the poisonous principle of these is known as phallin, one of the tox-albumins, the poison found in rattlesnake venom, for example, or the poison producing death in cholera and diphtheria. And—er—there's no known antidote by which the effects of phallin may be counteracted—"

I personally devoted myself to brooding over that simple sentence, while Luther ran on glibly about phallin acting directly on the blood corpuscles, dissolving the erythrocytes, so thinning the serum that it escaped from the blood vessels into the alimentary canal, draining the whole system of its vitality, and so forth and so on. I didn't even know what most of it meant.

Even Agatha looked pretty depressed. "Of all the horrid things," she said coldly. "Of all the horrid ways to die—"

Luther assured her that it was even horrider than that.

"You see, there aren't any symptoms, Miss Penrose, for at least—oh, say, six to thirteen hours—"

I looked at the clock. Katy was apparently safe.

"By which time," Luther continued briskly, "the fate of the person is practically sealed, as you might say. The poison doesn't reach the blood stream until the food reaches the small intestines, when it's too late for any known methods to remove it. The symptoms are nausea and dizziness, followed by convulsions and raving insanity."

Katy let out a blood curdling shriek you could have heard for fifty miles.

"Oh, I'm dyin', Mrs. Penrose, I'm dyin', I know I am!"

"Nothing of the sort," Agatha said crisply. "If you'd been going to die, you'd be dead now. Bev, give her an aspirin or something. I hardly blame her for feeling upset."

Mr. Grosgrain produced a small tin of aspirin tablets and two of them silenced Katy for the time being.

"Yes," he said, "it's really a very unpleasant death. The liver atrophies, and in—I think it's sixty-two per cent of the cases, death follows within forty-eight hours.

Sometimes even handling the specimens and breathing in the spores affects some people."

As one man, all of us backed away from the table. We were still staring at those mushrooms when Jo drove up in the roadster, which was practically obliterated from view by her luggage.

"I got everything," she said happily. "I got—what *is* the matter? Playing concentration?"

Agatha told her. "Obviously aimed at me, Jo. I'm the only one here who really loves mushrooms."

"I do too," Jo said. "I'd have gobbled—dear me, madness, raving insanity! Maybe I should have stayed sedately home with Eleo. What're you going to do with 'em?"

"Remove 'em from sight." Asey speared them, one by one, with a long handled fork, and put them back in the basket. "I happen," he observed dryly, "to be fond of mushrooms myself. Huh. What's the plain kind these is like, Grosgrain?"

"Agaricus campestris," he announced without batting an eye. "It's a gill fungus with brown spores. Many on the Cape. The Death Cup is found here, too. In woods, on lawns. You can tell it from the other by the white spores, and the presence of a bulb or volvus at the base. A careless person, or one who didn't happen to know, could very easily mistake them. As a matter of fact, the reason I devoted some time to the study of mushrooms is because my sister, who was very fond of them indeed, once picked by mistake some of the amanita muscaria, which resembles the Death Cup, but is not, fortunately, as deadly. That paralyzes the nerves controlling the action of the heart—"

"Sounds," Asey murmured, "deadly enough for me. How'd you save her from the—whatever it was?"

"She complained of not feeling well, and I called a doctor. He injected atropine, which is used as an antidote, and of course employed the most powerful emetics and purges. It was a harrowing experience for her, and for me, too. I determined that no one else should suffer if I could help it."

"Amen," Agatha said. "Amen, and thank you, Mr. Grosgrain. I feel exceptionally futile, saying thank you, it was so nice of you, after you've saved us from what I should unhesitatingly call worse than death, but it's all I can say. Later, possibly, I may muster words enough for a really good speech. Asey, how'd this fellow, this mushroom changer, get in?"

"I been tryin' to figure that out. Not through the g'rage, not through—you know, I'm stupid! 'Course. He come in through an upstairs window. Shinned up one of the elm trees. Come, I'll show you, Hanson."

There were no screens in the boys' bedroom, directly over mine, nor in two other windows at the back of the house. And there were four elms and a willow, all old and branchy and bent invitingly toward the house.

"But you'd have to be a trapeze artist," Jo said. "You—"

"Nonsense," I told her. "The twins have crawled up those trees and onto the ridge poles since they were four years old. You wouldn't swing directly to the window, silly, but to the roof. Watch Asey."

In two steps Asey was up the trunk of the nearest elm. Without the slightest effort he walked along one branch, steadying himself with a casual hand on the branch above. He stepped off the branch on to the weather-beaten shingles, hugged the peak of the dormer, lifted the window easily, and then, sliding one foot along the wooden gutter, thrust the other foot through the open window.

"An' there you be, ladies an' gents," he announced with a grin. "R'verse the process—you p'ceive I have abs'lutely nothin' up my sleeves, an'—oho. Here's a splotch of putty. Take it, Hanson. Catch. Maybe it's a clue."

Hanson caught the jagged, irregular blob of putty— it was about the size of my thumb nail, a little larger than a marble—and sniffed.

"It's the hell of a clue," he said. "Asey, now you're up there, wander around and see if you can't find something worth while. Maybe he came in a back window."

"He didn't." Asey crossed to the tree and jumped lightly down. "He didn't, 'cause they's marks where the bark's scraped off, an' some shingles scraped. More scored than scraped. He had rubber soles. Well, I s'pose some one of us can perch up in the tree to-night an' hope he'll come back with a bag of ars'nic or maybe a little ground glass an' strychnine. Let's see that hunk of putty."

"If you think that's a clue," I said, "you're doomed

to disappointment. The boys spent half the summer making putty balls for their sling shot. That's why we have to get our eggs from Logan's. They caught old Timmy Rich simultaneously on the back of the neck and the seat of his trousers, at ten feet, and he dropped a basket with five dozen eggs in it. He resented the whole affair at considerable length. Anyway, that's why that's no clue, Asey. It's just a piece of putty they slung before it hardened, that's all."

Asey chuckled. "I'd like to of seen Tim an'—his sense of humor always was ingrowin'. Too bad. Too bad about this putty, too. Seemed to me it was a real nice clue. 'Twasn't from the window pane, an' it seemed a real c'mpanion piece to a cat's bell an' a—God A'mighty, Bev, see what Pegleg's bringin' you!"

Limping up from the orchard came Jethro, bearing triumphantly in one hand an enormous puff ball.

He beamed at me. "Here y'are, Mrs. Penrose! Don't see why it's growin' so late, but here 'tis. You told me the other day your aunt liked puff balls, an' to find one if I could, an' I just found this—"

Of course it was funny, but only Jo laughed. Aunt Agatha distinctly shuddered.

I appealed to Asey. "Make him drag out his ear trumpet, please, and thank him kindly for me, but add that I want that puff ball conveyed to Crooked Cliff and hurled out into the current!"

After many false starts, Jethro got the idea. He looked his disappointment.

"But you told me you liked—"

"It's this way," Asey shouted manfully. "Y'see, last night—"

Half way through, Agatha gripped me by the arm.

"My ear drums are split," she whispered, "and if I have to hear 'mushroom' yelled in my ear again, I'm going to do some yelling myself. That man reminds me of great-uncle Stafford and the man named Dusenberry. Kyle's probably told you."

I told her, as Jo and I followed her back into the house, that Kyle hadn't.

"My dear, it's a family legend. Can't see how you missed it. Aunt Ruth was always bringing waifs and strays home. One of them stole the best Lowestoft pitcher. Anyway, one day she appeared with a tatterdemalion who said his name was Dusenberry. Uncle Staff happened on Dusenberry, loathed him at sight, and promptly asked Aunt Ruth who the creature was. She said he was a poor unfortunate, and so on and so on, and finally Uncle Staff demanded his name. 'Dusenberry,' Aunt Ruth yelled. 'Dusenberry, Stafford. It's DUSENBERRY!'"

Agatha cleared her throat and lighted a cigarette.

"And then Uncle Staff said, 'What say? What say, Ruth?' And she told him again, and again, and again. In fact, my father, when he told this, never screamed it any less than ten times, but my throat is sore already. Anyway, after a great period of time, Uncle Stafford unfurled his ear trumpet and tucked it away in his pocket. 'No use,' he said, casting a malicious look at the tramp. 'No use. No matter how hard you yell or how hard I listen, it still sounds just like Dusenberry to me.'"

Asey came in while we were still laughing, and Agatha had to tell the story all over again.

"R'minds me of a feller I knew in Calcutta," he said, "but I'm too hoarse to tell you about him right now. Bev, you'n Miss Ag'tha get your things. We're goin' out."

"Where?" Jo demanded.

"Goin' to the Inn for lunch," Asey said. "Seems to me it ought to taste better, no—no need for you to come along, Jo."

"So you don't care whether or not I'm poisoned, huh? That's a nice Christian sentiment, Asey! That's a nice—"

"You got a job. You're goin' through Kay Truman's things that Bob an' I packed away, an' see if you can find anythin' that'll help us on this. Anythin' that might hint about her death. You knew her, knew her way of thinkin' an' speakin', an' it's poss'ble you might find somethin' Dave an' I passed over. Yup, we went through 'em all, after it happened. Bob'll help you. Protect you with his life, if anyone tries to give you a ham sandwich with ars'nic dressin'."

Jo frowned. "I'm not thinking of that, Asey. I hate to prowl through her things, though."

"I know, Jo, but you got to. May help us a lot. You're the only one who can, in that matter."

"D'you think," Agatha asked him half an hour later while the three of us were hungrily gobbling down luncheon at the Inn—and their daily special, by the way, was nothing more nor less than creamed mushrooms on toast! "Do you think Jo'll find anything?"

"Nope." Asey shook his head. "But I had things to do that I didn't want her messin' with, an'—well, you can't never tell. She might."

"Are you going back to see Eleo?" I asked.

Jo's words about her mother being the sort who might possibly poison someone, whereas she would never shoot or stab, had been floating through my mind for some time.

"Yup. Though it don't seem to me I could see her scurryin' up trees an' slinkin' through houses any more'n I could see her rowin' boats. But she could of thought it out, an' had someone else do the dirty work for her."

I thought instantly of Creel Friar. "But it can't be Friar," I said. "Not with a broken arm. Asey, why d'you suppose Jo went out with him night before last, and then ditched him so suddenly last night? She said she had to, but that doesn't get us anywhere."

"Her mother would be my guess, Bev. I kind of think Mrs. Dwight suspected Jo'd gone back to Dave's on Thursday aft'noon, when she got mad an' left the car. Prob'ly said, if you don't be nice to Creel, I'll tell you went back. You'll r'call Jo came right out with her bein' there as soon as she come over last night."

"Another thing," Agatha said, "Jo told us the reason she didn't actually go into the house to see Dave that day was that the window shades were pulled down, or crooked. D'you think Dave was waiting for someone, or expected someone? Wouldn't it help if we could find out who?"

"I don't think he expected a soul," Asey said. "He

seemed to of been sittin' at his desk, writin', or goin' through papers. Bright day, that was. An' that desk gets the full sun in the aft'noon. My guess'd be that he just yanked the shades down because the sun bothered him."

"But what makes you so sure he wasn't expecting company?" Agatha persisted.

" 'Cause," Asey smiled, "he was a fussy sort about his clothes, an' he had on his oldest flannel pants, with paint spots an' grease, an' a dirty shirt. I guess, if you're all through, we'll go call on Creel Friar. 'Less, 'fore we set out, either of you wants the daily special. Okay, don't maul me, Bev! Seems to me Friar's got more to do with this than he seems to have on the surface. Anyone as common, everyday, upright, downright an' forthwith as unpleasant as that boy is, ought to be mixed up in a murder anyway, whether he is or not. An' if worse comes to worse, we can always find out a lot about Jo's mother. P'vidin'," he added as an afterthought, "that he's sober."

Mrs. Howes, who runs the glorified boarding house— only she calls it a Motorist's Rest and Guest House— where Luther and Creel Friar stayed, met us at the foot of the oystershell walk by the white picket fence.

She never, she told us before the car fairly stopped, never in all her life had passed such astounding days in her life.

"There never was such a month, not with that Friar boy, drinkin' an' drinkin'—why, his closet's always full of bottles! An' so untidy in the bathroom—you wouldn't believe it! Never cleans out the tub, an' just throws wet towels around. An' when I was over to Orleans, that

Mr. Walters and that Miss Snaith just up an' left, owin' me a week apiece. An' that Grosgrain man, he's broken everything breakable in his room, an' a lot of things I didn't think *could* be broken!"

"How?" Agatha demanded. This was a new light on Luther.

"Playin' golf, he says, though I told him with six golf courses in the vicin'ty, it seemed to me like he might go to one of the six, an' leave my bric-a-brac out of it. Though I must say he seemed real apologetic an' paid me real lib'ral for everything."

"Through the nose, if I know you," Asey murmured.

"What say, Asey? Oh, you want to see that Friar? Well, let me tell you if you can arrest him, I wish you would! I never would let him stay in this house, but he paid in advance, an' I can't help it. Say, Asey, was that woman in the Henderson house, the young lookin' one with the daughter, was she mixed up in this? This business of Dave Truman?"

"Why?" Asey countered.

"I'll tell you why." Mrs. Howes leaned over Agatha and me till she was nearly inside the roadster. "I'll tell you why. That Portygee woman, that Corregio woman that cleans for me, she's done work for Dave Truman since he let all his help go, an' she says," Mrs. Howes lowered her voice dramatically, "she says, that woman from the Henderson house pestered him all the time. Came there, an' called him up, an' asked him to lunch, an' for dinner, an' for all I know, to breakfast as well. Lina Corregio, she says she thinks the woman wanted him to marry her! An' she said, too, she didn't think he cared for her a bit!"

"You mean," the indiscriminate use of "she" and "her" had me confused, "you mean, Mrs. Dwight was in love with David Truman, but he didn't like her?"

Mrs. Howes nodded and smacked her lips. "That's just what I mean. An' when I heard about this, I thought about that, an' I said to myself, Hell hath no fury like a woman scorned. D'you want me to tell Friar you're here?"

"I'll break it to him gently myself," Asey told her. "Huh. Sure that ain't just a lot of talk, Lyddy?"

"You can go ask Lina."

Asey slid out of his seat. "Mind settin' here, you two?"

"Not," Agatha said, "if you faithfully promise to call us at the first hint of anything exciting."

Asey promised and left.

"Some man, ain't he?" Lyddy asked as he strode up the drive to the house. "I always say, whenever I need help, from fixin' the pump to helpin' with the church fair, there's no one like Asey to call on. You ever hear— oh, my goodness, there's Milly now, an' I haven't even got my beach plum jelly wrapped—"

Why the jelly should be wrapped, or what for, we never knew. Lyddy scampered across the lawn, called something we couldn't hear to Milly Adams, and disappeared from sight.

"Much as I like Lyddy," I said, "I'm always glad to see her go before she gets fairly started on one of her recitals. Once, when Kyle was new to North Weesit, he politely stood and let two quarts of ice cream drip to a thin trickle, listening to her tell about what the new minister said to the organist. He calls her the Mighty Ocean, because she rolls on and on."

"Have you thought about Mr. Grosgrain?" Aunt Agatha asked unexpectedly.

"Thought about him?" I repeated. "What do you mean, thought about him? I thought we had finished with Luther years ago, had him all tagged as innocent and honest. After all, Monty Walker said he was genuine, they've proved him nearsighted and gun shy, out of the picture entirely as the one who shot at Asey, on a bus when Dave was killed—what more can you think about Luther?"

"Only that the knife in the back of Asey's car was more of a threat than anything else. When you think it over, so were those mushrooms. I mean, it seems odd to me that he should have happened to be at your elbow when the mushrooms, so to speak, came up. In a sense, don't you see, it was rather like the knife business, something that might have ended tragically, but didn't. And don't you remember what Asey said? About it's being more sensible to harry someone than to kill?"

"You yourself were one of the first, Agatha Penrose, to say Luther was innocent!"

"True. As things stand now, he had nothing to do with killing Dave, or shooting at Asey. Still, he did row over to Ike Smalley's after we left for there, and he heard Asey say we were going there. Doesn't it occur to you, Bev, that we're being harried rather neatly? We've barely had time to try to find out anything. As soon as we seem to hit a track, something happens that makes you want to sheer off from the whole thing. There—oh, Asey's beckoning from the window!"

We scurried out of the car and up to Creel Friar's room on the second floor.

It was a mess. No details I could throw in would make it any messier. And the smell!

"Takes me back," I said reminiscently, "that smell. Back room of Jack and Charlie's, about four o'clock of a morning. But where's Creel?"

Asey nodded towards the bed. "He's in it. That lump you hear snoring. He wouldn't talk to me, so I poured him out another drink, an' he drank it, an' subs'quent p'rceedin' int'rested him no more, like the poet said. Look, I'm goin' through his things. I need help. Every pocket, every drawer, everythin' you see. Papers, letters, all. 'Course it ain't legal an' proper an' p'lite, but from what I seen of Friend Friar, I don't think he'd hes'tate under sim'lar circ'mstances."

Agatha wanted to know what we were hunting for.

"I don't care. Just anythin'. This is the Where-There's-Smoke-There's-Fire Club."

Asey took pockets, suitcases and drawers, and Agatha and I went through the letters and papers.

"All I have to say," Agatha snorted indignantly as she tossed a bunch of letters back on the desk, "is that this creature's private life resembles a vast seething sewer. Asey, this is manuscript, and it looks to me like a novel.

It *is* a novel. Has chapter headings—how conventional of him! It's—oh, my. Oh, dear me, Asey, I'm as liberal and free thinking a Boston spinster as I know, but you can't ask me to read that! Bev, the—"

"You don't have to," Asey said jubilantly. "Just cast your eyes on what Sherlock's got—"

He held out a tiny blob of lead.

"The lost bullet!" Agatha crowed. Then her face darkened. "So it didn't pop into his leg after all! What a pity, what a profound pity!"

CHAPTER TEN

AUNT AGATHA'S complacent glow and my delighted feeling of having finally achieved something lasted just exactly one hour and eighteen minutes
by the clock. It took us that time to track down Forman
at the police barracks and have him assure us that the blob
of lead from Creel's pocket couldn't possibly have been
fired from Dave's gun. It was a thirty-eight, and Dave's
gun was a forty-five. Or maybe it was a forty-four and a
thirty-eight. I always get measurements wrong.

Asey didn't appear at all disconcerted by the infor-
mation, but I began to understand how a balloon feels
when someone pricks it.

"Aunt Agatha," I said with a sigh, "I'm more disappointed than you look. He was such an ideal—Asey,
isn't there the least bit of hope that that bullet can mix
him up in this somewhere? Couldn't have come from the
other gun, the one Grosgrain says he found?"

Forman shook his head and launched into an explanation of which I understood not a single solitary
word. Ballistics, it seems, has its own language. Anyway,

we did manage to grasp that Creel's bullet was, in every-day speech, a blank.

"What about that gun that Grosgrain found?" Asey asked. "Any luck trackin' that down? I sort of hoped you might be able to get us somewhere with that, Forman. It's 'bout the only thing we got in all this so far."

Forman slapped his thigh. "Asey, so help me, I forgot all about it. They called me up to Boston yesterday on the Riley case, and I never— I'll phone up right away and get you all the dope just as soon as I can. That is, I'll get it if it's to be got."

"But you have to register guns, don't you?" Agatha asked. "I'm sure you'll find out a lot, Mr. Forman. That—"

"There ought to be a record of the gun if it was bought in this state, Miss Penrose," Forman said, "but not every place has the same laws. I'll tend to it right away, Asey."

We walked out to the roadster.

"Now, where?" I demanded.

Asey smiled. "I kind of think we can't work in friend Friar, no matter how nice 'twould be. I couldn't r'member the caliber of Dave's gun, but I had a nasty feelin' we wouldn't git nowhere, like my cousin Maria told me when I took her out in a car for the first time. That was in 1900, an' we had six flats in twenty yards. Huh. Well, ain't no use in tryin' to pump Friar for any tidin's for a day or two. Guess we better see what we can do about Jo's mother. Somehow I feel like tacklin' her this aft'noon, but I'm goin' to get me a Big Stick before we b'gin."

His search for the Big Stick led us first of all to Lina Corregio's house in Pochet. I call it a house, but it's more of a strange architectural nightmare, a sort of glorified lean-to composed of tar paper and lots of second-hand clapboards. I never look on it without thinking of Jericho's tumbling walls.

Lina had apparently been washing since the break of dawn; the grass was covered with drying sheets, and garments of every color and description fluttered from a dozen lines. Unconsciously I found myself picking out individual pieces—Sam Brigham's favorite pink striped shirts, and Bronson Shepherd's oversize plus fours, and Maida Shepherd's insidious mauve nightdresses.

In the back yard, Lina cheerfully sloshed clothes in two huge wooden tubs. I admired her carefree air. She possesses fourteen children according to my calculations and sixteen according to Kyle's, and there are those who put the figure even higher. But whatever the exact number, she manages them with far greater ease and much less worry than I cope with two.

Wiping her hands on the faded cotton dress of the nearest child, she walked over to the car.

"I hope you don't come for the sheets, Mrs. Penrose. They ain't dry. You said Monday, an' I—"

"I don't want the sheets," I assured her. "Mr. Mayo has some questions to ask you."

Lina beamed. "I bet I know. You come to ask me about Mrs. Dwight, hey? An' Mr. David Truman? I think to myself, sometimes sooner or later, they come to me an' ask about them two. At least," she displayed two large dimples, "at least about her, hey?"

Now Lina is Portuguese, according to her, but the manipulation of her eyebrows is purely Gallic. Mae West would have been proud to say those few sentences as well as Lina said them. They were, like editorials, fraught with import. They practically quivered with it.

"That's just about the size of it," Asey told her with a grin. "S'pose you just tell us what you know. I got a notion you can pack it into a few words without losin' a thing."

Lina crooked her finger at a small boy who stared in open-mouthed wonder at the car. "You, Oscar, you get me a chair!"

Aunt Agatha looked curiously at Oscar as he darted off. In direct contrast to the other Corregios, Oscar was blond and definitely Scandinavian.

"He's not one of yours, is he?" Agatha asked.

Lina's eyebrows went up and down. "Yes," she said tenderly, "it's funny he is so light, hey? But he is mine, all right."

We didn't go into the matter.

"Now," Lina plumped herself down in the chair Oscar brought out, "now I tell you all I know. First of the summer, I just do Truman's washing. Then, when he fire his help, I go there three times a week, to clean and cook. First part of the summer, I see Mrs. Dwight around once in a while, always with other people. Then, since— oh, four or five weeks, maybe, Mrs. Dwight is there every day I come. Sometimes twice a day. Sometimes," she added demurely, "sometimes maybe more. I don't know about that."

"How is it," Asey asked me, "that you didn't know she was over to Dave's so much? She'd have to go through your drive to get there."

"Until Agatha came," I explained, "I've hardly been home one hour in the twenty-four. And if I was, I was sewing fifty thousand pieces of Cash's woven names on to shorts and shirts and a million towels. And the twins were awf'ly strenuous their last days home. And Kyle almost lived on the 'Flotsam,' and couldn't see why I wouldn't help him varnish the cabin and make new port-hole curtains, and odd items like that. I'd hardly time for people who came up the drive to see me, let alone time to gape at Dave's guests. I rarely notice cars coming and going—there's always the ice man or the grocery boy, or something."

"Okay. Carry on, Lina."

Lina obediently carried on.

Mrs. Dwight, it appeared, was practically underfoot. If Lina wanted to get at the laundry, Mrs. Dwight would be mending Dave's socks or sewing buttons on shirts. Not with expert fingers, either, Lina added. If there was a room to be swept, Mrs. Dwight was in it, scattering cigarette ashes on the floor. If Lina polished the furniture, Mrs. Dwight would be filling the vases with flowers and dripping water all over everything.

"She was about everywhere. She was a bother." Lina made a face. "One day, when she walk on my clean kitchen floor with muddy boots, I tell her so. I say, 'Mrs. Dwight, you are a dam' bother!' "

Asey wanted to know how Eleo took that.

"How? She say I lose my job, and I say all right, she find someone else to wash her old green sheets—see, look at them!"

She jerked a scornful thumb at the pale green crêpe de chine sheets hanging from one of the lines.

"I say, you find someone else to wash them, someone that will hang them in the shade, and iron them careful, and charge as little as me. She," Lina smiled, "she shut up. But anyway, all the time she is after poor Mr. Truman. He don't want her. One day he even come to me and say, Lina, if that woman come, tell her I'm dead. Tell her what you want, but I won't see her to-day. But that don't do no good. She comes in anyway, and she hangs around till he come in, pretending he don't know she was there. He says to her at last one day, Eleo, you mustn't come here so much. People talk. And she walks up to him like Greta Gobbo," Lina's shoulders moved rhythmically up and down, "and she says, 'But you don't mind, Dave dear?' "

We all howled. Somehow Lina managed to inject into her imitation of Eleo's voice the honeyed sugarness that was its principal feature.

"He says he do mind," Lina went on. "He says he likes her, but not that way, and he don't want to put her in any place that might hurt her. She wants to know don't he love her, and he sort of waits, and then he says no. And my, did she ever get mad!" Lina closed her eyes and smiled. "If I call Pete just one of the names she calls him, he throw me out the window. I don't ever hear anyone that can get as mad like that but my Rosa. Rosa," she added for Agatha's benefit, "she is my oldest girl. She's a bad girl. She live down to Provincetown with a painter. And even Rosa, I don't think she could swear as good as that woman. It made me laugh. Her with her silk sheets and sweet voice and trying to get on with the Shepherds, and she talk like that. I told Pete that night, she was just like Rosa."

"'Member what day they had this bust-up?" Asey asked.

Lina nodded. "It was Tuesday this week, in the afternoon. You was there around noon, and you come back later. Yes, it was a pity she kill Mr. Truman. He was a nice man. Other people, they give me things and say, give 'em to the kids. Mr. Truman, he give me money and says, Lina, get yourself a present. He should been more careful. I told him that. I told him, it was a pity a woman like her should finish him."

We opened our mouths at that.

"What makes you think she killed him?" Asey demanded.

Lina shrugged. "Oh, she say so. She say so every other word all the time she is mad and calling him names. Mr. Truman just stands there and smiles all the time, and she says don't he think she means it? And he says, sure. Only she'll find some other man just as nice looking with some more hunting, and most likely one that's got more money."

"Go on," Asey told her. "Don't stop. We're hangin' on ev'ry word."

"So she says again, she will kill him, and he laughs and says he wishes she would, but he don't think so. He says better people than her said the same thing, but nothing happens, and he thinks nothing will. Then," Lina confessed amiably, "then they see me in the doorway, and she says for me to get the hell out, so I go into the next room, but she shut the door and I don't hear any more."

"She mention a knife?"

"Just like Rosa," Lina rocked back and forth placidly. "Just like Rosa, she say she'd like to have a knife to cut his heart out. It don't mean a thing, though. Rosa never cut her man's heart out yet, I never cut out Pete's. But it sound good, just the same."

Asey all but yodeled. "At last," he said, "at last I hear a woman tell the truth. Seems to me this world'd be a better place if more women admitted that half they said was just for the sound effects. Thank you kindly, Lina. You been more help than you know. Say—didn't Mrs. Dwight fire you after that? How come you still do her laundry?"

Lina giggled. "That Chink or whatever he is that works for her, he tell me I don't do the clothes any more. I say, so what? So who he get to do 'em? I tell him what the laundry do to them dam fool sheets. So we fix it up. He gives them to me and tells her he has got another woman, and then he tells her it will cost just twice as much as before, and I give him half the extra."

We were still chuckling when we left half an hour later.

"She reminds me," Agatha said, "of that lovely enormous bronze Buddha, that resigned and rather amiable one in Japan. It's fifty feet high and double that in girth. I've forgotten the name, though I once spent an hour gazing at it with admiration. I've a feeling that you couldn't beat Lina."

"You can't. Her husband, Pete, tried to," Asey said. "Last time was when Oscar there turned out blond. Even Pete thought that was sort of queer. After four months in the hosp'tal, he r'membered his great-grandfather was a sort of light c'mplected feller. Well, this is gettin' int'restin', ain't it, about Mrs. Dwight?"

"What are you going to do about it?"

"Goin' to check up on the time she got home Thursday, an' what she done later. Jo said somethin' about Friar bein' there, but if he was in his usual state, he'd never be sure about the month, let alone the day or the hour. Guess I'll have to chatter with that Filipino. Guess I still r'call enough of his lingo to get along. I'll leave you here in the car on the back road, an' try the kitchen door. Always seems to be a lot more inf'mation out of back doors than front. N'en, when I come back, we'll go turn the radio on in the front yard."

He'd been gone a scant five minutes when Mr. Grosgrain appeared from the other end of the lane. He looked at us and the car, hesitated, and then walked up to us.

"I—er—" he didn't seem to know just how to begin, "I—er—was taking a walk."

Aunt Agatha admitted that it was a nice afternoon for a walk.

"It is," Grosgrain agreed. "But I—I really didn't want to, myself. It was that Hanson. I was trying to be helpful and he said would I please do him a favor and take a walk. He said every time he thought of me and my story and what it would do to a jury, he was fit to eat grass. So I decided that I might as well take a walk. Has Mr. Mayo found out anything else?"

Agatha told him about the bullet and he sighed.

"I'd hoped, though it doesn't sound charitable, that he might be found to be the guilty one. It seemed to me that he—I mean, I think he—"

"He ought to be guilty of something," I finished for him. "But apparently he's not destined for the electric chair. He'll die in bed like a gentleman, of cirrhosis of the liver."

We brooded over the injustice of it all for half an hour, when Asey finally returned.

"One thing about them Filipinos," he remarked, "they like to be 'greeable. They'll agree with anyone. Did Mrs. Dwight get back at four-thirty? Yiss, sar. Was it maybe five? Yiss, sar. I went into a huddle with the cook after a while. She says it was well onto five that Mrs. Dwight got back, because she had popovers for tea, an' they fell. Huh." He became aware of Luther. "H'lo. Walkin', hey? How come you wandered over this way?"

"Why I just did, that's all. The road—"

"Yup. Road just spread out b'fore you an' led you here. You'n the children of Israel. Huh. Found out yet what I done this afternoon?"

"Why, why—Miss Penrose told me about Mr. Friar and the bullet, and—"

"An' everythin' else. Nice, ain't it, to be in the know?" I couldn't make out why Asey was so sharp with the little man.

"Look here," Agatha was plainly annoyed, "what's the idea of bullying Mr. Grosgrain and insinuating that I'm letting state secrets out of the bag?"

"Yup. I know. But brother Lute's gettin' kind of nick of timey, seem's if. We go to Smalley's an' he rows over in a boat. We have mushrooms, an' he's there to tell us they're poison."

Agatha had no comeback. After all, she'd said almost that to me a short time before.

"B'sides," Asey's hand shot out and grabbed Luther's right wrist, "b'sides, I'd kind of like to know why you're cuddlin' another gun, mister. Habit of yours. R'move it, Bev. That's it. Huh, I s'pose a kid in your boardin' house give you this, too? Or did you just find it settin' down b'side a spray of goldenrod? Maybe wild flowers was another hobby of yours, huh?"

Luther looked at Asey. Then he looked at the gun. His lips moved, but no words came.

"Get to it!" Asey ordered. "Don't stand there gaspin' like an expirin' pick'rel. What you trailin' me around for, armed to the teeth? Where'd you get that gun? Got a license for it? No?"

Luther clamped his lips firmly together.

"Got a license?" Asey repeated. "Bev, look in his wallet. None there? Then he ain't got one. If he had, it'd be there 'long with the orders an' clubs an' all. Okay. You crawl in an' drive, Bev, an' Luther'n' I'll ride the rumble."

In absolute silence, we drove back to the house.

"Here," Asey said to Hanson, "this time you got a real charge. Carryin' a gun without a license. He—"

Hanson took a long breath. "You wouldn't kid me, Asey? Honest, you wouldn't kid me?"

"I wouldn't," Asey assured him. "I'm tellin' you to book him for carryin' firearms without a license, or however it goes. Take him, Bob. Hanson, I want to talk with you."

Aunt Agatha looked at the pair curiously as they left the house.

"What in the world, Bev, has got into Asey? Why this quarterdeck manner?"

"You yourself," I retorted, "suggested to me that Luther might possibly be a little fishy. And after all, he may have saved us from poisoned mushrooms, but it's going to be cloying, having him forever in our hair. I get Asey's point."

"Yes," she admitted reluctantly, "but Asey—he's so different!"

"You ought to see him sometimes when he's really giving orders. You don't feel foremast handish then. You're just a fourth class apprentice who's stumbled into the scuppers. But he never raises his voice. He—"

Asey came back. "Okay," he said briskly. "I got to find my coat. Don't think I'm bein' hard on Luther. He's been clutchin' that gun since this mornin', an' I was scared he might let it go off at the wrong time. Be right back."

We were half way to Eleo's when Jo, in my roadster, passed us and jammed on the brakes to a quick stop.

"Sorry to stop the limited," she said, "but there's a telegram for Miss Penrose. Just phoned down from Hyannis. Bad news, I'm afraid."

Agatha reached out her hand for the message, read it and sighed.

"Aunt Nella— I've got to go to New York, Bev. How do I make connections?"

"Connections? God knows. The train service is just a flimsy pretense. Your best bet is to start from Boston—"

"Why not Providence?" Jo asked. "It's about the same distance, and you're that much nearer. If she can't pick up a plane, she can take a train. I'll see her on one or the other, and drive back."

"That'll do beautifully," Agatha said. "Hate to leave you, Bev, but I'll get back as soon as I can. No, don't bother coming back with me. I'll just toss a toothbrush in a bag and dart off with Jo, and there's not a thing you can do."

Asey solicitously helped her change cars, offered advice about trains, told Jo to be sure and get gas for the roadster, and then he and I went on our way.

Several minutes passed before I became aware of the

smile that played around his mouth. His quarterdeck manner had departed entirely.

"Asey!" I suddenly suspected that smile. "Asey, you wretch—"

"I'm no wretch," he returned, "I'm a fine upstandin' man, like Dorcas Winter said when she mistook me for a dead cousin an' wrote me up an obituary. A fine up-standin' man with a heart of gold, an'—"

"Asey, you know perfectly well that Aunt Nella never sent that telegram! You did it yourself!"

"Deary me," Asey murmured. "Deary me, I don't know what the world's comin' to. People gettin' so s'picious—"

"Asey, why did you? And why did you slap Luther into a cell, or its equivalent? What's the idea?"

He drew the car up by the side of the road.

"I'll tell you, Bev, an' you're about the only one I can tell. Every time we get set to do anythin', we seem to get jolted. Speakin' fancy-like, they's a leak. I set out to go somewhere, an' someone tosses knives into my car when I get there. They's a little mite too much of that goin' on. An' I can't find out where the op'sition's comin' from."

"You're not insinuating that Agatha's mixed up in this?"

"Nope, but she likes to speak her mind out loud. Like her tellin' Luther about that bullet. She don't mean to, but she does. So I called your husband's uncle over to Hyannis an' asked him what was a nice rel'tive to be in trouble, an' he told me, an' I told Jo, an' Jo wrote it down."

"What'll you say when she finds out and comes ripping back?"

"Wa-el," he drawled, "more strange things has happened in your house an' it's vicin'ty these last two days than a p'culiar telegram. B'sides, Harry Penrose says he'll see what he can do to keep her away. That's that. Luther's away for a while, too. Cabot, Lowell, Stunkenblock, Montgom'ry an' Cheesevitch can't get him out of that. That makes two folks elsewhere. Now we'll see if they's still a leak, an' how many more times we play leap frog with death."

"But Jo—"

"She's all right. She's off for a while. If she'd wanted to run away, she would of before. Guess she'll come back, but Bob's goin' to protect her. Ain't I kind?"

"Kind? You skunk! How is it you exempt me?"

"I need you, if ever we get far enough to need checkin' with what you three seen Thursday aft'noon. Giles would do, but he's busy at the boat yard. An' b'sides, he's got his own ideas about all this. Tells his story the same way each time. You kind of vary it."

"I do not!"

"Sure you do. Giles was too busy feelin' sore about Kay an' Dave to notice things. Miss Ag'tha noticed a lot, but she didn't know what was f'miliar, or what was strange, so the p'culiar things she stored up don't count. She's done a lot of her own thinkin', too. But you—you felt an 'you seen an' you listened, an'—well, you was gen'rally functionin' on all cylinders, an'—"

"And having few brains, I've not rationalized the whole business, and consequently I give you food for thought. I get it."

"Don't be silly. What I'm tryin' to say is that your story is worth more'n the others. Hey—ain't that the lady Eleo, now, comin' out of the Shepherds'?"

"Golly!" I said. "There was a whale of a tea party there to-day! I was asked, and accepted for Agatha, too. My, my, this is the end. I'm out of North Weesit society for good. Last time we were asked there for dinner, Kyle and the boys and I had the 'Glory Be' out in the afternoon, and got becalmed by Punkin Island. We got home in plenty of time to get there, but Kyle said we had such a nice excuse that it was a pity to throw it away and go. And his friend Greg Dunn was up at the Playhouse, so we had a sandwich and tore up there, and of course the whole Shepherd party came in later. We thought it was funny, but they didn't a bit."

"You could always drop in now," Asey suggested. "You got an alibi—Agatha called away—"

"Not on your life. They always have peanut butter sandwiches, and what's more, they make you eat the damn things, and peanut butter and I've been enemies for years."

Asey swung the roadster into the drive before Eleo's house just as she walked up her front steps.

She hailed us as pleasantly and gayly as though we were her nearest and dearest friends.

"Come in and have a drink. I need a flock after that party—you were clever to stay away, Bev. Somewhere in this bag I have a key, I hope. I'm going out to dinner and the servants have the night off—"

We waited while she prodded around in the entrails of an overstuffed white bag.

"Damn, there goes my lipstick! Thanks," Asey leaned over and picked it up, "this is so *full!*"

Something else fell and hit the top step with a tinkle. Asey's hand was over it in a flash.

He picked it up, smiled, and held it out for me to see.

It was a little silver bell, like the one on Sully's collar.

CHAPTER ELEVEN

WHILE Asey and I stared at the bell, Eleo found her latch key and swung open the heavy paneled front door.

"Go on in by the fire while I find some drinks. Dear God, until I came back to New England I'd forgotten that you had tea at tea parties—"

"Asey," I said, dumbly following him into the long living room, "Asey, d'you suppose—can you beat it! Was it Eleo, and is that Sully's bell?"

"Sully's got his collar on," Asey tossed the bell from one hand to the other, "an' the bell's on the collar. I looked before we left. Ain't poss'ble this is his, but on the other hand, it's poss'ble more'n one bell's muddled up in this. You wasn't sure the bell you heard was Sully's, you know. Might of been two other bells, easy."

Eleo pranced back with a rolling bar and one of those fifty gallon shakers that look like an old-fashioned milking pail.

"My tongue is absolutely hanging out. Gather round, you two! I'm so glad to find someone I can talk to. I've been broad-A-ing for years and years, and listening to more broad-A-ing for centuries. Amazing how that A can get you down! You could cut the Shepherds' with a pair of scissors—"

She babbled on, mixing cocktails with an airy hand and not much care as to just what went in anyway. I saw Asey shudder as she tossed a fourth dash of absinthe into what I had fondly thought was a Sidecar variation, up to that point.

I tasted the result finally and looked around for the nearest plant. Asey was already sidling toward the Cape Cod fire lighter, whose top was invitingly open. Eleo, though, tossed off three glasses of the foul brew and was beginning on a fourth when Asey hurriedly brought up the subject of the little silver bell.

"Where'd you ever get it?" he asked casually. "Bell for a cat's collar, ain't it?"

"That? Oh, did that pop out of my bag?" Eleo's fingers shook as she lighted a cigarette, but after three doses out of the milk pail, that wasn't to be wondered at. "Party favor. I forget whose, just now. Couple of weeks ago. Put it in my bag and it's been there ever since."

"You can do better than that," Asey told her. "Where'd you get it?"

"My God, why brood about it? I tell you it was a party favor. Look, is Jo really mad? Pablo came over to the Shepherds' before he went out and sent in a note saying she'd got her clothes."

"Tell us," Asey said firmly, "where you got that bell."

"I've told you fifty times, it was a party favor. Sort

of a glorified Jack Horner pie at someone's. Brighams' maybe. Call 'em up if it's so important. Phone's in the hall."

Asey left the room, still bearing his glass—he hadn't quite been able to reach the fire lighter. When he returned a few minutes later, he set his empty glass down on the table and grinned at me.

"She's right on that. They's a name stamped on the bell, an' Mrs. Brigham got hers an' read it to me. Same as this. Wa-el, that's that. Now, what time did you get back here from Mrs. Penrose's on Thursday?"

Eleo's diamonds flashed as she made a glib gesture of annoyance.

"Are you pumping me again? Thought I'd got off that. What time? Around four-thirty." She finished the fourth cocktail and poured out another. "Four-thirty. Why?"

"Your cook," Asey told her, "thought it was nearer five, if not after."

In a few brief, well chosen words, Eleo presented us with her opinion of cooks in general and her own model in particular. It was, as Asey remarked later, almost Friar.

"Just the samey," he pulled out his pipe, "she was pretty sure about her popovers fallin', an' bein' a cook of sorts, I kind of cling to her ideas. Jo went back to Dave's after she left you, an' I thought you maybe had, too. You know, to cut his heart out like you promised you would."

Eleo stiffened as though someone had poured a pail of solder down her backbone. Then without further warning, she burst into tears.

They were genuine, those tears. I knew they were, half by sheer intuition, and half by the whole-hearted way she gave in to them. And besides, an old campaigner like Eleo Dwight would never let her eyes get red just before a dinner party unless she was indulging in a pretty heartfelt emotional debauch.

Rather uncomfortably, Asey and I sat and watched her beautiful golden tan that I'd so envied all summer drizzle down her cheeks in little rivulets. It trickled down her chin, splashed greasily on the front of her dress and on the tips of her immaculate white pumps. Her mascara smudged and got in her eyes. It must have smarted, for she cried harder than ever.

I turned my head away. It seemed almost sacrilegious to watch the ravage go any further. I thought, too, of my father's favorite comment: "Women over twenty-one should confine their tears to the privacy of their own pillows."

"So you really cared for Dave," Asey said gently. "Huh. Was that why you tried your level best to keep Jo away from him?"

Eleo sniffed. "Well, it *was* pretty silly. A woman and her daughter both in love with the same man. Oh, lend me your handkerchief—my God, I'm a sight! If you really must know about Thursday, Asey, I pulled the car into Glover's Lane and bawled like a baby. Dave was as much of a swell as Giles said. I was as ashamed of contradicting him as I was of losing my temper. That was an awful afternoon. It's been awful ever since. I knew

Jo had gone back, and I've been frightened to death that you'd mix her in all this."

"That why you lied so hale an' hearty the other day?"

"Of course. Why else, d'you think? Much better you should worry about me than about Jo. She's just a sweet guileless infant, in spite of all I've tried to pound into her head. Ruin her to get in the papers. As for me, I've been in the papers too many times to—how'd you find out about me and Dave?"

"Roundabouts." Asey didn't favor her with the story of Lina. "Look, what about Friar?"

"What about him?" Eleo poured out another drink. "He's a frightful boy by anyone's standards, though he's amusing once in a while. I've thrown him and Jo at each other's heads. Thought it might sour her for a while on the new-art, new-writing crowd. If you run into the most unpleasant specimens of a bunch at the start, it doesn't flame and glitter half so much. Jo got awfully taken in by that crowd at college, and it seemed to me time for her to snap out of it."

Eleo's words were beginning to run into each other just a little, but it seemed to me that she was, for the first time in all the years I'd known her, actually telling the truth, saying what she felt without regard for effect or effects.

"What about the bell?" she went on. "What's a bell got to do with Dave's murder? I know it has, so don't say it hasn't. Things are awf'ly clear right now. You and Bev shouldn't have pitched your drinks out. A few of

these, Asey, and you'd have your murderer in your
pocket within the hour."

"If I wasn't in the pocket first. Tell you, I don't
know about that bell. Somehow, it seems to have a lot
to do with things. Our bell, that is. Not yours. It rings
when the cat that has it on its collar ain't around, an'
when the cat's around, it don't, an'—"

Eleo shook her head. "Don't, please. Don't spoil the
clear, crystal, lucid flow of my thoughts. Just leave the
bell where it is. Only, if you're after a bell, you've got
the hell of a hunt ahead of you." She liked the end of
her sentence so well that she repeated it two or three
times. "The hell of a hunt ahead of you. The hell of a
hunt ahead of you. The hell of a hunt—where was I, I
wonder? Oh, I know. The hell of a hunt ahead of you
for the bell. Lots of people at the Brighams' that night.
Tenwy—I mean, twenty, thirty, forty. Jo. Creel. Giles
Hopkins. You know why I don't like Giles Hopkins,
Bev? He's so damn worthy. If he married a woman,
she'd never get away from him till one or the other of
'em died. It was a Jack Horner pie. Bells at the end of
ribbons. Jo—is Jo really mad, Bev?"

I didn't know whether she wanted the truth or not,
but it seemed the easiest way out. "I rather think she is."

"Well, she'll get along all right. She's met enough
horrible examples of humanity among my friends to
steer fairly straight. It's a mistake guarding children,
Bev. Don't. More unpleasant things they see and hear,
more nasty people they meet, more they make for a safe,
sane life. Jeff Dwight was essen-essen— He was middle-

class. Jo's like him. Show 'em the devil and they want to go to Heaven and strum harps. I think I'll go to India next week. Got friends in Simla."

"What about Jo?" I demanded.

Eleo shrugged and set her glass in an ash tray, changed her mind and dropped both, very carefully, into the top of the milk pail shaker.

"Jo'll be okay. She'll go to New York and sell sports clothes at Macy's or Best's. Marry some nice section manager or a bond clerk and feel she's escaped the hell of a life with me. Ought to be the making of her, now I think of it."

"An' what about you, Mrs. Dwight?"

"Me, Asey? Oh, I'll prob'ly corrupt all the sub'lterns in Simla, marry a colonel who wants a little cottage in Kent. All British colonels want little cottages in Kent. All our colonels want to start little military schools, and all French colonels—oh, all the French army's the same. Look after Jo, will you, Bev? Till she gets a job. She's got plenty of money. Don't let her sponge. The Dwights were a bunch of spongers. Now, beat it. I've got just an hour to snap out of this and get over to Chatham, and if you ever mention me without my face on, so help me God, I will cut your hearts out!"

"Funny," Asey said as he helped me into the roadster, "funny how folks choose to live their lives, ain't it? Funny how—"

"Can't we do something?" I asked. "Really, I've got to like Eleo in the last half hour. Couldn't we do something about her?"

Asey shook his head. "We could, but it wouldn't help. Everyone's got the right to go to hell in their own way, as ole Cap'n Porter used to say. B'sides, Mrs. Dwight's fond of playin' around. She couldn't stop, not more'n ten minutes or so at a time, an' not more'n once a year. R'minds me of a feller I used to know in Samoa. Kept a store. You know his brother's fam'ly—one of the Nickersons over in Wellfleet. Well, sir, ev'ry time he seen anyone from civ'lization, c'mparatively speakin', he'd moan an' groan about how he wanted to get back, an' see the packet come into Wellfleet harbor b'fore he died, an' go to church an' hear one of ole Pepper Freeman's sermons, an' have an oyster stew in Higgins's oyster saloon in Boston. One day my uncle Howland Mayo says to him that he'd had enough of it. Told him to pack up his chest an' sail with him that night. Nickerson said he would, but he showed up that night without his chest. He just plain couldn't leave. Well, it's kind of like that. An' I ain't sure Mrs. Dwight wants to do anythin' but what she's doin' anyway. I think India'll be a nice place for her."

"Why?"

"Oh, seems to me she'd fit right square into anythin' from a second Mut'ny to the Viceroy's ball."

"Maybe," I said. "Only, keeping up your figure, I trust she stays out of Black Holes. Asey, what's to be done? What about Grosgrain?"

Asey laughed. "I still can't help thinkin' how funny that runt's goin' to look in plus fours."

"But what about him?" I told him Agatha's comments about the harrying. "Do you suppose, even if he had nothing to do with Dave's murder, that he's behind the harrying? He's certainly popped in at opportune moments!"

"Forget the harryin'," Asey advised. "No one's tried to kill us for," he squinted at the clock, "a good six or seven hours, if the Porter timepiece ain't lyin'."

"But suppose it was Luther?" I persisted. "Suppose Luther was here all the time, and that someone else dressed like him came down in the train and on the bus? As you said, he's a common type. I've thought of thousands of people he reminds me of. There was an elevator starter in an apartment Kyle and I had one winter in New York, and he's a dead ringer for the street cleaner who's always brushing around Elise Harding's. And Kyle once had an assistant when he was on the 'Courier'— there's no end to the people Luther's like. Suppose he had a double? Suppose he was here before? Before we knew of him, that is."

"Nice thought," Asey admitted. "Somethin' to toy with in the long winter evenin's."

"And a swell elegant alibi! It's such an easy, simple, cinchy plan, Asey. It's just as simple and naïve as Luther is himself. It fits with him. It fits with the way his mind works. Wherever are you taking us?"

"Over to Yarmouth to get fed. I kind of want to haul off an' think in quiet, an' Hanson 'n' Bob'll see to it I don't get no op'tunity if we go back to your house. Just r'lax an' enjoy the ride, Bev. Let the ole duffer here take a few practice swings at the ole gray matter."

I was perfectly willing. My brain hadn't taken such a beating in years as it had in the last few days. I can cope with missing sheets from the laundry, dinner for ten at half an hour's notice, bloody noses and broken bones and green apple stomach aches, and I can lie magnificently when Kyle's editors yowl for articles that Kyle has never even begun, with Kyle himself off on one boat or another, completely out of reach as he was right now. Domestic problems, in other words, leave me unmoved, but I'd quite forgotten how to attack anything less material. When I'm faced with something which requires sheer, unadulterated logic, I have to have a pen and a pencil and a lot of clean white paper, and a room to myself and a lot of absolute peace. None of those items had been handy in the last two days, and I rather seriously doubted if I'd get anywhere with them anyway.

It all reminded me of a problem in a final astronomy exam at college. The only thing, I thought regretfully, that I recalled out of the entire course. "The declension of a certain star is zero. The declension of the sun is also zero. Where will the star and its constellation be on May 24th?" Or was it some other date altogether? Anyway, there was about this business of Dave Truman and cat's bells, and missing bullets, and shots out of the night, and poisoned mushrooms, and knives stuck in car seats— there was much the same general haze and murk as far as I was concerned. Of course the answer to the astronomy problem had been a snap for those with the wit to get behind words and find out just what the question was in simple language. Probably, even possibly, the answer to this was just as easy. But I knew well that my mind was no spryer now than it had been eighteen years ago.

"What you sighin' so lusty for?" Asey demanded with a chuckle.

"Just resigning myself to the fact that mine is no mammoth intellect, that's all. In another five years I'll probably be joining the Thursday Morning Hollyhock Club. What's worse, I'll probably listen to Q-U-I-K-L-I-N-O ballyhoo and buy the damned stuff. I—"

"What," Asey deftly cut ahead of two trailer-trucks and miraculously escaped annihilating us both when another truck barged in from a side road, "just what's brought on this sad an' mel'ncholy streak?"

I told him. "And," I added, "don't lose sight of the fact that I'm a wife and mother. Slow down just a bit, won't you?"

"Pish-tush. An' you was the kid that drove my ole Bear Cat at seventy-nine—"

"That was in my youth," I defended myself. "Now I'm a sedate old hag. Asey, what about Katy and Giles and Jethro, if you're plugging leaks? Don't they count?"

"Wa-el," he grinned, "I don't think Katy'd understand enough to do much leakin', an' Pegleg couldn't hear enough, an' Giles wouldn't have the sense to smell anythin' nor be able to talk lucid-like about it if he did. You know, like them fool three monkeys."

I laughed. "But what have we actually got to go on anyway? That's what bothers me."

He admitted that we had little enough. The gun

from which the bullet had come that nearly finished him, the same gun Grosgrain said he found, was of no value as yet.

"All up in the air, an' chances is we'll never find out a thing about it. 'Course they can track it back to the fac'try, but that's like havin' a stray Ford traced back to Detroit. You can go that far, an' then work back, but it's long, hard work, an' sooner or later you'd lose the trail. An' the knife we got, the one Grosgrain says belongs to the kid in his boardin' house—well, s'pose it does? I told Hanson to check that, but Luther's told us what sounds like truth so far, even if it is sort of quaint like."

"That's the appalling thing about the truth." I found a crumpled cigarette in my pocket and fumbled with the dash lighter. "It always—my God, Asey, the perfect car! Your lighter works. Well, well, and I'd given up hope. The truth is always silly. I won a set of new tires from my favorite garage man in Boston on an election bet. Four tires versus a new suit. And Kyle wouldn't believe it. He said, sanely enough, that no garage man ever gave away four new tires. He even went around and forced Al to take a check for them. He didn't even believe Al. Of course it did sound absurd, having your garage man give you a set of tires, but—"

"What happened to the check?" Asey asked.

"In the same manner as Lina Corregio and the silk sheets, Al and I split it. But the truth is silly."

"Not so much silly," Asey said thoughtfully, "as that somehow folks expect the truth to be kind of gray an' drab. They c'nsider things that's poss'ble, but they don't seem to be able to let their minds an' 'magination stray towards things that's poss'ble an' prob'ble too. They say, such an' such a thing *can* happen, but. An' when the truth sounds silly, it's just that they ain't gone beyond that but. Or else they work it the other way an' ask—"

"Help!" I said. "Help!"

"They say," Asey went on serenely, "this has happened, this is the way it prob'ly did happen, an' they won't take other poss'bilities into account. Now—"

"As Eleo said, let my mind remain in its reasonably lucid and crystal state, Asey. You may think you're being intelligible, but you're simply talking Greek. Or ballistics. You—"

"There," Asey said triumphantly, as we turned up the drive of the old tavern, "see what I mean? They's a poss'bility you might get c'nfused, but you take it as a prob'bility, whereas if you—"

I got out of the car.

"This," I told him, "is where we eat. Give the gray matter a change and indulge the red corpuscles. I want lobster thermidor."

Just as we got up to go, Jo Dwight dashed in, looking very windblown and vivid and picturesque. She waved us back into our seats.

"I'm starved, absolutely starved, and you're going to plank yourselves down and watch me eat. What luck, finding—"

"You didn't get all the way to Providence and back?"

"No, Bev. I forgot to get gas, and stopped in New Bedford, and there was that Don what's-his-name. You know, the one whose family have that awful house and all the tennis courts in Orleans. He was going to take his plane in Providence, bound for New York, and he said he'd take Agatha if she'd go. She said yes, and there wasn't any need of my going any further, so I dumped her into his low backed car, and off they whizzed."

"Did she suspect anything?"

"Don't know. Maybe. She was all for calling Aunt Nella in New Bedford, but I said it was a waste of time, we couldn't stop to blither around with telephones, and there weren't any available except in nasty little cigar and tonic stores, and lunch counters, and dog wagons. In her heart of hearts, she thinks my mother's the guilty soul. Is she, Asey?"

"We been to see your mother," he told her. "No, she ain't in this. Look, would you do somethin' for me? Go make peace with her before either of you goes away, an' don't mention Dave if you can help it."

Jo downed an enormous bowl of clam chowder before she answered.

"I suppose I might as well. You ever know grandmother, Bev? Too bad. You'd understand mother. After all, if people set out to bring their children up a certain way, there's little hope for the poor devils. I'll hand it to mother that she showed me the worst and let me do my own thinking. And—how did you find out she was in love with Dave?"

"We didn't. Was she?" Asey caught my eye and shook his head ever so slightly.

"I hoped you'd tell me. I wondered. Asey, I went

through most of Kay's papers this afternoon. I can tell you something I didn't know and didn't understand much. Why Kay went around with Creel."

"Giles?" Asey asked.

"Yes. How did you guess? She never said so, out and out."

"Nope, but I'm an ole b'tween the lines reader. Giles got Cape Coddy an' ind'pendent ev'ry time he thought of her money an' c'mpared it to the boat yard profits, an' she kind of wanted to jog him, huh?"

"I think. It got Giles mad, all right, but it didn't get her anywhere. I'm beginning to think she cared more for Giles than he did—Asey, I think that cliff business and Kay's death have something to do with Dave's murder. I can't find anything that would back me up, but I do feel so. And if you read those things, doesn't it seem to you that Kay hadn't any intention in the world of killing herself? She wasn't the kind to jump off a cliff or go into a decline just because she couldn't get the man she wanted."

"I've thought about it," Asey said, "till I—go ahead an' snicker, Bev. Till I get all balled up. An' the more I think of it, the more it seems like I was right in the b'ginnin'. I think Kay an' them others was killed. Pushed off by someone. I know it don't hitch up. None of them girls had been in any struggle. None of 'em'd been raped or even touched. Dave, after a while, swung around to thinkin' it was all an accident. They's a couple of dangerous places there, where you could catch your foot an' go over. But Kay knew 'em. Dave set out to walk up to the cliff with her that night, an' then his bad knee started to hurt an' he went back. He didn't wait up for her. Now, him an' me, we went over that trip as far as he went, again an' again. Kay was as happy as a lark. She had on flat-soled shoes that'd never trip her. There you be. I kind of agree with you, Jo, though I ain't got any reason for it. Somethin' to do with her an' the rest caused Dave's death."

"Perhaps he found out something," I said. "Perhaps he had some clue."

"Maybe. Only he told me all the ideas he had. I wish he'd let me in on this one, if there was one. Seems to me he would have, too, if there'd been. But you can't tell. I—well, well. Thought the days of raidin' this place was over. What's the matter with you, Forman? How come you're here?"

Forman crossed over to our table.

"Luck, Asey, is the thing you keep in your pocket like a handkerchief. I was going down to Weesit to see you, but I'd been to Boston and back, and I needed food. Asey, I've got something. Tracked down that gun. Checked it, too."

He paused in that irritating fashion people always do when they have something important to say and know everyone's ears are falling off in an effort to hear.

"Well?" Asey demanded.

"That gun Grosgrain says he found was bought and registered by Giles Hopkins, Junior, of North Weesit. How's that hit you?"

CHAPTER TWELVE

"IT'S incredible," I told Asey angrily a few minutes later, as we raced back to North Weesit—we'd left Jo finishing, and Forman beginning, their respective meals. "It's absolutely impossible, Asey! Forman's made some stupid mistake!"

"I'm 'fraid he hasn't," Asey replied. "He's a careful sort. Cautious. He won't even say outright that two bullets come from the same gun even if they do. Says instead, 'This bullet's got six thousand dozen an' forty sim'lar markin's an' aspects to this bullet B.' B'sides, he went up to Boston an' checked it up himself."

I gritted inches of enamel off my teeth till we got to the neat, box-like Cape Cod house where Giles and his father live.

We found Giles Senior cheerfully scouring pans out in the kitchen.

"Hi, you two. Don't mind the mess. I had baked finnan haddie for supper—"

"Not beans?" Asey asked in mock horror. I remembered that it was Saturday, after all.

"I cheated, Asey. I'm sick of beans. Anyway, I've

staved off cleaning up as long as I could. I hate fish pans. Giles always has to do 'em for me. Sit down and tell me the news. I meant to get over to-day, but we're working like horses. If I go away, things don't seem to hustle the way they should."

"Giles out?" Asey asked.

"He went off yesterday with Sam Murdock to try out the new boat I built for Dykes. I don't expect to see 'em back till to-morrow."

"To-morrow?" I could have cried. "Oh, Uncle Giles, not until to-morrow?"

"Yes. The boy's been pretty much worked up over this business of Kay Truman, and Dave's death near finished him. He fiddled around, stood on one foot and then the other, and finally I told Sam to take him out and keep him away as long as possible. I'm terribly sorry, Bev, that he couldn't have gone with Kyle to Bermuda. A little North Weesit goes a long ways, and he's stuck it out here for over a year since college. He's a serious minded boy, and he needs changes more than he thinks. Asey, toss me that towel, will you? Look—Giles isn't involved in this affair, is he? He's not in trouble?"

Asey drew a long breath. "Yes an' no, Giles. I—"

"No," I interrupted, "no. Asey, he can't be, if he's been away since yesterday afternoon. He couldn't have had anything to do with the knife in your car, or the mushrooms. And he was beside me on the steps the night you got shot at. And certainly he had nothing to do with that gun!"

"Gun?" Giles hung up the dish towels and came

over to where we sat by the kitchen table. "Gun? You mean, the one that was—"

"Don't get worked up," Asey said. "It ain't that. Listen, did the boy have a .45 automatic Colt, d'you know?"

"He did have. Bought it with some birthday money while he was in college. Sold it a year ago to young Shepherd—what's his name, Bev?"

"Palmer?"

"That's the fellow. Yes, Giles sold it or swapped it, I don't recall just which. It was probably a swap. There's a lot of his tin peddling great-grandfather in him. Remember old Edmund, Asey?"

Asey grinned. "He was the feller that set out with a handful of rusty nails one mornin' an' come home trundlin' a wheelbarrow full of grain, an' leadin' two cows by a rope around his waist. Yes-yes. I still got a lot of pewter plates to home that my grandmother took for a whetstone an' three beehives. So he swapped it to young Shepherd. Huh. He home now, Bev?"

"Probably. He usually comes down week ends."

"Then we'll pop over an' see him. You see, Giles," Asey recounted the story of the gun Grosgrain said he found, and Forman's check-up on it, "that's how it stands, an' I don't mind tellin' you I'm mighty glad to see the buck passed. Tell Giles to come over when he gets home —oh, an' if Jo Dwight or Forman should come bustlin' in here, tell 'em we've gone elsewhere, but you don't know which elsewhere. We can do without 'em."

We caught Palmer Shepherd just as he was leaving

for some party or other up the Cape. Palmer is the sort of person Creel Friar hopes he looks like. If you met him bouncing on the top of a camel in the middle of the Sahara Desert, wearing whatever the natives in that part of the world happen to wear, you would instinctively expect to find a copy of the *Boston Evening Transcript* in his pocket. Just ten words, and you'd know his prep school, his year at Cambridge, his clubs, and just which brokerage house his grandfather founded, and he thinks he works in.

He instantly and honestly admitted that he had swapped an old chamois jacket, a pair of French horns from his car, and a set of old golf clubs—with bag, balls, and an old pair of spiked shoes, for the .45 Colt.

"Oh, yes," he added. "And a pile of old magazines and a couple of dozen books. Old ones."

The shadow of a smile flickered across Asey's face. I knew that he, too, was thinking of old Edmund and the rusty nails.

"Still got the gun?" Asey asked.

Palmer shook his head. "No, Asey, I haven't. Last spring I had a bunch down one weekend, and Tony Kent took the gun out to pot at a target on the beach. And then he and Amy took a walk up to the life saving station, and somehow," he grinned, "when they got back they discovered that they'd lost the gun. Of course we all went out and tried to find it, but we couldn't. After all, there are four good miles of dunes from our place to the station—anyway, Tony bought me another. Why d'you ask?"

Asey told him. "I s'pose," he added, "you can prove you was in Siam on Thursday?"

"Last Thursday? I stayed at the office," Palmer stated with a touch of bitterness, "till ten at night, trying to find three items my worthy father lost. I got there at nine-twelve, for which my worthy parent docked me. You can check that with the greatest of ease. Sorry about the gun, Asey, but it's just plain lost. Anyone could have picked it up."

And that, so to speak, was that.

"Huh," Asey muttered as we climbed into the roadster again. "This is a nice, log'cal mess, ain't it? Only honest, up an' down clue we got turns out like this. You know any nice haystacks, Bev, where I could hunt needles? It'd be a cinch. It'd be a pleasure."

"At least you can do a little rationalizing, anyway," I remarked. "You can figure out that the person you're after knows Dave Truman, is either a native or a summer person—don't laugh, you wretch! What I mean is, it's not a tourist! Anyhow, he's a good shot, a good knife thrower, he knows all about mushrooms, and he knows a lot about us."

Asey wrinkled up his forehead. "Maybe so, an' maybe not so. I'll 'gree with you on some points. He knew Dave, an' he wanted to get rid of him. As for his bein' either a native or a summer person, I don't think so, Bev. Not nes'sarily. If you went at it ambitious-like, you could learn all you wanted to know about the layout of the place in a day or so, or even less. As for a good knife thrower, yes an' no. Didn't take any skill to kill Dave, or jam a knife in my car seat. First just took strength, an' a sort of cowardly spirit, an' the last didn't take much of anythin'."

"He was a good shot," I said defensively.

"Yup, but he didn't hit me," Asey pointed out. "As for the mushrooms, you wouldn't really have to know as much as Luther did to be able to switch 'em. 'Course, he'd have to be an active sort to go poppin' in through your windows—"

"You certainly can't deny," I broke in, "that he knows you, knows me, knows what we're planning, what we think, what we do—"

"I wouldn't say 'Know,'" Asey observed thoughtfully. "May be splittin' hairs, but I'd say 'Observe.' Someone sittin' up in a tree, or watchin' us with a pair of glasses, they could get just as far. What I mean is, it don't have to be someone we're int'mate with, or someone that's int'mate with us. Well, I got you under my eye, an' Miss Ag'tha's elsewhere, an' Jo's goin' to be looked after by Bob. An' Hanson's kind of a chump in some ways, but he's honest enough, an' so's Bob. Giles is out, an' the rest of Hanson's men is all right, an' Luther— well," he smiled, "you kind of have to b'lieve him. He's out of the way, anyway. 'Stead of drawin' a big circle an' narrowin' down, you sort of got to work out from the middle, here."

"But if it's someone who's intimately connected with us, or," I amended hastily, "someone who's got a chance to do a lot of observing, what about Katy or Jethro?"

Asey chuckled. "Sure, Katy knows a Death Cup from

a plain mushroom! Sure she knew Dave, owned Truman stock, an' shot at me!"

"Well, there's Jethro. You thought of him first of all!"

"D'you see Pegleg scramblin' up trees with that wooden pin of his, leapin' around your roof, waltzin' in gutters? B'sides, how'd that deaf ole haddock hear anythin' to b'gin with? Lord, he couldn't prowl around tinklin' a bell, Bev! Take more'n a dinky little bell for him to hear. Bell—it'd take a dynamite blast an' a couple trench mortars, an' then he'd prob'ly ask if they was a moskeeter in the room! No, I don't count either of 'em in this. Nor Jo's mother, nor Creel."

"Then possibly you can tell me just how we're going to enlarge your circle," I demanded. "Where do you go from here?"

"Jimmy Porter's still goin' through crank lists, an' stock lists, an' I'm hopin' for a little news from him sooner or later. Now we sort of 'counted for the in'cent by-standers, we'll get to branchin' out. Take the folks that live round. Let's see. Like the Logans, f'r instance."

I snorted. "Old man Logan is nearly stone blind, and the boy is a half wit, generously speaking."

"Well, take Tommy Dawson. You saw him wanderin' about the inlet with a flounder spear."

"But Ike Smalley alibied him. Don't you remember? You've got to do better than that, Asey."

"Maybe. Just the samey, I think I'll swing over an' chat with Tommy. He may have seen somethin' that'd help. This is the Catchin'-At-Straws Club, Bev."

"Instead of talking with Tommy," I was impatient,

"why don't you go working back to Kay, if you think her death had something to do with Dave's?"

"I worked on that since she died," Asey said, "an' if I couldn't get any place in all these weeks, I don't think I can make any mammoth discov'ries to-night."

We found the Dawson family in their dining room, listening to a radio sketch of New England life; I gathered they bore it for the sheer joy of panning the dialect. Personally I've wondered what sort of explosion will occur on the day broadcasters discover that most New Englanders gave up wheezing through their noses before I was born.

Elisha Dawson greeted us cheerfully and then turned on his son. "There, Tommy, see? I told you what'd happen if you didn't go to Asey right away and tell him about that woman!"

"Aw, pa," Tommy said wearily, "I told you a thousand times I wasn't even sure if I seen a woman—honest, Asey, did you come for that?"

"Certainly did," Asey told him blandly. "What time was it you seen her? Can you make a guess?"

Tommy shook his head. "Honest, Asey, I don't know. I tell you, I didn't pay much attention to things, an' it might not have been a woman in white I seen—"

I almost fell off the edge of my chair. A woman in white couldn't have been Jo, as I'd thought at first. No mistaking Jo in her flaming red shorts and jersey for any woman in white. Yet Eleo had worn white that day. A white knitted dress, and a woolly white polo coat.

"Might of been a man in white pants and a white

shirt. Anyway it was—oh, gee, Asey, I'm not a bit sure! I thought for a second I seen someone back of Truman's house, but honest, I never thought of it till we heard about his bein' killed, an' it might just be imagination. I ain't a bit sure!"

And under an hour of Asey's ruthless cross-examination, Tommy stuck to his guns. He thought he might have seen a figure dressed in white behind Dave's house, some time after four o'clock. He wasn't sure, wouldn't swear to it in court, didn't remember any distinguishing features, thought it was probably his imagination after all.

"But," I said to Asey after we left, "isn't that something? Lord, it does my soul good to hear such a vague tale as that! Anything to work this business away from us. But couldn't there have been someone?"

"Whyn't Giles see?"

"Giles was the only one in any position to do any seeing," I admitted, "but you said yourself that he might not have the wit to smell everything out, or the sense to mention everything. Besides all that, he wasn't thinking of making time checks on incipient murderers! And why couldn't this figure in white have gone to Dave's house hours before? Why couldn't it have been the departure that Tommy saw? Giles was out of the tree when the person went. He and Agatha and I were all out in front of Dave's. The person might have come and gone at random, with a brass band, and we'd never have known at that point."

"It's food for thought," Asey agreed, "if it ain't anythin' else, an' course I'm still broodin' over some of the dif'rences in your three stories of that day. What were they? God A'mighty, ain't you listened to 'em often enough to know? No, I—my golly," he added as we swung up to my house, "look at Hanson, sittin' on the back steps! Man alive, what are you, gettin' into the mood to pose for a 'B'fore' an' after sufferin' picture for somebody's liver pills?"

Bob Raymond appeared at the kitchen door in time to hear the last of Asey's comment.

"Don't say a word," he pleaded. "Just go away and let us be. We're sick at heart. And when I say we're sick at heart, I mean that we're sick at heart. Luther trouble again."

"Don't tell me," Asey said, "that ole Monty an' his five-piece firm has wangled that pint of cider out of jail already?"

"Not now, but they've begun to raise hell so soon. I don't know what that bunch has on the Governor, but from what his secretary said half an hour ago, I'd say the pardon was already blotted. No, he's not out yet, but he'll be out on the crack of dawn Monday morning."

"But listen here, Hanson," Asey began.

"It would be kinder not to speak to Hanson," Bob said. "He's ready to burst into tears. No, Luther hasn't said where he got the gun, if that's what you wanted to know. He didn't say a word during the trip, only that he wanted Mr. Montgomery. Just like a baby yelling for his bottle. Boston had no records of the gun at all. I pulled the old line and said probably if he told all, he'd be let off, but he looked more than ever as though he'd blub and kept calling for Mr. Montgomery. It got tiresome."

Asey nodded. "I can see where just the sound of it would git on your nerves. It was like to have got on mine just the other afternoon. Is Jo back?"

"Inside. Oh, and Parker's been here, Asey."

"Any message for me?"

"No. He just said for you to take your own sweet time and go at things your own sweet way, and to let him know if you needed aid. He said not to let Walker, Adams, Meredith and the rest of 'em spoil your sleep, and to pay even less attention to the Governor and the papers. But that didn't cheer Hanson."

"I know," Hanson announced gloomily, "what he meant. So does Asey."

Bob raised his eyebrows. "What he meant?"

"Yup." Asey got out of the car. "You're too new to get it. When Parker b'gins tellin' you to go slow an' easy, an' not to bother about pol'ticians an' the press, what he means is he wants action quick. Looky, Hanson, ain't you got any notions? Ain't you found anythin' to-day at all?"

Hanson reached into the pocket of his blue coat and brought out a handful of things.

"I raked the lawn like you said, and I raked back of the house, and I went through the inside on hands and knees, and this is all I got."

Under the kitchen light, we examined the miscellaneous assortment. There were half a dozen hairpins—

one I recognized as mine, a marble that the boys must have lost, a pin in the shape of a basketball, with Kay's initials and class engraved on the back, a small bakelite cigar holder and a small blob of putty.

"Why, Asey," I said, "this is like the one you found in the roof gutter yesterday! Those wretched twins—they promised me they'd never use those sling shots anywhere but on their own land!"

Asey picked up the little irregular hunk and looked at it curiously.

"Got any putty around, Bev?"

"Gobs. Tins in the boathouse, in the garage, and probably in the cellar. But why—you can't think those two pieces of putty mean anything? You're cracked. I tell you, the twins made hundreds of balls during the summer!"

Just the same, in spite of my protests, Asey went rambling off with a flashlight. I went inside and found Jo disconsolately playing double Napoleon before the fire.

"There's something wrong," she said peevishly. "I can't even get started."

I leaned over her shoulder. "Let me see—dear child, you've got hold of the cards the twins play with! One pack's got no aces. They used 'em for targets after they saw a western where the hero pierced four aces through the heart—I'm *not* consciously punning—in four shots. But you haven't even asked about Giles!"

Jo shrugged. "You'd have been in here hours ago, yelping it to the skies, if there'd been anything in that. Besides, I knew he hadn't—what happened, did he lose the gun?"

I told her about Palmer Shepherd, but she interrupted me before I was half through.

"I know. Tony Kent lost it. Kay was on that party and told me all about it. Mostly because Mrs. Shepherd was at a complete loss to understand how dear Tony and dear Amy *could* have lost the gun, and why they didn't find it out till so long afterwards. It was very touching."

Asey strode in with his arms full of cans.

"What are you playing?" Jo asked with a laugh. "The Fuller Putty Man?"

"This," Asey informed her, "is a practical an' inform'tive little talk on silly things you run across. Provin' that even if you're faced with fact, an' the fact seems prob'bly to have a def'nite origin, you don't want to state the fact as havin' that base alone till you've broke down an' fiddled with some of the un-prob'ble poss'bilities. Now—"

"All men eat to live," Jo chanted mournfully. "A eats to live, therefore A is a man. All men live to eat, A lives to eat, therefore—"

"He's not showing off," I said. "He's just rubbing it in for my benefit. Go on, Sherlock. Tell us about the little putty hunks—"

Not in the least disconcerted, Asey held up a mangy looking putty can. "We got here," he said, "exhibit A. Typ'cal of the sort of putty tins you keep in your boat house. Your husband ain't no Cape Codder, that's a cinch. All the putty's been mixed with white paint—"

"For the boat, of course—"

"Just so. Wasteful. Mix it when you want it. Exhibit

B's from the cellar. This is a del'cate blushin' pink. Why, I don't know. You ain't got any pink boats, have you?"

I laughed. "That came from a rainy day when the boys decided to make marionettes or puppets or something. They gave it up before they used the putty—I think they found a box of plastic wood that held more charms. Go on."

"Exhibit C. Putty from g'rage. Some is punkin colored—"

"Floors in dining room and—"

"An' blue. Your blinds, I guess. An' green—but it really don't matter, except that you're a wasteful fam'ly with putty. Point is, you ain't got a speck of putty in the house that ain't had colored paint mixed in. I found a tin can of plain putty balls down in the boat house, but they'd been painted afterwards. Now, these we found—"

"You know, Asey," Jo's irony was delightful, "you know, we've almost guessed. The one from the gutter and the one Hanson found are NOT painted. Isn't it amazing?"

Asey grinned amiably. "It is, an' if your mighty brain can explain 'em, I'll give you all my ole shoes an' socks an' throw in a lemon an' a piece of coal."

We brooded over those two foolish chunks of putty till we became maudlin.

"Sure a little bit of putty fell from out the clouds one day," Jo warbled in a feeble soprano, strumming an imaginary piano, "and settled on the roof-top of the house of Penrose, K—"

"Putty bad, putty bad." Asey shook his head mournfully. "I c'n do better than that. I—"

"You can't," I interrupted proudly. "I've got a better one still. 'A putty in the hand is worth two'—"

It took several minutes to extricate myself from the avalanche of pillows.

"Now," Jo said, "let's be serious. Asey, what do you think the things mean?"

Asey flashed a look at her and hauled out his pipe.

"I don't know," he said, "any more'n I know what about rel'tivity or what about the League of Nations, or what about Russia. If—"

An idea hit me with such force that I screamed.

"Fingerprints, Asey! Fingerprints! You don't make putty balls with gloves on—"

"You don't, but this feller did. Leastways, Hanson an' Bob had a session with the one Hanson found, an' they wasn't any, an' I couldn't find any on the piece I found in the gutter. That's why I didn't think even then you was right about it's bein' one of the twins's pieces of sling shot am'nition, Bev."

I felt indescribably dumb.

"It ain't even much of a ball," Asey went on, "or even a good beginnin' of one. I been sort of grapplin' with it all day. Now the ones the twins had in their tin can was real round an' smooth."

"You mean," I said, "you've been thinking about that hunk of putty all day and never mentioned it?"

The phone rang, that eternal one-two-three-four-five! Asey got up and answered it.

"Aunt Agatha, I bet," I whispered to Jo. "And my, will she burn up the wires!"

But it wasn't Agatha, although the call came from New York. And Asey was glowing when he finally set down the receiver.

"Jimmy Porter—"

"Bill's brother?"

"Uh-huh. An' he's all worked up. Says he's been plowin' through files since early mornin'—had a lot of trouble gettin' p'mission to get at the records an' into the firm's files. That's why he's not r'ported b'fore. Says he's on the trail of somethin' hot, is on the verge of takin' a special plane to Boston, has got everythin' fixed up so's he can get into the comp'ny files here, even to-morrow, an' he'll let me know just's soon's he can when he's checked up."

"But didn't he tell you names?" I demanded. "Didn't he even drop a hint?"

"He don't know names, yet. That's what he was comin' here for. Just m'randums he'd happened on, in Dave's own private files. Said to 'C.F. Boston office,' so Jimmy's goin' to c.f."

There was nothing to do but to possess our souls with patience till Jimmy Porter should come to Boston and settle the matter. But we were pretty discouraged when Sunday noon rolled around with no word from him.

"Prob'ly," Asey sounded disappointed, too, "prob'ly some hitch in his gettin' hold of the things on Sunday. Ho-hum—"

Just at that moment Hanson appeared with Jimmy Porter. Usually Jimmy resembles a tailor's dummy; that day he looked like a soap-box haranguer out of Union Square.

"I'm here," he said. "Hi—I'm here, and I'm a wreck! No sleep since God knows when, but I got a clue, and it was too good to let go. I didn't call you because I wanted you to see the stuff, and God bless Parker—"

"He see you through? I phoned him to—"

"Four of his men leaped on me at the airport. Thought I was being pinched. Bev, get something like a cup of coffee or a pail of soup, will you, like an angel? Where—here's the briefcase. Here are your papers—d'you know it's cost me a thousand dollars in bribes alone, getting at these things? Treat 'em with care. And if you don't think this is something—"

"Tell us while you show him!" I demanded.

"Right. There were any number of crank letters, but all the usual illiterate stuff. All westerners, too. Thing that led me on the right track was a memo of Dave's saying 'What about North Weesit crank? Send correspondence from Boston.' But it hadn't been. Here you are. The heftiest crank in the records; ninety-four letters, and he owned just exactly one share, that was a transfer from an estate. He hadn't even bought the share. And just see how near and convenient it is!"

Jo and I cracked our heads together as both of us leaned over to see the signature, and we hit Hanson's jaw as we backed away.

The signature on the letters was Ike Smalley's.

CHAPTER THIRTEEN

"NO, you don't!" Jimmy yelled as we all scrambled for the door. "No, you don't run away till I'm properly fed and some of the dust is removed from my palate! Bev, Kyle never used to keep a house without a spot of whisky for weary wayfarers! And consider, if Ike Smalley has kept this long, he'll keep an hour or two longer. After all my research, I want to be in at the kill—"

"Sorry," Asey apologized. "We didn't mean to run out on you, only this five star headline news has sort of d'moralized us. While Bev finds you a drink, I'll go make Katy hustle dinner."

"We might as well wait anyway," I said a few minutes later to the accompaniment of Jimmy's gentle swallows. "It's the Smalley dinner hour. Think, Asey, what happened the last time we burst into one of their meals. Think of those cancerous ads, and the anæmic Currier and Iveses, and that horsehair furniture—"

Katy outdid herself for the title of the cook of the world's worst Sunday dinner, but we hardly noticed it. I personally felt the way a whippet looks before a race.

"Ike fits!" I said excitedly. "He fits so beautifully! You said 'observe,' Asey. And think of Ike and his binoculars, and—"

"And lazy as he is," Jo broke in, "he's plenty active. Slow, but agile just the same. He could have shinnied up the roof—"

"And from the looks of those letters," Jimmy said, "he certainly felt he had a motive, all right. Honestly, I can't get over it. One share, and that's his reaction to losing it. What'd he have done if he'd owned Union Atlas, or Kreuger—"

"May be an expl'nation of what happened to Kreuger," Asey suggested. "Maybe Ike wrote letters to him. I didn't know the feller had gumption enough to write letters like these. Set him to work with a party platform, an' he'd make a third party with sixty words."

"He must have walked along the shore," I gabbled happily, "in the shadow of the bushes. Couldn't have used a boat to cross over, or Tommy'd have seen him. I wonder why Jethro didn't?"

"Pegleg?" Jimmy asked with a laugh. "Was he around? Up in the potato patch? Oh, that's easy, Bev. Old Pegleg Black wouldn't have heard anything, so he wouldn't have seen anything either. Someone sneaked in my garage last year and stole two blankets out of the car, and Pegleg was hoeing ten feet away, but he didn't hear or see a thing."

"And he's a native," I said. "He knows layouts and the lay of the land. He'd know about mushrooms. Kyle says Ike's a superb shot. Oh, it's all fitting in at last!"

"Think of his sitting there," Jo got up and stalked around the room, "sitting there, watching Dave through his binoculars, seeing Dave live in what must be utter luxury to him, brooding about his lost share!"

"Depression complex," Bob Raymond suggested. "Probably he didn't really get upset at first, and then he got to thinking about the things he could have done with the money from that share, and then it achieved such proportions that he began to feel downtrodden, and all."

"And on one share!" Jimmy, who'd probably lost fifty thousand in the Truman crash alone, shook his head and sighed. "Beats me. Why, if I felt that way about one share, most of my friends would have been dead and cut up into small choice tidbits years ago."

"Yet," Asey said thoughtfully, "Smalleys've had a d'pression on their hands all their lives. Lived on gov'-ment butter an' pork an' coal the last two winters. Lived higher'n they ever did before, too. Maybe that's the answer, though. Maybe that pork give 'em a taste for the better things they might of got from that share."

Before we left the house, we had Ike Smalley pretty well sewed in a sack. Jo and Jimmy and Bob and Hanson and I planned the whole business out. It was so simple, so incredibly simple! I began to think that if I'd only thought a bit more on that old astronomy problem, I might have got that, too. It worked out so nicely, so smoothly!

Ike had of course slipped over to Dave's and hidden, probably while Jethro was having his lunch, or even while

Jet was digging the potatoes. Somehow Ike had got hold of Sully, taken off his collar, and used the bell to hide any noise he might make, knowing that Dave would ascribe any strange sounds to the cat gamboling about.

Probably, if Dave was at his desk, as his half begun letter to Grosgrain and some pages of figures and lists indicated, then Ike had no chance to enter the living room unobserved. The desk faced both doors. Ike, therefore, must have followed Dave to the front of the house when Dave came outdoors with his gun, and become panicky at the sight of it, thinking Dave suspected something wrong. Then, as Dave lingered on the top step, Ike had lunged forward and driven home the knife.

"Then," Jo said, "he got Sully and replaced the bell and left, while Bev and Giles and Agatha were there. Then, later, when he saw the police, he got excited, came over here that night and prowled around to see what he could find out. Saw Asey, realized his chances of not being discovered were about a thousand per cent better if Asey were out of the way, and shot at him when he left. Knowing that the gun couldn't be traced to him— of course, Ike easily could have picked up the Giles-Palmer-Tony Kent model on the beach—he left it behind. Grosgrain found it."

"Then," Hanson added happily, "he found Grosgrain's knife, and took that along with him. Then, when Asey called next morning, he—"

"He pretended to go after sody," I finished, "but in reality, stuck the knife into the seat of the car, thinking it would give Asey food for thought, and a few bad moments. Then he probably thought of the mushrooms, crawled into our house night before last—using another bell, or Sully's, and switched the mushrooms Mike left, for his own Death Cups. But Asey, isn't it too late to find mushrooms around?"

Asey, who'd been listening to our narrative with a strangely immobile face, inclined his head.

"Yup. But once about five years ago, Ike an' Sophy d'cided to raise 'em for a livin' in their cellar. No effort. They got one of them dinky little round cellars, an' like I said when I seen it, after Ike asked my advice, they could raise 'em without even plantin' 'em. 'Nough fungus growth in that cellar to feed the unemployed in comfort for ten years. But—"

"There you are!" I said triumphantly. "There you are. It all fits in. Asey, aren't you pleased?"

He tapped on his pipe carefully before replying.

"Seems to fit," he said at last, "but what do you make of Dave's last word? Where's the ink fit in?"

I sighed. "Are you still harping on that? Asey, don't be a nitwit! He was trying to say 'Ike,' of course! Now I suppose you'll ask what about those silly pieces of putty? Well, I don't know. But it seems to me perfectly possible that the twins got hold of some of the putty before paint was mixed in it, and rolled it with a putty knife. Come on—you can't possibly eat any more, Jimmy. You've gone beyond bad manners. More would just mean indigestion. Come on, let's go. Come on, Asey. We can all go in your car, and Hanson and Bob can take theirs, and we'll get to Ike's."

"We ain't goin' to Ike's," Asey said surprisingly.

"Not going to Ike's?" Jimmy Porter stared at him. "What? Why not?"

"Oh, we're goin' there 'ventually, but not now. I want to see Washy Wheeler first an' do a little checkin'."

There was something in his tone which invited no opposition. We went to Washy's weatherbeaten little half house, on the other end of Ike's lane.

Washy, dressed in his best Sunday serge, puffing an after dinner cigar, pumped Asey by the hand and nodded to the rest of us.

"Glad to see you, glad to see you," he said hospitably. "Hullo, Hanson. Say, there's a strange boat runnin' up the east channel three times a week. Same route Regan used to use for his rum fleet. Seem to be landin' in the cove somewheres. Maybe you'd like to look into it."

Hanson nodded gratefully. "Sure would. I had a feeling Regan wouldn't give up so easy, and he knows they've cut the coast guard down off here. Shouldn't wonder if he wasn't running more than liquor. Okay. Thanks. Go on, Asey."

Asey came to the point at once. "This business of Dave Truman, Washy. We want to know what you know about Ike Smalley's goin's on that aft'noon. Thursday. Around fourish to fiveish."

Washy looked puzzled. "I dunno nothin' about him that time, Asey. I come over to his fish house round half past five, an' he was settin' there with his glasses—"

"He said you come at four or four-thirty," Asey said.

"Never in this world! No, sireebob. I know it was

half past five anyhow, because I had his mail an' paper, an' Betsey told me to run down an' take it so's to get back b'fore suppertime. She said, 'It's near five-thirty. Hurry an' get back.' "

"What'd Ike have to say?" Asey demanded. "Give us the works. Tell us what he said, an' what happened till you took him back to his house."

Washy puffed at his cigar for a minute.

"Gosh, it's hard to think back. That aft'noon wasn't any dif'ferent from any other I went down there. Yes, it was." He looked at Jo and grinned, and then turned pink. "Ike told me to look through the glasses over to Truman's landin', and I seen you—uh—take a swim—"

"What time was that?" Asey asked Jo.

"I didn't have a watch with me, but it must have been near five-thirty, Asey, because it's a good thirty-five minutes' walk home, and I was home by six-thirty. I mean, after I took my dip and got dressed again, it must have been easily quarter to six. Chilly."

"I can't remember much more about that day," Washy said. "I—I'm sorry, Miss Dwight—"

"Perfectly all right," Jo said. "If I choose to go swimming in spots that aren't secluded, it's no one's fault but my own that I get looked at. Don't be upset about it. I didn't know you were gazing at the time, and I'm fully clothed now, so there's no sense in my getting worked up, now, if you get the idea."

Washy didn't follow her involved reasoning, but he appeared to be somewhat relieved.

"I told my wife," he confessed, "an' she said I ought

to be ashamed of myself. I—uh—honest, Asey, that's about all I remember. Ike and I talked about things in gen'ral. That is, he beefed about the gov'ment, an' cap'talism, an' war debts." Washy grinned. "Like I always tell him, I can see where he's int'rested in debts. Ain't five folks in this town he don't owe money to."

"He say anythin' about Dave?"

"Did he?" Washy smiled. "I told him, when I was tellin' him about the murder, I said, 'If I didn't know you had the guts of a dead fish, I'd think you killed Dave Truman yourself.' Why, Asey, he owned a lot of Truman stock, see—"

Jimmy Porter let out a muffled roar.

"An' when that comp'ny folded up, he was fit to be tied. I tried to argue with him, made him admit he'd got as much in div'dends as he ever invested, with their bonuses an' all durin' prosperity, but he wouldn't see things that way. I told him, I said, 'If you had the money in a bank, most likely the bank'd of failed.' Not," he added hastily, "that any bank down here failed, but you know Ike. Him an' hard luck is—"

"First cousins," Asey nodded. "I know. He just missed catchin' that rich widow woman that come to town thirty years ago, an' he just missed connectin' with the Spanish war, else he'd been a hero, he says, with a good pension. An' he spent ten years savin' to buy a good motor boat, an' didn't moor it proper, an' it drifted away to sea the first week he had it. I know."

"Well, he seemed to think it was all Dave's fault that he lost his share. I said, I told him, 'Dave ain't no more to blame for you losin' your money than Pres'dent Hoover was r'spons'ble for the d'pression, or Calvin Coolidge for prosperity. You just be reas'n'ble.' But," Washy concluded briefly, "he wa'n't."

"Did Ike ever say, out an' out, that he'd like to kill Dave, or anythin' like that?"

Washy hesitated. "Well," he said lamely, "he never exactly said he'd like to murder Dave, but he said about everythin' else. He ain't said much, though, since Dave went. Come to think of it, he ain't even talked much about war debts. He's all hipped on Huey Long now. Thinks he might move down to Huey's country where the poor's r'lieved an' the rich is soaked. You don't honestly think Ike was mixed up in that business of Dave, do you?"

Asey shrugged.

"Golly!" Washy came near swallowing his cigar. "Dave was stabbed in the back, wa'n't he? An' Ike's the sort—by George!"

"Happen to know if he's still raisin' mushrooms?" Asey wanted to know.

"I dunno. If you know that cellar of his, you'd know he'd raise 'em whether he wanted to or not. He give me some once, but I never et 'em. He said it was a pity to have so many, but it wouldn't pay him to sell 'em. He'd just lose money. He even had it figgered out how much money he saved not raisin' 'em. An' Sophy said they wasn't fit to eat. Not fit for human bein's. Just the same, Sophy was fryin' some yest'day. Nice big ones, they was."

It was all I could do to keep from howling. So Ike,

after leaving us a little gift of Death Cups, had placidly taken my mushrooms home! And Sophy, forsooth, had fried them in butter!

Asey grinned as he looked at me. "Thanks, Washy," he said. "You been a help. I guess we'll go have a little talk with Ike himself, now."

But Ike, Sophy told us in surly tones, was not at home.

"An' what do *they* want?" she demanded, looking suspiciously toward Hanson and Bob Raymond.

"Where's Ike?" Asey asked.

"I don't know. Out. What do they want?"

"When'll he be back?"

"I don't know." Sophy started to close the door, but Asey wedged his foot between the door and the casing.

"Look here, Sophy, I want Ike. I want to know where he is, an' when he'll be back. An' if you won't tell me, you can maybe answer a few questions yourself. Where's that gun of his he found on the beach?"

Sophy's eyes narrowed. "He never found any gun on the beach."

"Okay. You still raisin' mushrooms?"

"No!"

"Where'd you get the ones you cooked yest'day?" Asey asked smoothly. "They drop out of a nice white cloud, or wash up on the beach?"

Sophy just glared at him. I'd never thought of her before as being anything but a rather drab, commonplace, untidy looking woman. That day, as she stood there gripping the old battered kitchen door, I began to be afraid of her.

Little things I'd never noticed before seemed to leap out and hit me in the face. I found myself ticking them off mentally, one by one.

There were the little streaks of dirt ground into the wrinkles at her throat, the stains on her fingers with their dirty, cracked nails, the grease spots and smudges on her mussed apron, the disgusting grayness of her shirt, which showed above the collar of her faded dress. There was something sinister about her yellow pointed teeth, and something more than sinister about the way her lips curled back over them, displaying hideously wrinkled gums. But her eyes were really what frightened me. They weren't the eyes of a normal person who was simply angry; they were the eyes of a fanatic. They—

Jo slipped her arm in mine. "I'm scared of her," she whispered in my ear. "Thank God we're surrounded by strong, able-bodied men! Bev, she's a witch!"

I was almost ready to agree.

"Okay," Asey said calmly, "if you don't want to help us, Sophy, you don't have to. Only it's a pity about that gun. We found it, an' I was goin' to give it back to Ike. But if you'd rather I didn't, it's all the same to me. I'll tell Ike when I see him that you didn't seem to want him to have it back."

Sophy moistened her lips. "I'll take it if you found it," she said, falling into Asey's trap. "You didn't tell me you found that gun."

"Didn't I?"

She looked at him. "You ain't got it," she said. "You—" her mouth worked.

"I just made you say he had a gun he found on the beach," Asey told her. "That's right. That's all I wanted to know, Sophy. Thank ye kindly."

"Wait," Sophy said as Asey turned away and started back to the roadster. "Wait!"

Asey kept right on.

Sophy hesitated, then relinquished her grip on the door and ran after him.

"Asey—"

He turned around.

"Well, what is it?"

"Asey, Ike—he ain't—Asey, Ike didn't have nothin' to do with Dave Truman's murder, did he? He ain't got nothin' to do with it?"

Asey pushed her hand off his arm. "I didn't say he had."

"But you think—Asey, did he?"

Asey sighed. "Look here, Sophy. I come here an' asked you as p'lite as I know how, where was Ike. You was just as unpleasant as you could be. You wouldn't tell me anythin'. I don't see no reason why at this point I should stop an' answer your questions. Leave go of my elbow!"

But she wouldn't let him get away.

"You got to tell me! Asey, I been almost sick, I have! He talked so much about Dave Truman, an' what he thought of him, an' how he wished all rich men could be murdered, an'—an' all." She began to sob, great racking dry sobs that shook her frail figure. "You got to tell me—do you think he did?"

"Was he home Thursday night?" Asey demanded.

She shook her head. "He went uptown. He didn't come home till late."

"An' Friday night?"

"I don't know. I went over to Ella's an' stayed with her, that night."

"Did he say where he got the mushrooms he brought home, the ones you cooked yest'day? He tell you where they come from?"

"No."

"They wasn't like those in your cellar?"

"No," Sophy said again. "But he told me to cook 'em. He said he knew they was good."

"Okay. Huh, I guess he did. Now, where's Ike? Where was he goin'?"

"He said he was just goin' to take a walk. I don't know where. Asey, he shouldn't have said those things against Dave Truman. Not after he paid Ike."

"Paid? You—tell us the whole thing!"

Brokenly, sometimes speaking so low I could hear her only with difficulty, Sophy told us about the share of Truman and Company stock.

It had come to them as a bequest from an uncle in Boston who'd died some ten years before. Ike had wanted to spend it all, then and there, but she had persuaded him not to touch it. After a while, the thought of owning stock in such a company had rather gone to Ike's head.

He bought the evening paper just to see how the share was doing.

"Night after night," Sophy said. "I told him it was a waste of money. I told him he could read Washy's paper the next day. But no, he had to see what that share was worth every day!"

Beside me, Jo was swallowing hard.

Sophy went on with the story. She'd tried to make Ike sell the share when it was near its highest point, but Ike had just laughed, and each day as it jumped a little higher, he began to plan on what he'd do with the money from it, when it went just a little higher yet.

Jimmy Porter laughed a rather sour laugh. "He wasn't alone," he said bitterly. "So did lots of others."

And then the market had crashed. Ike didn't get so worked up about it at first, but as time went on and the stock showed no signs of ever recovering, Ike began to take it harder and harder. That was when he began to write letters to the company, and to curse Dave Truman. Then someone told him the company would come back, and he cheered up for a while. Then the company had gone on the rocks completely.

Ike kept on writing letters, and then one day about two months ago, he had gone over to see Dave.

"He had a speech he'd written out an' learned," Sophy said. "Parts of it he got out of the Bible, an' parts out of a book about Russia someone give him. I told him he ought to be ashamed to talk like that, but he went over and said it to Dave Truman. Dave give him a hundred dollars. That was what the stock was really worth, he said. I thought Ike would keep still an' mind his business after that, but he was mad Dave hadn't give him as much as it was back in the time it was so much more."

"There are those," Jimmy Porter observed, "who would be happy, those who would actually ring bells and blow whistles and ride on a merry-go-round, to have salvaged as much as that out of Truman stock. And they had more than one share, too. I've got a bundle of stock you could paper your house with, and I'd be delighted to sell it at twenty cents a yard, seven cents cash!"

Sophy looked at him as though he were speaking a different language.

"Then Dave was killed," Sophy said, "an' since then, Ike's been a dif'rent body. Almost cheerful. I—I didn't dare say nothin'—but Asey—did he have anythin' to do with it?"

Asey looked at her tear blotched face. "'Course not," he said reassuringly. "'Course he ain't. You—you just stay here an' I'll run down to the boathouse an' see if I can find him."

It was a good attempt, but it didn't fool Sophy. She wept and wailed until Bob Raymond had to carry her into the house.

I offered to help, but Asey waved me aside.

"I'll see if I can't calm her down, an' Bob'll stay till I get Washy's wife or someone to look after her. Can't leave her here alone—no, Bev. No need for you to do anythin'. Look, you an' Jo an' Jimmy an' Hanson sort of work your way down to the boathouse. If Ike's there, just engage him in cheery an' in'cent conv'sation till I get there. Don't give him no hints about nothin'. Just sort of ramble on an' even let him tell you about war debts an' Huey Long, if he wants."

Obediently the four of us set off in the direction of the narrow foot path to the shore.

Jimmy caught his foot in a rusty wagon wheel and tumbled headlong.

"If Ike wanted to kill anyone," he remarked, "I should think he'd just ask him out to the back of his house some dark night, and let him wander. Talk about mazes! And Bev, you and Jo be careful of those bushes. They're all grown over with poison ivy. Better let me go ahead. Hanson, you hold the branches aside when I shove 'em back—"

"Here goes the first pair of stockings I've worn in months," Jo grumbled. "Try to dress up and be a lady, and then you get into blackberry brambles—"

She stopped short at Jimmy's exclamation—he was at the end of the path, where the long sandy beach began.

Quietly, we picked our way out of the underbrush and stood beside him.

Ike Smalley was sitting in a broken chair on the near end of his ramshackle wharf. In either hand he held a hunting knife—the blades sparkled in the sun. With a quick motion he hurled both at once toward the back wall of the fish house. Both of them thudded, not more than an inch apart, into a crude circle drawn on the wall.

CHAPTER FOURTEEN

STUNNED into a fascinated silence, we watched Ike pull himself, one joint at a time, out of the broken chair. Lazily he ambled over to the side of the shack and withdrew the knives.

Once again he returned to his seat, and once again he hurled the knives into the circle.

"Seems," Asey coolly murmured in my ear, "like this was a nice time to act, while he's still pryin' himself out of that chair—"

And Asey went into action. Before Ike had time to brace himself for the effort of rising, Asey had yanked the knives out of the wall and stuck them into his own belt. Then he swung around.

"Stay put," he advised Ike crisply. "Just don't even bother to start hoistin' yourself up. Just set there nice an' placid like. You're goin' to set for some little time, an' it'd be a pity to dis'pate s'perfluous en'gy."

The rest of us crowded on to the rickety wharf and stood there with our mouths gaping open at the two of them.

"Now," Asey said, "I was sort of feelin' that this was

all a sort of by-path, but it looks like it led us into some-thin'. Ike, might I inquire if it's a reg'lar habit of yours, this knife thowin' practice?"

Ike stammered and stuttered and finally admitted that once in a while he kind of liked to see if his eyes was failin' any.

Asey smiled. "I'd say offhand that if your oc'list d'pended on you for s'port, chances was he'd starve to death, if he wasn't already dead. Pretty nifty knife thrower, ain't you?"

"So-so," Ike said. "Just so-so. In the book I learned from, there was the picture of the feller that wrote it, an' he could hit a target, standin' back to it, blindfolded, an' throwin' underhand. 'Course, I ain't in that class."

"P'raps not," Asey said, "but you're good enough to suit me. Ike, you're a pretty good shot, too, ain't you?"

"Well, I gen'rally manage to hit what I'm aimin' at most of the time."

His slow, deliberate nasal drawl amazed me. He didn't in the least seem to realize what Asey was talking about. He didn't, in fact, seem to care very much. I marveled that such a mental tortoise could have roused himself to the penning of such fiery epistles as Jimmy Porter had shown us an hour or so before. It just didn't seem credible.

"Huh." Asey sounded confused, too. "Well, Ike, I guess this is the place where we arrest you for the murder of Dave Truman, an' a lot of little inc'dentals like tryin' to shoot me, an' tryin' to poison us all over at Bev's—"

The expression on Ike Smalley's face just took me

back to the old days of silent movies and slow motion slap-stick comedies. It was the way Ben Turpin used to look when he began to emerge from the splatterings of the accurately aimed custard pie. It was the expression of that wide eyed Mack Sennett bathing girl when the expected hot shower turned out to be a cascade of snow. It combined, in short, blank, thunderstruck bewilderment with the dawn of bitter indignation and of acute unhappiness.

"Wha-wha's that, Asey?" Ike asked feebly.

Asey said it all over again.

"Wha—what—what's that?"

"No." Asey shook his head. "No, I ain't goin' to say it more'n twice. You heard."

"Sure I heard." Ike blinked. "But I dunno what you *mean,* Asey. What you mean, anyway?"

Slowly, in simple monosyllables, Asey explained what he meant.

"Oh." Ike sounded vastly relieved. "Oh, I see. You don't mean me, though, do you, Asey? You don't think I killed Dave?"

Asey sighed. "Ike, I wouldn't for the world dis'range the marvelous an' curious workin's of what you most likely refer to as a brain. I wouldn't want to get you mad or upset—"

"I ain't mad," Ike assured him earnestly. "I ain't mad. I'm just hurt you should think that way. Why, Asey, you're a kind of r'lation to me, you are, an' you know me since—why, you known me all your life, I guess. An'—"

"Listen, Asey," Hanson had stood it just as long as

he could, "you let me snap these bracelets on him, an'
we'll break the news afterwards. We'd be here till we
died if we waited for him to get it now. Look here, you.
See these? There. That's it. These are handcuffs. I'm
puttin' 'em on your wrists, see? Don't yell. They won't
hurt if you keep still. Now, I'm putting those on you
because I'm going to cart you off to jail for murdering
Dave Truman. That make it any clearer?"

Ike stared stupidly at the handcuffs.

"But I didn't," he said after a while. "I didn't kill
Dave. Asey, tell him to take these things off me!"

"First," Asey told him, "we're goin' to take up a little
unfinished business. Ike, you told us Washy come over
here to the fish house round four, Thursday aft'noon.
An' it—"

"Why, Asey Mayo," Ike said righteously, "I never
said any such thing. I said he was there round five-thirty,
same time as we seen this girl here." He moved his head
toward Jo.

"What you do b'fore Washy come?"

"Just set," Ike responded. "Set. An'," he added as an
afterthought, "an' sort of pondered, as you might say.
You take the way the world is now, an' you can ponder
real easy. Jimmy, what you think about things? How you
think these new-fangled ideas is doin'? You—"

"Didn't run over an' stab Dave in the back, in that
time b'fore Washy come?" Asey asked.

"'Course not. Don't talk so wild. Jimmy, how's Wall
Street feel about Huey Long an'—"

"Never threatened Dave?" Asey went on. "Never said

you'd like to kill him? Never wrote no threatenin' letters
to him an' his comp'ny, nor went over an' bullied him
into payin' you for your lost share?"

"I wrote letters to Dave," Ike admitted, "an' to that
comp'ny, an' I told him I thought he ought to pay me
for that share. Sure I did. Why, you take ole Cap'n Phin
Newcomb, when that quahaug cannin' works of his bust
up. Phin, he paid up ev'ry penny, didn't he? An' Dave
Truman had more after Truman an' Comp'ny went,
more, mind you, than Phin ever had. But I never said I
wanted to kill Dave. Dave was all right. He was just
a—a mizzled cap'tlist."

"A which?"

"A mizzled cap'tlist," Ike repeated serenely. "Mizzled.
M-i-s-l-e-d. He meant well, Dave did, only he was
mizzled."

Ike waited until our laughter had died down.

"Well," he said, "that's what he was, even if you
think it's funny."

"How about this .45 Colt you found on the beach
between Shepherds' an' the life savin' station?" Asey
leaned against the railing and pulled out his pipe. "Tell
us 'bout that."

"I didn't find it on the beach, Asey. It was in the
beach grass 'longside that high dune. You know the one
I mean. It's the one that's kind of in back of the others.
Where—"

"Where Pegleg Black used to have a gunnin' camp.
I know. But git back to the gun."

"I lost it last week. I tell you, it's been a great

trib'lation, that gun. I put it in the woodshed, I did, same as I always do, but I can't seem to find it. Sophy, she says she don't r'member seein' it there, but I always put it there. 'Course, it might of dropped over b'hind where the wall sort of slants out, down under the floor. But to look there proper, you'd have to take the floor up, an' like I told Sophy—"

"Yup, you said it wasn't hardly worth the effort," Asey grinned and squinted at the end of his pipe.

"How'd you know?" Ike demanded.

"Guessed. I'm a good guesser, I am. Once won an oil lamp with a genuine hand-painted shade for guessin' the number of beans in a bottle at the Ladies' Aid fair—"

"In 1892," Ike said. "Yup. Or was it 1889? It was the year the old ice house burned down—"

"Say," Hanson broke in, "are you asking him questions, Asey, or is this Ole Home Week?"

"Sort of a mixture," Asey informed him gently. "Ike, you didn't stick a knife in the seat of my car when we was here the other day, did you? Say, 'bout the same time you got your sody?"

"What'n time," Ike looked at Asey as though he were a bit daft, "what'n time'd I do a thing like that for? In your nice shiny auto! What's the matter with you anyhow, Asey Mayo?"

"People been wonderin' for years," Asey said. "Now. 'Bout your mushroom cellar. Culled any mushrooms lately?"

"You *be* crazy," Ike stated flatly. " 'Course not. Why should I—"

"Where'd you get the mushrooms you give Sophy to cook yest'day?"

"Found 'em in a heap by the side o' the main road, over by Hopkins's place," Ike said. "I guessed they jounced out of that ole truck of Mike the fruit man's. It's an awful jouncy truck. Sophy got a watermelon once. 'Course, it was a little squashed, but she made pickle out of it. She makes awful good watermelon pickle, Sophy does. I often thought she ought to put it up to sell, but then like I said to her—"

"It wouldn't hardly pay you for the trouble," Asey finished for him.

"You are a good guesser," Ike said. "Yes, sir, you are. That's just what I said. I—"

"Look here," Hanson interrupted plaintively, "this's gone far enough, Asey. I'll just take him along to Parker. He can't prove a thing one way or another. He's lyin' like a rug. I'll take him up and then—"

"Wouldn't be in too much of a hurry," Asey scratched a match along the side of his corduroy trousers and held it over his pipe bowl. "I wouldn't hurry, Hanson. R'member the Maine."

"Remember what?" Hanson said.

"Oh," Asey puffed at his pipe, "oh—well, remember Grosgrain. Think of Luther, an' what happened."

"This guy," Hanson was beginning to regain some of his original jaunty cocksureness, "this guy ain't connected with lawyers. Won't be any trouble with him."

"Might."

"What d'you mean, might? Gee, he had his story all

ready, and he gave it like a shot. He can't prove he
picked up the mushrooms, or he lost the gun, or anything."

"Maybe not. Only let's, just for the fun of it, try an'
be a bit surer this trip, Hanson. Think—oho. H'lo, Doc.
Glad to see your bright an' shinin' face again."

The piles creaked as Dr. Cummings bustled out on
the wharf.

"Cheery or cherry? I'm speechless, Asey. Utterly
speechless. Believe it or not, I've done nothing but deliver
babies for the last forty hours—"

"Forty babies?" Jimmy Porter inquired.

"Five. Just five, Jimmy. But I tell you, in my next
incarnation I'm going to be a politician. Would it ever be
heaven to sit in a swivel chair day after day, with a
Corona Corona between my teeth, and my feet up on a
desk! My wife says she wishes mankind would stop eating
for two weeks so she could get a rest from meals. Let
me tell you, I wish womankind would stop enriching
the world for two weeks and give *me* a rest! For the love
of God, Asey, what's this poor idiot got handcuffs on
for?"

"Ask Hanson," Asey suggested. "It was his idea."

At great length, Hanson told the doctor why.

"There," he concluded, "that's why. Wouldn't you
put handcuffs on him yourself?"

Cummings snorted. "Put handcuffs on Ike Smalley?
I'd as soon think of putting handcuffs on the Venus de
Milo. Your story sounds well, Hanson, but man alive,
it's psychologically impossible!"

"But, doc, he can't prove—"

"Of course he can't prove anything! No one ever expected him to! Don't be foolish, Hanson. You don't ask Grant's Tomb to prove anything, do you? Or any other inanimate object? Certainly not! Ike hasn't the mental ability or the mental agility, or the wit, or the judgment. Even if he had, he still wouldn't have possessed the capacity or the gumption to have killed Dave! Asey, surely you haven't fallen for this? You're not chump enough to agree with Hanson?"

Asey smiled.

"Wa-el," he drawled, "if I'm driven to it, Doc, I'm 'fraid I'd have to up an' say that I might poss'bly maybe p'raps be sort of inclined to more'n half side with you."

Hanson and Jo and Bob Raymond received Asey's delightful understatement with badly concealed annoyance. I wasn't surprised. I'd felt all along that the enthusiasm for Ike's guilt was more or less entirely ours. Asey had been interested enough, but he lacked a certain glow.

"See here," Jimmy Porter said with some asperity, "you mean, Asey, that this trip of mine was just a wild goose chase?"

"I ain't c'mitted myself," Asey told him. "I just wandered along, tryin' to piece a lot of ragged bobtail together; sure it all sounds nice. Some of the figgerin' you done was what I been thinkin' myself. Only, I can't put Ike in it. I can't even now. I couldn't even when I seen those letters."

"Aw," Hanson said, "aw, Asey, for Pete's sake!

What's the matter with you? Of course he did it. If he didn't, who did?"

Asey shrugged elaborately.

"What about the mushrooms?" Hanson asked. "And this cellar business?"

"I think they come from Ike's cellar all right, Hanson. I never said they didn't. I know it. Only, they's a hook on their trap door outside into the cellar. An' some-one carefully picked the hook. Broke in. Stole the mush-rooms. I found that out while Bob was quietin' down Sophy."

"Phooey," Hanson said. "Phooey. Nuts. Plain nuts. He did it to make it look that way."

"Ike," Asey remarked, "never went to all that trou-ble. Nun—no. If he *thought* of makin' it seem like some-one'd broke in, he wouldn't of been able to go to all the work of actually makin' it look that way. N'en, they's other little items that don't c'nect."

" 'Ink,' " Hanson said. "I bet that's it. Well, 'ink' and 'Ike' sound a lot alike to me. And I think those hunks of putty belong to the Penrose kids, like Mrs. Penrose said."

"Poss'bly," Asey smiled amiably. "Poss'bly. Then they's this about Tommy Dawson's story. Sophy ain't got anythin' white. Nor has Ike. No white dresses for her, no white pants or shirts for him."

"That's a half-baked story anyhow," Hanson pro-tested. "Dawson's not sure if he saw anyone or not. And what about sheets? They got sheets, haven't they?"

"What about sheets in your house?" Asey asked Ike,

who was listening to the arguments for and against himself with only a modicum of interest.

"Sheets?" Ike allowed himself to grin. "Sheets? We ain't had any for years."

Hanson stuck his thumbs in his Sam Browne belt.

"Look, Asey, this is all foolishness!"

"Okay," Asey said, "take Ike with you. An'—well, I hate to say it, but the mare's nest you'll get around your ears'll beat anythin' Grosgrain ever started. I ain't got any lawyers, but deary me, won't I make you look silly!"

Hanson hesitated.

"I suppose Asey's right," Jimmy Porter said. "Perhaps you'd best wait, Hanson, though it burns me up. After all my time and effort! Dear God, I'll never try to be a public spirited citizen again!"

"Wouldn't say so, Jimmy," Asey remarked. "You helped a lot. We found out where the mushrooms come from, an'—"

"And you're back again to what I said," I interrupted. "Anyone who knew about them would have to be some local person. A native or a summer person. And it would have had to be one to find that gun."

"Find or steal," Bob Raymond corrected. "That's what you think, isn't it, Asey? That's how the gun went from the wood house?"

Asey nodded. "But it don't have to be someone from around here. If I was goin' to spy on Dave an' find out his habits, this neck over here's where I'd pick to park. An' if I happened to see Ike throwin' knives, I'd think real hard an' quick. An' with Ike out of the house a lot, an' Sophy out a lot, I don't know but what I might do a little stealthy reconnoiterin'.""

"But the gun was stolen last week!"

"Okay. No one's been doin' any noticin' or huntin' around for p'spective murd'rers of Dave Truman, has they? Long as anyone kept out of sight, who'd know how long they was here, or how long they stayed, or what they was doin'? If you got no reason to question anythin' that seems natural, you don't. Biled down, some up an' comin' feller with brains has taken advantage of a casual sort of layout to cover himself up real neat. He's used Ike's gun an' Ike's mushrooms, an' you can guess he might poss'bly know how Ike felt about a—a mizzled cap'tlist. He's used a cat's bell; that could ring in three or four. He's used knives that's common here. All in all, I'd call him a feller that adjusts himself real intel'gent to his surroundin's. But you could find out about Ike, if you was parked around here. You could find out maybe about Mrs. Dwight's fuss with Dave. Lina ain't close mouthed. If this lad's as clever as I think, I'm willin' to give him the ben'fit of the doubt an' say he's a clever smeller out of facts. Lots of clever smeller outers of facts hail from other places than North Weesit."

"There you be!" Ike turned to Hanson. "Now, let me out of these things!"

Hanson looked appealingly at Asey. "Can't I even take him along with us?"

"Yup, you can. Only unlock him. I want him for a number of reasons. No, don't fuss, Ike. You don't know how lucky you are. Lucky I think you're fool enough to speak the truth. You pop along. Soph's all right. Washy Wheeler's wife's with her. Come 'long."

All the way home I thought about the day that Kyle and I exploded the Santa Claus myth for the twins, at their own persistent requests. At first they'd felt rather grown-up and superior. Later, each one separately confided to me that it was really too bad to have found out, definitely.

"Santa Claus," Snuf informed me, "was a very good story and a very good idea. Everything fitted so nice."

Privately, in my own heart of hearts, I entertained much the same notion about Ike Smalley.

The trooper whom Hanson had left behind emerged precipitately from the kitchen as we rolled up the drive.

"No one's been here," he answered Hanson's query, "except Mrs. Penrose's aunt."

"How'd she get here?" I demanded, knowing that the Sunday train schedule was a thing of horror.

"Some young feller drove her. She'd flown back from New York to Providence with him, and then drove down here. Same one she went with, she said. And Mrs. Dwight was here and will come back later, and Giles Hopkins, the young one, he was here, and he'll come back later."

Katy appeared. "Miss Agatha left a note for Mr. Mayo," she said.

"Oh, Asey!" I laughed. "Asey, that note will probably tell you where to get off! Where is she now, Katy?"

"She took your roadster and went off to the Inn

about half an hour ago, to get dinner. She said for me not to bother."

"Thanks. Asey, what's it say?"

He grinned. "It says, 'Add first lines for stories: I was deceived by a blue-eyed ex-sailor.' That's all."

Jo screamed. "It's enough! Oh, it's superb! A blue-eyed ex-sailor! I love it!"

"See here." Cummings, who had trailed along with us, took hold of Asey's elbow. "This is all nice clean fun, but let's get on. Dave's 'Ink' comment is still a mystery, but let me see those little putty chunks. They're almost crazier than the cat's bell."

"Asey gave them to me for safe keeping," I said. "Come on indoors. They're in the living room, in Kyle's brass chest."

Self-consciously, with all eyes on me, I took from the mantel the three enormous keys which open the old chest, got them arranged in order, and pushed up the lid.

"Right here, and if you don't think they— Asey, my eye, Asey, they're gone!"

And they were gone, too. They weren't hidden in anything or under anything, or covered by anything. They were just plain gone.

Asey stroked his chin. "Er—Bev. When I asked you to put them in a nice safe place, why in time did you pick on this chest? Hasn't Kyle got a safe, down cellar?"

"He has. But he and I forgot the combination years ago. And the boys slammed it shut, one day. We always meant to have it opened, but we never got around to it. You see, we don't know what's in it, and we're afraid that if there is anything, it won't be worth the price of the opening process. I think there's some money and four of grandmother's coin silver teaspoons, but Kyle says he's sure he spent the money in it, and we've plenty of spoons. So—Asey, I never thought of your meaning that! Kyle always keeps money and everything right in this chest here!"

"With the keys square on the mantel in plain sight?"

"It's the purloined letter theory," I said defensively. "I—we—we never thought anyone would think there was anything valuable in it, if the keys were in plain sight. Oh, dear! Oh, damn, Asey, I'm sorry!"

"So'm I," he said. "Well, anyway, it seems like them putty pieces means somethin', that's one sure thing. Even if we don't know what."

"When were they taken?" I demanded. "When? And who took 'em? After all, we've all been here, and this afternoon—why, Hanson's man was here, and Katy!"

"An'," Asey added ironically, "Giles an' Mrs. Dwight an' Miss Ag'tha!"

"But you know perfectly well not one of them has a thing to do with this, you've ruled them out yourself! The one person who absolutely couldn't have stabbed Dave was Agatha; Giles was away during the last harrying, and Eleo—didn't we settle her?"

Jo got up and started to leave.

"What's wrong?" I asked.

"Little thought. Let you know later."

"D'tective instinct," Asey murmured. "Good ole curios'ty. I—"

"Stop being ironic and silky and mad!" I almost yelled at him. "What are you going to do? It's all my fault, and I admit it, but why don't you *do* something?"

"Never was a one to do much g'rage door padlockin' after the car'd gone. Jimmy, what do you know about someone financin' Dave to a new start?"

"Not a thing. Never heard a sniff about it. Almost impossible. Too impossible to consider."

"Uh-huh. But s'pose he had three times the backin' of Truman an' Comp'ny? Would he be washed up then?"

"He would not. But let me tell you, Asey, if someone offered to back Dave, even just enough to start another Truman's, and if his ex-business pals found out, I can understand why Dave was killed. Dave was a tremendous power. With adequate backing he'd be as powerful as—"

"Yup. But s'pose Dave'd been offered the job of playin' with just three times the money involved in Truman an' Comp'ny. Straight, that is, Jimmy. I know about it."

Jimmy thought for a moment. "Only one man would or could do it, Asey, and that's Amborough. But I've not even heard a whisper."

"S'posin' the news of that got out. Would Dave's pals try any dirty work on him then?"

"Never, if they knew Amborough was behind it. They'd have Dave a misunderstood financial genius with rotten luck and crooked underlings inside of a week. Dave'd have been the white-haired boy. You don't argue with anyone Amborough backs. Dave Truman least of all. If you're sure about that, Asey, and any offer he made Dave, you can bet your bottom dollar that's one reason why Dave wasn't killed. Or *not* the reason why he was."

Jo came back. "My turn next, Bev," she said. "Asey, you told me to lock Kay's diary up, when I wasn't reading it. This morning I took it out of that trunk, and when Jimmy came—well, the point is I forgot to put it back. And—"

"That's gone, too?"

"No. But someone's neatly sliced seven pages out. And it was okay just before we left."

CHAPTER FIFTEEN

"WHICH seven pages?" Asey demanded.

"The very last. I haven't an idea as to what was in 'em, either. I wasn't more than half way through that. Kay's writing—"

"Don't tell me," Asey said feelingly. "I know. Readin' it was sort of like d'cipherin' the Rosetta stone or the script of some drunken German. Had a touch of Ar'bic, almost. Real pretty to look at, 'tis, but makin' it out's a dif'rent matter. But I read those last pages. Wasn't anythin' in 'em to warrant their bein' cut out. Can't see what good it'd do anyone to take 'em now. If there'd been anythin' in 'em that'd of caught anyone, they'd of been caught b'fore this. I don't get it."

"But Asey, suppose there might have been something that I'd notice, and you wouldn't? And if someone knew I was reading it, perhaps they figured that out."

"Maybe." Asey got up and prowled restlessly around the room. "But if they had somethin' in 'em, wouldn't Dave of known, Jo?"

She shook her head. "Not necessarily. Loads of things, silly references to silly things, would have meant less than nothing to him. Take 'widgets.' Now Kay could say 'widgets' to me, and we'd both howl, remembering the time she and I sneaked out of Miss Lacey's and went to see the 'Beggar on Horseback.' At night. It was considered very daring, and we were nearly expelled. That sort of thing."

"I guess maybe you're right," Asey admitted. "I saw 'widgets' a couple of times, an' it didn't mean any more to me than it did to Dave. Fact was, both of us thought we'd read the word wrong. But them last pages, Jo, Dave an' I read about a hundred times apiece. It was just a sort of funny d'scription of havin' tea with ole lady Swett over in the Center. She'd written down all the Swett fam'ly stories, an' that's all them last pages was. All written the aft'noon of the day she died, an' was about the day b'fore. Must of been ten pages of little yarns. Dave an' I got the idea she thought of writin' a story about 'em some day, 'cause she'd taken pains to get ev'ry little detail just so."

"But there must be some reason for those pages being taken!" Jo insisted.

"Seem's if. But it'd take an expert to read 'em, first of all. Not ev'ry Tom, Dick an' Harry could make out two words a page."

"But if someone knew I was reading it," Jo argued, "he might feel that I might catch some reference to something that you and Dave might have missed that might— oh, dear, this is so complicated! Put it this way: X may never have read Kay's diary. X may not be able to make out a word. But X may suspect there may be something in it that would incriminate X. Moreover, X might think that I, knowing Kay so well, having so many private jokes with her, might pounce on something you and Dave passed over. And say, voilà!"

"Voilà what?" Asey asked. "You mean, about her death, or Dave's, or what?"

Jo shrugged. "I don't know. Just plain voilà. What's wrong with that reasoning that you scowl so and shake your head and practically mutter?"

"Didn't know I was," Asey returned. "Only thing is, if X suspected they was somethin' in that diary that might incrim'nate him in Kay's death, his cue was to keep quiet an' let it alone. He'd ought to of known it'd never be found out if it hadn't been up till now. An' even so, why swipe the last seven pages? Why take the trouble? Why not take the whole thing, burn it, an' scatter the ashes over the great blue an' rollin' Atlantic? Or just scatter it without any prelim'naries?"

"Are you being rhetorical?" Jimmy Porter inquired, "or d'you expect us to answer?"

"Just wonderin' out loud," Asey told him. "This's the first move on the part of friend X that seems dumb. Other things he done had nice reasons b'hind 'em. He shot at me b'cause he felt I was encumberin' the earth, an' he'd be better off without me. Everythin's been done was nice an' straightforward, with nice motives b'hind. But this was plum, out an' out dum foolish."

"I don't see why," Hanson said. "Seems to me it was a good idea."

Asey sat down on the arm of a chair.

"Listen, Hanson. The business of Kay Truman's death is officially over, ain't it? Then why rake it up? Why not r'move all the ev'dence, if you thought the diary *was* ev'dence, huh? Chances is Jo'd have read it an' thought like Dave an' I did, that if anythin' was troublin' Kay, it wasn't important enough for her to put even in a diary that had a lock an' key. It's sort of like a small kid commentin' on the big choc'late disappearin'. If he sat tight an' said nothin', prob'ly no one'd ever notice it. Once he calls attention to it, an' father starts investigatin', an' they's trouble. Better let it ride, an' then be real amazed like if the candy's found missin'. Gee, any ten-year-old knows that!"

That was, I reflected, true enough. But it didn't satisfy Hanson.

"Don't it show you that Kay's death and her father's was hitched up?" he asked.

"How? Why? An' if they was, why make us a present of the fact? 'Course," he added reflectively, "someone might just be wantin' to get us off on another false trail, an' steal the diary to make us do some more wanderin'. But I don't think so. Anyone that'd play around reckless with guns an' knives an' poison an' all that, he ain't goin' to be so sissy as to steal a few pages out of a diary to throw us off the track. No siree. Not while he's still got nitroglycerin an' mustard gas left!"

"Well," I said, "what about the putty chunks?"

"Even sillier. They'd sort of roused my curiosity in a mild way, like Siamese twins or a six-legged calf. But I couldn't of sworn they had anythin' to do with this really. I felt so, but I wasn't sure. Yet if they didn't, why'd the feller take 'em? 'Course they's always the other side of thinkin' they're more blind trails, but like the diary, it ain't worthy. Not of X, anyhows. If the putty pieces an' the pages was stole in what you might call good faith, then we ain't up against the master mind I thought. If they're a trick, it's a punk trick. I—"

Aunt Agatha burst in, grinned at Asey and greeted the rest of us.

"And Jimmy Porter, even! What brought you? Obviously things have been happening, and I shall sit and scream till I've been caught up. Asey, I still can't figure why I was sent away, but you've no idea what distance does to a muddled brain. I've a new perspective entirely. Now, go on and sum up, quickly, before I throw things."

"I'll sum," Asey said, "if you'll take your eyes off the iron woodbasket. But it's goin' to be brief."

When he came to the final bits about the missing putty balls, Agatha really did scream.

"Asey—Bev, my child, and the rest of you, this is awful! Oh, dear Lord, I should have stayed in New York! Practically the first thing I did on arriving home was to open the brass chest as I always do, and stuff in my money and check book. Didn't you find 'em, in the corner?"

We'd been so busy hunting the putty chunks that we hadn't noticed anything else, but her money and papers and check book were undeniably there.

"But—"

"Let me get it out, Bev. I'm bursting! When I

jammed my things in, I knocked down an envelope from the tray, and those pieces of putty rolled out! They were there then, and now of course you'll never believe that I didn't remove 'em. Oh, Asey, and I know Monty Walker, but Monty'd never get me out of jail!"

"Then those were taken," Asey pulled at his chin, "b'tween the time you left an' the time we come back. Half an hour, Katy said."

"You believe me?" Agatha sounded disappointed.

"For a blue-eyed ex-sailor," Asey informed her with a grin, "I'm a real credulous soul. Half an hour. Well, Hanson, that proves one thing. Ike couldn't of had anythin' to do with it. You saved yourself a black eye by goin' easy on him. He's out."

Reluctantly Hanson admitted that such was probably the case.

"An' if Dave was already stabbed when Giles an' Bev found him, then Miss Ag'tha's out."

Hanson nodded. "Yeah. But Katy said Mrs. Dwight'd been and gone, and Giles too. What about them?"

Katy was called in and put through another of Asey's cross-examinations. It cheered me to find that she was actually learning how to answer a direct question. Perhaps—it was a daring thought—perhaps, some day, when I asked her if we needed butter, she'd really say yes or no, and not embark first on a lengthy explanation of where the last pound went, ounce by ounce.

But both Katy and the trooper who'd been left behind swore up and down that neither Eleo nor Giles could have stolen anything. Both had come in cars, both left at once after asking what time we'd return. The doors were locked. The—

"What about the windows?" I asked. "Perhaps our pal made another second story entrance."

"I don't think." Asey sounded positive. "I wedged 'em good an' solid. Now listen. How'd you two spend the time after Miss Ag'tha come an' left till we come?"

Katy blushed, and the trooper stared industriously at the cross-eyed Hessian andiron.

"Oh," Asey said. "Whyn't you say so? Where was you?"

The trooper gruffly confessed that he and Katy had taken a little walk in the orchard. Only the kitchen door had been left unlocked, though, he added defensively.

"Queer," Asey remarked, "how sometimes folks don't need more'n just one unlocked door to get into a house by. Pers'nally, one door at a time is just about all I'm able to manage. Deary me, run away, both of you, b'fore I tell you how mad I am with the two of you. Ind'vidually, sep'rately an' t'gether. Vamoose!"

Katy fled, but the trooper paused on the threshold.

"What about Smalley? He says he wants to go home."

"Let him," Asey said. "Kiss him on both cheeks an' let him go. Any objections, Hanson?"

Hanson flicked a cigarette into the fireplace.

"No." He sighed like a steam engine. "I suppose not. Only Grosgrain'll wiggle out by to-morrow. Seems too bad we ain't got anything at all to give Parker."

"Bear up," Asey advised. "Maybe he'd rather have

one real good solid murd'rer than half a dozen punk guesses. Run 'long, Hanson, an' thank Ike for bein' so amiable an' nice. Be as tactful as you can, an' maybe he won't toss a knife at you some day for puttin' them handcuffs on. They hurt Ike's pride somethin' awful."

"I can't get over seeing those pieces of putty," Agatha said, "and now they're gone! I feel as though I were shining in a reflected glory. 'The last person to see the murdered man was a Lemuel F. Smith.' That sort of thing. I didn't begin to recall the blob of putty Asey found in the gutter, Bev. I thought they belonged to the twins, and you were keeping them in the chest for some big purpose. I even wondered if you were going to have them bronzed, the same way Natalie West had all her children's first shoes bronzed and made into paper weights. I almost saw them mounted on paper weights, all engraved—'Budge and Snuf: first marble attempt.' Hm. If Katy and her boy friend were in the orchard twenty minutes, it's possible someone might have come in a car, gone into the house, and then departed without their being a whit the wiser, isn't it?"

"Prob'ly," Asey said, "someone's been watchin' for just this op'tunity. They most likely was in before Katy an' her pal was ten feet away. I—my, my! A guest! Where'd you get it, Hanson?"

Hanson steered Creel Friar into the room.

"This? He says he wants to see you, Asey."

Creel, more nearly sober than I'd ever seen him before, shrugged Hanson's hand off his shoulder and edged down on the couch. Both arms were in splints, heavily taped and bandaged, and bound close to his body, with his hands folded over his stomach. It gave him a peculiarly benevolent aspect, slightly Oriental in spite of his stubble of beard and thrown-on looking clothes.

"See here, Mayo," Creel, as usual, wasted no time on polite preliminaries, "that bloody little stinker swiped my gun and I want it back before I leave!"

"Any p'ticular stinker?" Asey asked in silken tones.

Creel described the stinker at some length. Out of the blurry maze of adjectives, expletives and just plain nasty language, I began to feel that he was referring to Luther.

"You may be a writer," Asey said, "but you ain't much shakes at d'scription. No credit to the p'fession. Can't even recognize a stinker when you take five minutes to tell about him. Friar, you go in for white suits, don't you?"

"And just what has my choice of raiment to do with Grosgrain's pinching my gun?"

"An' even if you hadn't two broken arms—say, where was you Thursday aft'noon? From four o'clock till you went to the Dwight's? You was whole then."

Boiled down to its barest essentials, Creel felt that his whereabouts at any time was no affair of Asey's. He was extremely definite about it.

"Uh-huh. You didn't happen to kill Dave Truman, did you?"

"For Christ's sakes!" Creel really began to lose his temper. "For Christ's sakes! I—"

"Yup, but did you?"

Creel answered with a brief résumé of Asey's ancestry, immediate and remote, which would have startled anyone who felt, with Darwin, that the fittest survived. From Asey he proceeded to the Truman family, and in two sentences had every one of us in the room boiling and frothing. I saw Agatha's hand curl over a wrought iron book end, and Jimmy and the doctor were both ready to spring from their chairs to Creel's throat. Jo was what Kyle calls "white mad," so infuriated that she trembled.

"That'll do," Asey said quietly. "Hanson, c'mere." He wrote a few words on a piece of paper. "See to this. I told you that'd do, Friar! I meant it! One more word out of you, 'less it's asked for, an' I'll show you how much funnier you'd look with a broken nose an' two black eyes an' a couple of split lips. What type of gun did Grosgrain take from your room?"

"A .38 something or other. I—"

"That's all I asked you. Don't 'laborate, don't add, don't frost it. Have you a license to carry that gun?"

"I say the hell—"

"Yes'r no."

"All right." Creel got up. "It wasn't my gun, and I didn't lose it. All right, all right! I'll run along, and how—"

"Think twice," Asey said. "You spoke before witnesses an'—Peewee, you flew, all right! Oh, on your way here anyhow? Here's your boy friend, Peewee. He carries guns without licenses."

"You've got to prove it was my gun." Creel started

for the door. "And I'll never admit it. I won't admit anything at all. Little too previous, Mayo! Tough luck, Peewee. You've no right to hold me, and I'll be gone before you can summon me. Can't arrest me without a warrant, and it's Sunday. I know a thing or two, Mayo!"

"You're a real bright lad," Asey said. "Brilliant, Wonder to me a brain like yours ain't produced somethin' in best seller lists from coast to coast of this fair country. No, don't stop him, Hanson. No, Jimmy! We'll see you out to the car, Friar. Yes, indeed. This fair country an' others includin' the Scandinavian. Let me help you down the steps. There!"

The rest of us trailed along while Asey helped Creel down the steps in the direction of Hank Green's aged Buick, which serves as North Weesit's only taxi.

"He's got something up his sleeve," Agatha murmured. "Hanson and Peewee know—"

Asey let go of Creel's arm at the edge of the drive, and Creel stumbled—or, as Jo asked later, was he pushed? At all events, Creel swayed, fell against one of the peach trees Kyle and I had put out the previous spring and nursed through the drought—and snapped it in two.

"There," Asey said suavely. "Go on, Peewee, an' take the laddie. Help it up!"

Creel began to splutter.

"You know a lot of lawr," Asey told him, his blue eyes twinkling, "but you ain't up on the fine points. This is my version of the old fruit tree game. Whosoever trespasses an' wilfully defaces or mut'lates a fruit tree in this grand an' glorious Commonwealth, of a Sunday, may be held without warrant an' tucked into jail till Monday mornin'. You wasn't invited here, so you're a trespasser, an' the lawr was built for the likes of you. By to-morrow mornin', we'll get this gun business with Grosgrain fixed up, an' then we'll get you for bein' without a gun license, an' then—honest, if you say a word, I'll make my own charge of slander, Friar! You slandered me b'fore a bunch of folks, an' Lord knows the damage you done. May never live it down. I f'get the max'mum you can sue for slander, but it's a lot. An'," Asey smiled sweetly, "a night in jail may p'raps teach you somethin'. Think it over."

Peewee, his face one broad grin, shoved Creel into the car, and off they went.

"Do—"

"Don't ask me if I think he killed Dave," Asey said. "I know he didn't. Bob did some checkin' for me yest'day an' found he was in P—town Thursday till five. Even got sober witnesses to prove it. But after his r'marks about Kay an' Dave, it seemed to me it would be fun to be nasty. B'sides, it'll clear up Luther's silence about that gun in his pocket. Friar d'serves jail on princ'ple. Think of all the words he'll scrawl on the walls—huh, he can't, can he, with his busted arms? Well, think of all the words he'd scrawl if he could. Hanson, I want you. Bev, in about half an hour I want a scrambled egg or two. An' would you let Katy have the night off?"

"You shall have a dozen, scrambled in my best manner," I promised. "Jo, go over to Logan's—Bob, you go

with her, and get enough for all of us. Count noses and
multiply by four, and divide by twelve and get that many
dozen."

"Bev," Aunt Agatha began a few minutes later, as
she and I milled around in the kitchen with coffee pots
and toasters, "Bev, what d'you—"

"Listen," I snapped, "if you ask me what I think, I
shall plunge my teeth in your ankle and pretend you're
a bone! Think. Think, forsooth! Asey may think whoever killed Dave is first cousin to the lowest variety of
imbecile, after this putty and diary affair, but he's still
a master mind to me. I don't even think of thinking. I
don't even think of thinking of thinking. I—"

Agatha said hurriedly that she got the idea. "But
Asey has something," she went on, "he knows something,
or feels something, or—"

"Or something. I get your idea, too. P'raps, beloved
aunt, he has, but I gave up and yelled 'uncle' long ago.
I admit it, what's more."

Agatha didn't choose to take the hint.

"I think," she said, "that the same person who's done
all of what they call the harrying, is the one who stabbed
Dave. Now, you and I are out. So is Giles. So is Creel
Friar, if Asey told the truth about his alibi. Grosgrain's
out. If he's in jail now, he couldn't have stolen the putty
and the pages. Eleo and Jo are out. And—"

"And Katy and Jethro and Hanson and Bob Raymond and Jimmy Porter and the other state cop," I said
wearily. "I know the list. I've gone over it so many times
that it's like mounting a flight of familiar, well worn

steps. Everyone's alibied at one point or another in the harrying business. And what've you got left? Just—who killed Dave, who shot at Asey, who thrust the knife in the car, who switched the mushrooms, who tinkled Sully's bell, who stole the putty chunks and the diary pages? And what are the chunks and what do they mean, and why were the pages stolen? We haven't the knife that killed Dave. We can't find the bullet Dave fired out of his gun. Luther says the second knife belongs to a child in his boarding house on Dolphin road. Ike says the Colt that Grosgrain found got lost in his woodshed. Asey says someone broke in Ike's cellar and stole the mushrooms. There. You can make it much louder and funnier, but those are the essentials. You say all that, and then you go back and say it all over again. Even varying the words, the thoughts are just exactly the same. Gets tiresome, if you ask me."

But Agatha was still brooding when Jo and Bob returned with the eggs, bearing Giles with them.

"We found him," Jo said, "but don't look glum. We added on a dozen more eggs for him, and he's staying to supper. Look, Bev, what d'you think—"

I made a loud noise. "And that," I said, "is a staccato shriek, Giles. You asked what they were, once. Call me when you've finished scrambling and have things on the table, I can't bear this another minute!"

Jimmy Porter said he felt the same way, so he and I strolled out to the orchard and watched Nauset Light's three long blinks and three short ones, and followed the long sweep of Highland in the distance.

"Makes me dizzy," Jimmy said. "Like a six-day bike race. Mind feeding me again to-night, Bev? I'll pop up to the Inn later. Think I'll stay a few days and see how Asey clears this up."

"Few days?" I said. "Nonsense. You may spend a week here, Jimmy, but the next ten years you will have to spend at the Inn. Few days!"

"You don't know Asey as well as I do," Jimmy said. "He lived with us, you know, when dad was alive, and he practically brought Bill and me up. I'll admit I don't hold a candle to brother Bill in his estimation, but I know my Asey Mayo. He's puzzled, but he knows—"

"Fiddlesticks," I said. "Fiddle tailed rooster, as mother used to say. Bosh. Tosh. Pooh. In fact, pooh-pooh!"

"I'm right, Bev. Bill and I went to school down here one winter when we were kids, and Asey heard our lessons at home. I was a shark at math. Always got the answers to problems, but nine times out of ten, I never knew how I got 'em. It drove Asey mad. 'All right,' he'd say, 's'pose it *is* ten apples? How you goin' to prove it? No use gettin' the answer 'less you could prove to me I owed you ten apples, an' proved it so hard I'd give 'em to you! Go on, now. Piece by piece!' And really, Bev, it did me a lot of good. I'm still a shark at figures, but I can prove 'em. But the point is, Asey's got his answer. Now he's going at it piece by piece. Some step or other has got him sunk right now, but not for long. He's just given Hanson a fistful of telegrams. Now look here, Bev. You think this business through—"

I let out another staccato shriek and went indoors. After supper, I went to bed.

"And I'm going to stuff cotton in my ears," I said as I left the others, "just so I shan't be forced to hear anyone else mutter, 'Honestly, Bev, what do you THINK?'"

"Ostrich," Asey taunted. "Ostrich!"

"No ostrich about it! I'm just a plain simple home body, and from now on I act like one. To-morrow I'm going to darn socks and make quince jam and stop all this fol-de-rolling around with people who think!"

"Woozums," Jo said soothingly. "Woozums! That's right, Bev. Just you go to bed and forget it all. And if we find X, we shan't even wake you up to tell you about him! Probably, to-morrow morning, we shall be able to greet you in the famous words of Henry the Fourth to his pal Crillon—I think it was Henry the Fourth, anyway, and I'm hoping it was Crillon. You know. 'Hang yourself, brave Crillon! We fought at Arques, and you were not there!' Sleep well, darling!"

I sniffed. "I've heard of optimism," I said coldly, "but the supporters of the Asey-Mayo-Will-Get-Him-To-morrow Club go beyond optimism. You're even two steps beyond Utopia. I, too, can quote. 'This is the very coinage of your brain, this bodiless creation ecstasy.' I can do better—all right, I won't. But no more alarums and excursions for me!"

And the upshot of all that pooh-poohing and ranting about was that I felt pretty damned silly when I waked up during the night—the illuminated hands of my clock said it was 2:17—and found the window beside my bed open, the screen out and Jo's bed clothes pulled over the foot of her bed.

After a brief mental debate, I quietly slipped on my old sport shoes, yanked a scarf around my neck, girded a polo coat about me and crawled out of the window myself.

Once out in the cold damp air, I felt even sillier. Probably Jo had flipped out with Bob or Jimmy, gone to a party or something—I heard footsteps crunch for a second in the driveway. Dave's drive, for it was the crunch of gravel, and our drive is hard packed oyster shells. Keeping carefully on the grass, I followed along our drive to the hedge, then stopped and listened. There was little chance of seeing anything, for the fragment of a moon was hidden behind clouds. I couldn't hear a sound, but it seemed to me that I could make out a figure darting by the corner of Dave's house.

"Idiot," I muttered to myself, "she's making for the cliff—"

I didn't want to yell at her. She'd either hide, or the noise would rouse the house, and Jo would have a pile of explanations, and I would take a fearful beating for coming out by myself. So I scurried along noiselessly behind. I'd lost sight of her completely, but I knew where she was heading—Kay's lean-to near the cliff. And it was easy enough to follow the foot path, even in the dark. I'd used it since I was a child.

Half way up, I froze in my tracks. A voice, Jo's voice, yelled for help. Then she screamed, and the scream stopped suddenly in the middle.

CHAPTER SIXTEEN

I TOOK a long breath, jerked myself together and started forward just as two flashlights snapped on and began to hiccup about.

Asey's quarterdeck voice—and how I blessed the sound of it!—began to issue orders.

"Hanson! Never mind this! You train one light on the path to Truman's an' Penrose's! Whistle for Bob! Take Thompson an' start huntin', pronto! Beat it!"

As I staggered along I could see Asey bending over someone—Jo—stretched out on the ground ahead. Suddenly his light shot up and hit me in the face.

"It's only me!" I called out in a voice that was entirely strange to me. "It's Bev, Asey. You're blinding me!"

"What you doin'—"

"Get out of the way." I shoved him aside and knelt down beside Jo. "Let me—is she hurt? Is she dead? What happened?"

Jo wobbled her head, opened one eye and closed it again.

"I'm not dead," she informed us feebly. "Breath knocked out and the rest fright—wow! I was nearly number five, I guess. I'll be all right in a sec—"

Asey rose and towered over me. "Bev," he said sternly, "what's the idea of your bein' out here at this p'ticular time?"

"Why, I woke up and saw that she was gone and the window open— Jo, are you really all right, you crazy loon? Asey, what *is* this all about? What happened?"

"Go on with your yarn," he returned.

"My yarn? But Asey, it's no yarn! I found her gone, and after all my alarums and excursions chatter, it seemed too silly to start any hue and cry. I just followed her out and along the path up here. When I was half way up, I heard her cry out."

"Followed me up here, hell!" Jo said. "I've been here over half an hour!"

"Then who did I follow?" I demanded. "I certainly followed someone—oh!" My back began to prickle. "Oh —it was whoever frightened Jo—Asey, *what's* been going on?"

"God knows." His flash light swung out again and illuminated the figure of Giles, coming from the other end of the cliff. "Ole Home Week, huh? What you doin' here, Giles?"

Giles ignored Asey completely, ran to Jo's side and knelt down beside me.

"Jo," he said, "oh, my dear, what happened?"

Jo giggled feebly. But before she could answer, Asey gripped Giles by the shoulder.

"I said, what you doin' here?"

"Tell you later. Jo, are you hurt? What happened?

Can you walk? No, don't move. I'll carry you back to the house."

"No need to carry me," Jo told him. "I can walk. Wah! Guess I can't, either. Can't even move. No, I'm not hurt, silly! I—I guess I'm still scared. I know what I want to do, but my arms and legs don't get the idea. Asey, who was he? Hadn't you better help Hanson, and let Giles take me back?"

"He'n Bob have as much chance of gettin' anyone as I have. Pick her up, Giles, an' we'll roll along. I'll throw the light for you, an' when she gets heavy, let me know. Bev, grab on to my left arm an' hold hard."

For the first time I noticed the enormous old-fashioned forty-five he held in his right hand.

"Look," I said, "what—Asey, tell me what's been going on, will you?"

"Later, an' then we'll have the whole works. All at once. Where's that craft off the bar headin'?"

I turned and peered out over the cliff, through the pitch darkness. "I can't see any lights, Asey. But there is a boat—yes. I hear. Let's see, with the tide," I thought rapidly, trying to remember Kyle's various routes, "only way he can get around the bar, and that's the east shoal. He'll have to show a light to pick up the buoy. There— see? He's heading for Provincetown, Asey."

"Wait," he said, "no—you hustle along, Giles. Now Bev—oho. Here come the rest."

In the shaft of light from the powerful flash Hanson had left perched on a rock, pointed down toward the houses, I could see Agatha and Jimmy Porter racing toward us.

"With all of you," Asey said, "you'd ought to be all right. Leggo, Bev. I got to run an' do some phonin'. I want that boat picked up. You hold the light. I can see plenty."

He was off like a shot. Giles and I made our way down the path to Dave's garden, along the side of the garage to Dave's house. Aunt Agatha and Jimmy caught up with us there, and began to pepper us with questions.

"Let 'em ride," I said. "Giles and I don't know a thing. Just wait."

Jimmy offered to carry Jo, but Giles refused with a curt nod. He had on his stern-and-rockbound-coast look again, but I noticed that it melted as Jo's cheek occasionally came in contact with his.

Asey was still at the phone when we finally got back to the house.

"That's what I think, Parker," he was saying. "So have 'em try to get a whack at that boat, anyway. No, I ain't got the whole story, but I'll let you know. Yup, come along. Glad to have you."

Giles put Jo down on the couch. I noticed that the curtains in the living room were drawn, and the shades pulled down below the sills. The front door lock snapped, and Asey came in.

"Well," he observed, "we're bar'caded as much as we can be. Now, let's get this straight. Bev, on your word of honor, was the only reason you went up on the cliff to-night that you thought you was followin' Jo to bring her home?"

"Word of honor, Asey."

"Giles, why was you there?"

"I'll tell you—Bev, won't you get Jo some whisky or something?"

"I think," I said, "we'd all benefit by a spot. Wait up."

"Well," Giles went on hesitantly a few minutes later, as Jo gulped down half a glass of straight whisky as though it were a Coca Cola, "well, it sounds crazy, Asey. But I haven't been home since I left here. I—well, once in a while I've gone up there on the cliff and just sat, at night, trying to piece things out. We'd talked so much to-night about Kay and Dave and everything, that I didn't feel like going home to bed. I went up there and stayed. I was starting home around the other side when I heard someone cry out. That's all."

"Didn't see anyone or hear anything?"

"I wasn't looking or listening," Giles answered simply. "I was thinking."

"Hear a boat?"

"Yes, I thought I did, but I couldn't see any lights. I thought it must have been a car running somewhere on the beach road."

"Giles, you tellin' me the abs'lute gospel truth?"

Giles nodded. There wasn't any doubt in my mind but what he was, either, and apparently Asey felt the same way.

"Okay. Now, Jo, feel like givin' us the works?"

Jo lighted a cigarette and grinned. "I feel," she remarked, "like floating around the ceiling, but at least I can talk without jittering, and move without shaking like a leaf. Asey, who was he?"

"You're a better judge of that than me, right now. How come you went out?"

Jo blew a mammoth cloud of smoke under the shade of the Sandwich glass lamp.

"Asey, as God is my witness, I don't know. I haven't the faintest idea in the world. I woke up about an hour ago—it was a bit after one, anyway, and listened to the waves, and got to thinking about Kay, and all of a sudden something told me to go to the cliff. Call it what you want to, intuition or sheer insanity. I didn't really want to go, very much, but I put on my shoes, and worked off the screen—I knew you'd be in the living room, and I didn't want to let you know I was going out. Anyway, I popped out the window and started up the cliff. I sat up there—I don't know how long, but it seemed like years."

"You loon," I said, "you absolute loon! All by yourself—"

"You went too," Jo retorted. "You've no come-back. And I had more sense than you. I took along one of the walking sticks."

The umbrella stand full of walking sticks is an important fixture of our front lawn. Kyle thinks it's heresy to walk without a stick, and his collection of homemade ones got too large for the front hall to hold.

"That saved you, I cal'late," Asey commented.

"Saved me? Saved me! I'm going to salvage that stick to-morrow and have it framed. Gilded. Bronzed, as Agatha said about the woman's baby shoes. Anyway, I was starting back, and I saw a flashlight flick for a split second, as though it were under someone's coat. So—"

"Weren't you frightened to death?" Agatha asked breathlessly.

"Strangely enough, no. Not then. Kay used to go there at night, and she often ran into some of the local boys and girls. Favorite parking place, that cliff. Anyway I called out and said not to be alarmed, I was just taking a stroll and not to disturb themselves on my account, and then instead of the usual humorous answer like Kay used to get, there was just silence, with a swish of grass as though someone were creeping up on me. Then, I can tell you, I began to be scared plenty!"

She lighted another cigarette from the stub in her hand. "And thank God I'm left handed, too. That was the thing that really mattered."

"Why?" Jimmy demanded.

"Because I gripped the stick in my left hand, automatically. I could feel someone near me, then. And by the way, let me tell you right now that all this to-do about seeing your life in a news reel in your last moment is a lot of tosh. All I could think of was what a chump I was not to have eaten that scrambled egg that was left over from supper. It seemed a pity to die knowing that I'd let at least three good eggs go to waste. So I gripped the stick and waited. And then a gorilla, or King Kong, or something, loomed beside me and someone started to shove me over the cliff. King Kong was on my right, see, and I braced myself with the stick, jamming it into the ground with my left hand. And the man pushed harder, and then I yelled like fury for help, and gave way a little, to the left. He stuck his hand over my mouth, pushed harder, and I dug the stick down harder and shoved myself back and to the right. Caught him off balance. I fell on my back, and he too—"

"How? Why'd' he go down?" Agatha asked.

"Oh," Jo explained airily, "when he stuck his hand over my mouth, I got my teeth into it. Pah, it was nasty tasting. Like a barn smells. As I went down, I kept on biting. You know, same idea as the lady in the circus that swings from a rope by her teeth. I just hung on. His hand and arm went with me, in other words, and gravity did the rest. He came down on top of me, kerplunk. That's what knocked out my breath. He was up like a rubber ball and away like a cat. I would have got him for you, if I hadn't given myself such a bang, and if he hadn't landed so hard. But only part of him hit me, from about the middle up, I'd say. If I'd got a chance to get hold of his legs—they learned us a little practical jiu jitsu in college, I think I might have got him. Of course the honest truth of the matter was that I was too scared to think quickly, or I'd have tried to get a hold on him before."

"Yup," Asey agreed with a twinkle in his eye. "Yup. Pretty slow brain of yours. Pers'nly, I'd say you done just about all you could do. Jo, didn't you get a thing about the feller that'd tell us who he was?"

She shook her head. "Truly, no. He seemed huge, but Luther would have seemed huge at that point. He was strong, quick, and he didn't utter a word, not even when my bicuspids were at work. But what was the idea, Asey? He didn't try to maul me. He just up and started to shove me over the cliff. Just like that!"

The tip of Asey's shoe traced out the pattern of faded roses on the old hooked rug before the fire.

"Huh," he looked up and shook his head. "I ain't got all of it yet. Miss Ag'tha, you an' Jimmy didn't go out, did you, till you heard Hanson's whistle goin'?"

"She waked me," Jimmy said. "I didn't hear a thing."

"B'sides, the doors was locked, an' that light was playin' down here. Yup. Well, this is my side. 'Member what Washy Wheeler said, about a boat comin' in the harbor three nights a week, reg'lar? Thought it was Regan's. Regan," he added for Agatha's benefit, "was one of the best rum runners on the coast. Have Bev take you some day along the little wood roads that lead any which way to the ocean or the bay, an' wonder casual why they're so well worn, an' so broad, just's if a truck with double tires was makin' the ruts. Regan run enough likker on the Cape to sink it. Anyhows, b'fore Dave bought his house, it b'longed to a queer little feller named Norcross, that come here 'bout once a summer for a week-end. An' Regan's fellers d'cided the cliff was a swell place for a come-on or stay-out signal. Used it always, only no one knew till Dave moved here from the Center that it was goin' on. Dave figgered it out. He couldn't get anythin' done about it. That was b'fore the days of Parker, an' Regan was tied up with a lot of folks. So Dave went an' seen Regan himself, an' told him that as a pers'nal favor, he wished he'd signal from somewheres else. It sort of tickled Regan, to have someone with nerve enough to up an' tell him that, an' he said he'd lay off the cliff. He did, too."

"What—" Jimmy began, "then what—"

"I'm gettin' to it, by d'grees. Y'see, about two years ago, the fed'ral boys got up on their hind legs an' barged in an' nabbed Regan for runnin' dope. But they didn't get the rest of his boys, an' they done about as much good as if they'd cut off one of Regan's finger nails. Hanson told me last year that they was still runnin' dope in here somewhere, but they couldn't find where. Anyway, to get down to it, when Washy said that, I begun to wonder if whoever was runnin' Regan's business for him wasn't maybe usin' the cliff. Hanson run over there to Washy's to-night an' found out it was Tuesday, Thursday an' Sunday that the boat come in. An'—"

"Kay was killed on a Sunday!" Jo interrupted.

"Just so. So was Nan Dawson. Other two girls they found on a Wednesday an' a Friday mornin'. So Hanson an' I set off to-night to go up there an' see what we could see, prowlin' around. I guess we got the answer."

"You mean," Giles said dully, "that someone—that someone just pushed Kay and the others off, the way they would have pushed Jo to-night, just because they thought their signaling was being interfered with?"

"That's it. I think, after Kay left Dave that night,

she went up to her lean-to, an' I think on her way back, she maybe seen the light Jo seen, an' called out, thinkin' it was some kids, an' got treated the way Jo was. Only she didn't have any stick. Nan Dawson was sort of cracked, used to wander anywhere any time of night or day. Prob'ly she just wandered there an' got into the same thing."

"But what about the other girls?" Agatha asked.

"I went over all them cases," Asey told her, "with Parker, after we found Kay. The servant girl had left her beau down the line an' was walkin' home by herself. That's what the boy said, an' he proved it. They was at a dance hall together, an' folks was with him from ten minutes after the time she an' him left, till he come back, an' then on through the next day when she was found. Why she come here, God knows. Feller admitted they'd parked up here any number of times. Sneaked in over Dave's fence, an' cut across his back lots. Maybe she thought the feller would follow her. No one knows much about the other girl. Her car was parked down the road a bit. P'raps she just come up here for the fun of it. Never will know. But it sort of explains what's been happenin' here."

Jo shivered. "And to think of the times Kay and I came up," her voice cracked, "oh—I'm sorry. But this has me jittering again. Why haven't more people run into it?"

"Prob'ly b'cause they wasn't here late enough, for one thing. Prob'ly b'cause a couple up there'd never no-tice a light flash for just a second, nor make any talk about it to other folks if they did. Take too much explainin'. Prob'ly, if they ever heard or seen anythin', they'd think it was others like themselves."

"But why should they be so—so drastic?" Jo twisted her wrist watch strap nervously. "Why shove people off the cliff? Wouldn't that call attention to it?"

"In a way, yes. In a way, it'd scare folks off. At least, people wouldn't tramp around at night for fun. I mean, older people. Kids didn't count. You see, this game ain't like bootleggin' or rum runnin'. It's a damn sight more expensive business, an' when the narcotic squad get you, they get you good an' proper. 'Parently whoever give the signal up there was told to take no chances. He didn't." Asey played with his pipe. "N'then, if the signaller happened to be a nervous sort, scared of bein' found out, he'd prob'ly push first an' think later."

"And I," I said, "followed him up there! My eye. My God! Asey, then if this is what happened to Kay, she certainly never wrote anything about it in her diary."

"But X might think," Jo said, "that Kay might have caught on to something going on up there, and perhaps made some comment about it. Perhaps she had an inkling, but hadn't mentioned it to Dave. Still the whole book would have been a better bet, as Asey said. I can't think any more. I'm exhausted. But I'm scared to go to bed."

"I'll carry you in," Giles offered.

"I can—oh, all right. Thanks." Jo was equally diffident, but Aunt Agatha flicked her eyebrow at me and waited a good two minutes before she followed them.

"I'll go see what's b'come of Hanson an' the rest," Asey said. "Jimmy, take this gun an' hold the fort, will you, till I get back? Bev, next time you don't feel like alarums an' excursions, don't move till you yell for re'nforcements. You're right handed as blazes."

I followed him to the front door and snapped on the lock behind him. Giles, glowing a little, accosted me as I went back to the living room.

"Look, Bev, what's Jo planning to do after she leaves here?"

"Probably," I quoted Eleo, "probably sell sports clothes at Macy's, and fall in love with a section manager. Why? I thought you loathed the sight of her."

"I thought so too," Giles said honestly, "till I saw her there on the cliff to-night. Then I knew I didn't at all. On the contrariwise."

"What about Kay?" I demanded.

"Kay was the best friend I ever had," Giles said seriously. "But say—Bev, d'you think I've—"

"Go ask Jimmy about your chances," I told him. "I— well, of course you have, idiot! If you don't let yourself go stern-and-rockbound too much! Now, run along. I want some sleep myself. Help Jimmy guard."

But even after I got to bed, I couldn't sleep, and I couldn't tell whether Jo was awake or not. I coughed tentatively, and she giggled.

"I know what you're thinking, Bev. You're wondering what mother'll say. She won't be surprised. She—"

"Jo!" I said. "You—my dear child, don't tell me

you've always wanted that clod of a cousin of mine? I can't believe it!"

She chuckled. "Now you know. Lots of gals have wanted him, darling. Go 'long to sleep. I shan't go out again. Uh. Say, Bev, don't you think he's good looking?"

"Oatmeal ad," I said with a yawn. "Oatmeal ad—oh, I'm tired!"

None of us was exactly radiant the next morning.

"Pick out a whole cast for 'Ten Nights in a Bar Room,'" Asey murmured to me at breakfast, "without leavin' this room. Even Hanson—look at him comin' up the walk. Might be ole Hezekiah Lawson over to Chatham, the feller that never smiled."

Hanson sat down, refused a cup of coffee and sighed.

"Not a trace of the boat, Asey. Nope, we ain't got anythin' more on anythin'. Friar come through and they let Grosgrain go. Gee, Peewee's happy. Judge give Friar two weeks and a fine for contempt. Night in a cell didn't make him any happier, I guess. Now what?"

"Didn't you even catch sight of the man last night?" Aunt Agatha asked.

"Not a sight or a sound. You know what I think, Asey? I think he pulled the Statue of Liberty on us. Just stood still till we got away, and then made off." He shrugged. "I guess I will have a cup of coffee after all, Mrs. Penrose. I ate my breakfast six hours ago. Asey, what now? Parker's coming down, isn't he?"

Asey nodded. "Stay 'round an' wait for him. I'm goin' over to Dave's an' hunt some more for the bullet that come out of his gun. Tell you what, you come, an' help, soon's you're ready. Anyone else comin'?"

I said I would, but Jo shook her head, and Aunt Agatha nodded towards the kitchen.

"I'm going to superintend your quince jam before the quinces die a natural death. Seems to me I heard you murmur something about quince jam and darning baskets last night, Bev?"

I made a face at her and followed Asey out of the side door. Jimmy Porter came along with us.

"Not that I'll be any great help," he admitted, "but I don't seem to be able to sit still. Asey—control yourself, Bev—but Asey, what leads d'you really think you've got?"

"I had two nice little chunks of putty," Asey told him, "but I ain't got 'em any more."

We strolled across to Dave's house in silence. Asey unlocked the door and pointed to the millstone as we entered.

"From there, I think the bullet from Dave's gun ric'chetted. But that's guess work. No sense peekin' around, Jimmy. Ev'ry inch of this front doorway here's been gone over by state experts."

He led the way into the big living room and sat down at Dave's desk.

"Here's where he sat," he said almost to himself, "an' balanced his 'counts, an' started to write to Luther. An' then he heard Sully's bell an' got up. Or maybe he thought he smelled a skunk, an' set out to pot it. Anyways, he went out. Stood in the doorway, an' got stabbed, firin' his own gun as he was. N'en he told you an' Giles an' Miss Ag'tha, that he didn't shoot himself at all, it was murder—"

"What d'you mean, he told us that? He didn't say anything like it, Asey!"

"He did, Bev. 'I didn't' an' just 'm' for murder. N'en he said 'Ink.' An'—" Asey stopped short and banged his fist against the desk top, then he leaned forward and flipped open the inkwell. After staring at it a moment, he reached up, opened the doors of the secretary, and fingered the odds and ends on the first shelf. Then, methodically, he bent down and pulled out drawer after drawer, until he came upon a half empty ink bottle.

His eyes narrowed as he twisted it around and around in his hand.

"Huh," he said, "huh. I'm kind of a dummed ole fool. 'Course Dave meant ink when he said ink. Just plain ink!"

"Asey Mayo, what are you talking about?" I demanded.

"Yessiree, I know I'm right now. Thought I'd kind of got on the track, but how in time it *is* the track is more'n I see even yet."

He got up from the desk and walked to the window, with Jimmy and me following him like a couple of robots. He drew aside the curtains, and all three of us looked out over the lawn.

Hanson was strolling along the drive towards us, with Giles and Eleo Dwight and Jo. Behind them, with Grosgrain trotting along beside him, came Jethro, trundling Dave's old wheelbarrow back. I thought, with a stab of shame, that it was high time we invested in one ourselves; we'd been borrowing that wheelbarrow for five years.

Sully the cat slithered through the hedge and started galloping after the procession, his tail waving majestically in the breeze. Asey swung around to us suddenly.

"Jimmy," he said quietly—but there was a note of triumph in his voice, "please stroll casual through that bunch, an' soon's you get b'yond the hedge, run like blazes for Bob Raymond an' Thompson. Be ready to come hoppin' back, too. Git!"

"Asey!" I whacked his shoulder in my excitement as Jimmy left. "Asey, you can't tell me you've actually got this business!"

"Two minutes ago, I'd of said yes'n no, Bev, but now I sort of think I can maybe say yes. I b'gun to catch on yest'day, but now, by golly, it's all here with all the trimmin's. An' I can't hardly swallow it even now. Honest, I can't b'lieve—bless that cat!"

CHAPTER SEVENTEEN

"BLESS what cat? Asey—"

Paying not the slightest bit of attention to my maunderings, he strode jauntily across the room to the back window. With a flick of his forefinger, he unlocked it and pulled down the upper half.

Casually, he drew his big, old-fashioned forty-five from one of the pockets of his canvas coat and aimed it carefully out the open window. Before I had time to utter another word, he cocked it and fired three shots in quick succession.

Then he turned around and spoke to me.

"That get 'em? Are they all comin' in?"

There was no need to answer him. Hanson, Giles, Jo, Eleo, Jethro, Grosgrain—the whole bunch of them tumbled into the room at once.

Asey silenced their flood of questions with a wave of his forty-five.

"Just set for a second, if you don't mind. All nice an' quiet like."

We waited in a silence so complete that the proverbial dropping pin would have sounded like a presidential salute. We could hear the dust settle, atom by atom.

Jimmy, with Bob and Thompson, pounded in; Katy and Aunt Agatha weren't many inches off their heels.

"Now," Asey said, "Bob, you take the front door, please, an' Thompson, you stand over here. Yup. Keep your guns out. Any signs of Parker, Jimmy? Too bad. We'll have to settle as much of this as we can without him. Hanson, grab Jet's arm. Giles, take the other. Fine. Now, Bob, the bracelets, please. One hand to Hanson an'—c'mere, Thompson. One to you. Set? That's fine." Asey returned the big forty-five to his belt. "Fine. Now we can stop actin' like a dime novel an' r'lax. Don't like to wave guns around, but I didn't want no variations of all this shootin' an' knifin' an' poisonin' that's been goin' on."

We just stared from Asey, who lounged against the piano, filling his pipe, to Jethro, handcuffed between the two officers. Now that all the what-d'you-thinks were over at last, not one of us had a word to say. We couldn't speak. We were too dumbfounded.

"See here, Asey," Aunt Agatha's calm was completely shattered. It was the first, and the last, time in my life I ever knew her to raise her voice. "Asey, you don't mean that deaf old haddock—"

"He ain't deaf."

That quiet announcement struck us, as Jimmy said later to Kyle, like mustard gas after a bombardment.

"Nope," Asey went on coolly. "That's what kept makin' me think I was cracked. Hanson an' Bob—they thought I was cracked, too—all of us been tryin' to trap him since I got this bright idea yesterday. No 'mount of mutterin's an' murmurin's an' whisperin's b'hind his back done any good. Nor car horns, nor footsteps, nor nothin'. I give up hope c'mplete in one way till that blessed cat—y'see, Bev," he turned to me, "when Sully come through that hedge just a while ago, he had his collar an' bell on. I seen the orange ribbon Miss Ag'tha tied on it this mornin'. Giles turned around as the cat come through, an' so did Grosgrain, an' some of the others of you. But Jethro turned first. Funny, for a deaf person to hear the tinkle of the bell first. I'm goin' to buy Sully a porterhouse steak for supper an' broil it m'self."

"Why'd he pretend to be deaf?" I demanded.

"Really was, for a time, I guess. After he had typhoid. How long ago was that, Jet?"

Jethro didn't answer.

"Fifteen, twenty years, anyways," Asey continued. "I s'pose he just kept up pretendin' after it wore off. Good idea. Lots of fun for him. It's one of them afflictions that come in awful handy. Ever think of the number of things you say under your breath to deaf folks—if you're sure they can't read lips? Think of all the names you call 'em, an' all the things you let out, knowin' you're safe. God A'mighty, think of the names we called him in the last few days. I bet you'd never of called him a deaf haddock, Miss Ag'tha, if you knew he could hear! An'—just set an' ponder on the things we let him in on! Deary me, no wonder there seemed to be a kind of leak! Why, right from the b'ginnin'—'member that night he shot at me? Just as he went out of the room, after bringin' Sully in, I said Dave'd called me over an' said he was sort of scared about things. That's why I got shot at. Anyhows, my first guess was the right one, an' that makes me feel a lot better."

Giles opened and closed his mouth a couple of times.

"But Asey, I saw him all the time, Thursday aft'noon! It's not possible!"

Asey puffed at his pipe. "That's what *you* said, ev'ry time you told your story. Bev said you seen him in his blue shirt. See what I meant about dif'rent stories, Bev? Yup, Giles, you prob'ly did see the blue shirt all right. Think it out. 'Member what Ike Smalley told us the first day we went over to see him? He said, he watched Jet a long time, an' Jet was slowin' up. Sure he was. You seen the blue shirt, Giles, an' Jet *was* slowin' up. He was inside the house, an' the shirt was stickin' on a box, or made up somehow as though it would seem he was up there, bendin' over the potato patch. So—"

"But Tommy Dawson and his figure in white!"

"Just Pegleg," Asey said. "White overalls, like painters wear. Hangin' up on a hook in the barn, now. Least, they was the other day."

"Wouldn't it possibly be kinder," Aunt Agatha's voice was back to normal, "just to give us the whole story and then let us ask questions?"

"All right. Got to wait for Parker anyway. I'm hopin' he'll have the last nail to drive in this. So Jet leaves his shirt an' comes inside the house, tinklin' Sully's bell that he's swiped. Then Dave won't notice any noise. If he hears anythin', he'll think it's the cat. But Dave was at the desk here, mind you. In full sight of both doors. Wasn't a chance. Then, I think why Dave went out—r'member he told me he'd been feelin' uneasy—I think he kind of must of had the same experience you did, Bev. He heard the bell tinkle, an' seen Sully streak across the lawn to your house. I sort of think that might be why he went out, with his gun in his hand. N'en, when he come back, Jet was waitin' for him, at the door. N'en, Jet went off. 'Bout that time, r'member, Sully come back. Jet put the collar back on. Mistake, Jet. You'd ought to of left it on the table."

"But what about the bullet from Dave's gun?"

"I'm gettin' to it. First off, Jet went back to the potato patch—you was all over here, then. Now, the bullet—well, it ric'chetted off the millstone, like I thought. Went into Jet's leg too. Oney it was the wooden leg. An' I'm pleased an' proud to say I caught on to most of that before he stole the putty chunks, oney his bein' deaf made me think I was cracked."

"What had those putty pieces to do," I began.

"How in blazes," Jimmy chimed in, "did you figure that out?"

"Wa-el, it's simple now, but it wan't then. Putty— well, putty fills holes. Holes in wood. Okay. There was a hole in wood that was bein' filled, only the wood wasn't stationary, else we wouldn't of found one chunk on the lawn an' one in the gutter on the roof. First I thought 'cane', an' then I worked up to 'wooden leg.' N'en—well, we'd been huntin' for someone with a hole in their leg.

So it added up to Jethro bein' the one with a hole in his leg. So—"

"Is it still there?" Jo demanded breathlessly. "In his leg?"

"Take his leg off, Hanson." We had to smile at Asey's casual order. "Let's see."

Hanson unstrapped the pegleg, and examined it carefully.

"But it ain't, Asey!"

"Let's see. Sure 'tis. Got some plastic wood fin'ly, huh? Tough on you that Dave didn't have any, an' the Penrose kids'd left the cover off their box. An' you didn't dare take the chance of leggin' uptown, with your weak pin. Y'see, he had to use putty till he got a chance to get some plastic wood. Putty dropped out, 'course, what with him thumpin' around. Yup, you can dig it out, Bob, an' I'm pretty sure you'll find the bullet under it. Go easy. Where'd I got to? Oh. Well, on his way back Thursday aft'noon later, from diggin' potatoes, Jet come into Dave's barn an' stuck in putty. S'pose he was worried that the hole might be seen. N'en later he heard me say that about Dave callin' me over, an' he got more worried, so he took the gun he'd swiped from Ike Smalley's wood house, an' tried to plug me. That gun was an awful good idea, Pegleg. You hoped it'd go back to Ike, an' you knew Ike's talk about Dave. Planned to use it yourself, I bet, only you had to use a knife when you seen all the Penroses an' their friends in the orchard. No noise."

"How'd he get downstairs and out, to shoot you?" Giles wanted to know. "And how, if he's the one, how'd he climb trees and—and last night, Jo said the man was up like a cat. How could he do that with his leg?"

" 'Member I said his brother Nehemiah Black was a fancy shot with the circus, an' Pegleg helped? He done acr'batics, too. An' after, I got to thinkin' about a wooden legged feller I shipped with once out of Sydney. He could climb riggin' like a cat. So it wasn't impos'ble that Pegleg should climb them trees. Used a rubber cane tip on the end of the leg, didn't you? No noise again. Made them marks I seen on the roof. What say, Jo?"

"Just muttering about Long John Silver," she said. "Giles, didn't you see 'Treasure Island' in the movies? Well, then!"

"So Pegleg opened the window of the garage loft," Asey went on, "come down the willow there, just like I come down the other when I was d'm'nstratin', an' potted at me. That didn't work. He tossed the gun away, hopin' again to get Ike, I think. N'en later he found the knife Grosgrain lost, an'—'course, he heard us say we was goin' to Ike's, so he went over an' done his knife stickin' act. N'en that didn't seem to get him anywhere, so he broke open Ike's cellar an' got the mushrooms, an' crawled in an' switched 'em. Masterly, Pegleg. Best of all was your timin', when you brought that puff ball up to Bev 'bout the time you hoped we'd be gorgin' ourselves with Death Cups. 'At was good."

Jethro continued to say nothing. Even Asey's obviously sincere comment on his master stroke left him entirely unmoved.

"But swipin' the putty pieces an' that diary," Asey

shook his head. "That was where you slipped. The diary p'ticularly was bad. Showed me you was losin' inspiration. That—"

"Is he," Jo asked, "the—Asey, was it Jet, last night on the cliff? If it was, what about his hand? Shouldn't it show traces of where I bit him?"

Hanson yanked Jethro toward him. "Only some scratches," he reported. "No bite."

"They ain't scratches," Asey looked at the hand. "You bit hard, Jo, but he's tough. When he got home, he took a razor an' cut the marks into scratches, an' then iodined 'em. Rubbed dirt in this mornin', huh? Oh, h'lo, Parker. Glad to see you."

"I came to tell you," he observed, "that your guess about the leg was right, but you seem to have got to Scotland before me. He was having a new pegleg made by a fellow in North Rolleston. Hullo, Porter. Usually, I—"

"For God's sakes," Jimmy said, "enlighten us, will you? Asey just skips from point to point, and he'd probably never think of going into details on this, if it was some of his own brain work."

"Asey figured," Parker answered, "that if the putty came from a hole in Jet's leg, Jet would eventually buy a new leg. So he thought he'd find out. Half my men have spent since last night tracking down people who make wooden legs. Luckily they're rare. We found the fellow who was making a new one for Jet, ordered for a rush job. Letter written Thursday night."

"Why didn't you just grab him and look?" Agatha said. "Why all this?"

" 'Cause he might have had a spare leg, an' worn the spare. 'Cause it all seemed silly, then. 'Cause it was nicer not to let him know. You got to r'member, Jet was deaf. An' if he was deaf, he wasn't the one. Lots of things. An' it seemed saner to get things settled first."

"I told you so," Jimmy whispered in my ear. "I told you so!"

"The motive," Eleo spoke for the first time, "why on earth—?"

"Well, the business of the girls on the cliff was just like Jo, last night. Only Jo was lucky. Them others got in Jet's way, or made him scared enough of bein' found out. As for his killin' Dave, I think Dave'd begun to suspect Jethro was more'n he seemed. Maybe he'd even seen the signalin', an' figgered it was Jet who was on Regan's pay roll, so—"

"Is he?"

"Are you, Pegleg?" Asey asked.

Jethro's face never moved a muscle.

"Dave didn't tell me," Asey continued, "so prob'ly it was nothin' more'n a suspicion. Prob'ly he felt the same way I did; Jet was just a deaf ole fool. But I guess, Pegleg was gettin' scared to death of bein' found out. P'raps he pushed the first girl off more or less by ac'dent, but they was all cold-blooded murders. An' Dave spent a lot of time up on the cliff, after Kay died. An' then," Asey tossed his empty pipe from hand to hand, "I think some of the business was r'verse blackmail."

"Was what?" I asked.

"Don't know no other name for it. Jet, I sort of think, heard Dave tellin' me about that Englishman an' the new comp'ny. He also sort of felt that Dave was catchin' on. He wanted Dave to beat it b'fore he got the cliff business figured out. So, he just sat around an' spread all the stories about Dave killin' himself, an' about Dave startin' out to walk with Kay that night earlier, an' hoped the talk would make Dave leave. Run him out of town. But Dave wouldn't be run, an' showed no signs of goin' ever. An' I think," Asey paid no attention at all to Jethro, who was watching him like a hawk, "I think Dave caught on an' said, 'Lay off, or I'll call in some of my r'porter friends, an' have 'em write you up as you are. Not the pict'resque feller, the artists' model, the touch of quaint ole Cape Cod, but a sort of second-rate village bum' "—

"He did not!" Jet yelled out angrily. "He did not! He told me he wasn't goin' to leave here, an' he was catchin' on about the cliff! He seen the light Tuesday night! An' Regan's man said if I didn't carry on an' keep my face closed—" he stopped short, looked around at us, and tried to spring forward on Asey.

"I get it. Both sides forcin' you, an' you was the slice of ham. Thanks."

"Take him out, Hanson," Parker said quietly. "That was nicely done, Asey. How'd you think of pulling it out that way?"

"Vanity," Asey told him gravely, "of vanities. Like the preacher saith. Pegleg's as proud as a pig about bein' a landmark. Even saves the press clippin's about himself an' pastes 'em in a book. I r'membered, sort of."

"Sort of," Agatha murmured. "Sort of! There's just one more thing, Asey. Just what in the world did Dave mean by 'Ink'?"

Asey grinned. "That was so easy, Miss Ag'tha, that I didn't get it till a little while ago when I come over here with Bev an' Jimmy, an' looked at the ink bottle. See, inkwell on the desk's full to brimmin'. Dave'd 'parently just filled it b'fore he begun his letter to Grosgrain. But he'd put the bottle back. See?"

He held out the half full ink bottle, and we all stared at it.

"At the risk of seeming even more stupid," Aunt Agatha announced, "I must frankly admit that I, for one, do not begin to see. Do any of you?"

We didn't.

Asey shook his head sadly. "Deary me, look at it! What's it *say*?"

"Say?" Agatha repeated, "say? Oh, you mean, on it. Oh!"

I was simple, too, in a Columbus-and-the-egg sort of way.

It just said, JET BLACK.

At four o'clock that afternoon we were still draped around the luncheon table, still hashing everything over for the millionth time.

There was an unaccountable second of silence, and

Luther, who had barely opened his mouth—he hadn't had a chance, really—grabbed it.

"Er—Mr. Mayo," he said apologetically, "I—well, as a matter of fact, this is the first opportunity I've had to speak to you about something I intended to thank you for this morning. It was about that gun you found in my pocket. I took it from Mr. Friar's room, that night he broke his other arm. He and his friend were so drunk, I rather hesitated to let them have it in their possession. They spoke of—really, I thought it best. Anyway, I'm very grateful to you for finding out about the matter, and for having me released. There was no need for you to—"

"I don't make a habit," Asey told him with a grin, "of makin' in'cent folks languish in jail. 'Course, I owe you an apol'gy in the first place for snatchin' you, but I did want you out of the way just then. I—"

"I see," Agatha said. "I get it. Aunt Nella, Aunt Nella, my eye! Now—"

"I've simply got to go." Eleo Dwight rose. "Bev, wasn't I right? I mean, in spirit. But she didn't even wait for a Macy section manager or a bond clerk. Giles, beat her occasionally and she'll do you nicely."

"How'd you know?" Giles asked in honest amazement. "We haven't said a thing—"

Eleo sighed. "I don't pretend to be any Asey Mayo, my children, but there are several departments in which I fairly shine. I'm sailing for India on Saturday, Jo. If you could dress that up, and teach it to tolerate me, you might get married and come along. I—please don't ruin my face, Jo! Bev and Asey have seen it at its worst, but

—oh, God, come along home, if you've got to be that way! At least no one will ever see!"

After the three of them left, Grosgrain got up.

"I—er—I must go, really, Mrs. Penrose. I—er—had an appointment with the golf professional at one, and—"

"But it's after four," I said.

"I know. Yes, yes, so it is! But to tell the truth," Luther blushed, "I—er—well, Mr. Montgomery sent me some clothes, proper golf clothes, and they came while I was—er—away—"

"I see," Asey said in a muffled voice. "I—huh, an' I intended to give 'em to you myself. Run along. Jimmy, you was murmurin' about golf. Go give him a lesson."

Jimmy took Luther by the arm, and Asey, Agatha and I were left alone.

"Well," Agatha said after a few minutes, "what now, Sherlock?"

Asey smiled. "What I really ought to do," he said, "is to get home to Wellfleet an' get some sleep. But—" he looked out of the window at his roadster. "But, I dunno. No, siree, I dunno. After all, I c'n sleep any time. I—"

"Do let's," Agatha said. "Shall we, Bev? We won't stay and bother. Just for one minute—"

We dashed for the roadster.

"Add first lines," Agatha said thoughtfully as she and I climbed in beside Asey. "No, I've run out of first lines. But I've got a grand last line—listen: 'So, with their eager faces turned to the radiance of the setting sun, with all nature seemingly aglow in harmony, after four days of dancing with trembling steps around the altar of death—' "

" 'After four days,' " I fell into the spirit of the thing, " 'of cheating death, though it came in many forms— silent as the wind, fleet as a falcon—' "

"That the knife?" Asey inquired drily.

"That's the knife. Um. 'Though it took the sound of the bumble bee, and—' "

"Funny bullet, Bev. Nev' heard one—"

"Stop, Asey! I'm just warming up. —'The sound of the bumble bee, small thunder from the skies, though it borrowed the speed of the forked lightning—' "

" 'Though,' " Agatha intoned, " 'it took the form of an asp, yet their leader—' "

"Took 'em," Asey finished with a chuckle, "to see Luther Charles Grosgrain of Dolphin Street, also of Walker, Adams, Saltonstall, Swish-swosh an' Foodelberg, all dressed up in a pair of plus fours!"

$6.00 MYSTERY

THE TINKLING SYMBOL

An Asey Mayo Cape Cod Mystery

Phoebe Atwood Taylor

"While the plot and characters are complex and satisfying, the atmosphere of 'Old Cape Cod' in the thirties adds another enjoyable dimension."
—*The News* (Stockbridge, MA)

The residents of West Weesit had good reason to start calling Crooked Cliff "Suicide Cliff." Four women's bodies had been found at its foot, Kay Truman's only last month. Her father, Dave Truman, had already been depressed after his wife left him and his business failed. So when the folks at the tea party across the bay saw him come out of his home with a gun and point it at himself, they naturally assumed that the gunshot did him in.

When it appeared that someone had actually stabbed him in the back with terrific force, however, it seemed time to send for Asey Mayo—who quickly became a ready target himself for a practiced and determined shooter!

A Foul Play Press Book

The Countryman Press, Inc.
Woodstock, Vermont

Cover by Leslie Fry

ISBN 0-88150-263-4

90000

9 780881 502633